# LOVE ONLINE

# PENELOPE WARD

First Edition
Copyright © 2018
By Penelope Ward
ISBN-10: 1942215894
ISBN-13: 978-1942215899

This book is a work of fiction. All names, characters, locations, and incidents are products of the author's imagination. Any resemblance to actual persons, things, living or dead, locales, or events is entirely coincidental.

Edited by: Jessica Royer Ocken
Proofreading and Formatting by: Elaine York
Cover Model: Eddy Putter, Touche Models Amsterdam
Cover Photographer: Nicole Langholz
Cover Design: Letitia Hasser, RBA Designs

# LOVE ONLINE

## CHAPTER 1

*Ryder*

Sip. Nod. Smile. Repeat.

I was a master at pretending to give a shit during conversations with fake people.

This blonde had been doing a pretty good job at looking like she was interested in *me*, and then she had to go and stick in a story about her recent audition on the Warner Brothers lot. That's when I began to tune her out.

All I could think about was how good it was going to feel to hit the sheets later and pass out alone in my bed—not with said blonde. Not with anyone in this room.

She batted her lashes. "So anyway, anytime you want to see my demo, I'd love to get your thoughts..."

*There it was.* These conversations always ended the same way, with a request for a favor.

"Sure, yeah. Just send it to my assistant, Alexa."

I didn't have an assistant.

I used the name Alexa to humor myself because it reminded me of the talking app.

"Will you excuse me?" I said, brushing past her.

One surefire way to ensure I never looked at your shit was to straight up ask me to in the middle of a conversation that was supposed to be about something else.

People were so ballsy.

On the outside, everyone probably thought I had the perfect life, the world at my fingertips—a good-looking dude with more money than I knew what to do with who threw the best parties in Beverly Hills, women falling at my feet everywhere I went.

I'm the son of one of Hollywood's biggest movie producers, so all of the wannabes in this city see me as a direct line to Sterling McNamara.

It must have seemed like I have it all, given that I live alone in this ten-million-dollar house, with walls of glass revealing a hillside view. But what people don't realize is how freaking tiring it is to never be seen for who you actually are, only for the things you own or the connections you have. It's real damn tiring. And honestly, lately, I've found myself *bored*—really bored with life. When everything is handed to you, there's nothing exciting to strive for, nothing to look forward to.

It isn't that I don't appreciate all I've been given. I have a great job working for my father's studio. I love my dad and respect how hard he's worked to get to where he is. But sometimes, it feels like a curse, a shadow I can't step out of. And I often wonder if I would have been better off not taking the opportunities handed to me, if I should've moved away and started from scratch. But I couldn't do that to my dad. He's always assumed I would take over his role someday. That's what he's always worked toward.

His business decisions are based around that scenario—to secure a spot for me, to set me up for when he eventually steps down. I'm his only child.

It was also hard for me to think about giving up that opportunity, so I went along with it all.

My house reeked of alcohol and cologne. I looked around at the fifty or so people congregating in my living room, mostly half-naked women and the men trying to sleep with them.

*Who are these people?*

I could probably name three people in the entire room. Everyone else was mainly here for the free booze, and by the end of the night, half of them would be drunk off their asses in my pool or passed out in the living room until my housekeeper, Lorena, kicked them out in the morning with—get this—a cowbell.

There's nothing funnier than listening from the comfort of my bed to her ringing that thing and yelling in Spanish for stragglers to get the hell out of the house. "¡Larguense de mi casa!"

Lorena is funny as hell and doesn't give a flying fuck what people think of her. She's tiny, but a force to be reckoned with. Her title may be housekeeper, but she's really keeper of the house. She takes that role very seriously. And I appreciate how protective she is.

I left the crowded living room, meaning to get myself a Sapporo beer, which I kept stocked in the fridge and not at the bar. But instead, I passed right by the kitchen, venturing into my bedroom.

When that door shut, I let out a long sigh of relief. The sounds from my party were now muffled, barely audible.

Peace and quiet.

*This.*

This was what I wanted.

No way was I going back out there tonight.

It had gotten to the point that lying in my bed and jerking off alone was more enticing than sex with a real woman. Because my hand wasn't a user—it expected nothing from me. And then I could just pass out right after. I could have had any woman in the house tonight, and that's exactly why I had no interest in a single one of them.

Tonight, all I wanted was to get off so I could fall sleep. Lately, I'd had trouble sleeping. Thoughts of Mallory were seeping into my brain again and keeping me from being able to relax. I couldn't let myself fall into that cycle of guilt tonight.

So, I knew I was gonna need a little help.

Not caring about the party going on outside, I locked the door and grabbed my laptop.

My back sank into my pillow as I logged in to my trusty porn site and perused the options on the menu. Pop-up ads flashed throughout the screen, with giant flopping dicks everywhere.

*What am I in the mood for tonight?*

MILF.

Blondes.

Asian.

Oral.

Anal.

Nothing was appealing to me.

On the bottom of the screen was a selection of cam girls. I always bypassed that option completely. The idea of competing with other men to interact live with a girl had never interested me. I preferred to not have to deal with my porn talking back to me. There were way more efficient ways to get my rocks off.

There was really nothing a cam girl was gonna do that I couldn't get in a previously recorded video without having to keep shelling out money to see so much as a fragment of her nipple. Although, I'm sure there are some lonely dudes who are easy targets to get sucked into something like that, because they needed attention even if it was fake.

*No thanks.*

I was about to move past that section as I normally did until one of the cam-girl images caught my eye. The preview featured a still shot of her playing a violin.

*A violin.*

I laughed.

*What the fuck?*

Had I come across the female Yo-Yo Ma of the porn world?

*Montana Lane.* That was her name.

*A violin.* Just when I thought I'd seen it all. If I wanted to listen to music, I'd go to the symphony—not a porn site. Not to mention, I preferred sex with "no strings."

That was bad, but I couldn't help myself.

Nevertheless, this whole thing made me curious. So I did what any bored dude avoiding a house full of people would do. I clicked on it.

*Famous last words.*

There she was, live in the flesh in real time. Unlike the preview, there was no violin in sight.

I laughed to myself. *False advertising!*

Instead, she was fully clothed and…singing. Well, fully clothed was a relative term in this case, since her boobs were busting out of her pale pink tank top, her nipples like buckshot pellets through the fabric. But she was covered.

I closed my eyes and listened to her acoustic performance for a moment.

*Her voice.*

Her voice was sick—breathy and completely in tune. Hypnotic. The song sounded familiar, and when I realized what it was, my body froze.

She was singing "Blue Skies" by Willie Nelson.

*No effing way.*

My heart thundered against my chest. That's the song my mother used to sing to me when I was a kid. Mom died a few years ago of a rare cancer. She sang it to me shortly before she died, too. I wasn't expecting to connect with my mother on a cam-girl site. Nevertheless, it was happening—no way I could turn away from this now.

Montana was really into it, closing her eyes to concentrate on hitting all the right notes. And it was flawless.

Several minutes went by as I listened to her smooth, buttery voice. It calmed me in a way very few things could lately. In a weird way, it felt like my mother was with me. (Although, I hoped to God Mom left before I started jerking off.)

Montana Lane was naturally beautiful in a way most women out here in L.A. were not. She wasn't wearing a drop of makeup, and yet her skin was flawless on camera. You could tell her breasts weren't fake, either. They dropped and bounced naturally as she moved. And her hair was a color of brown that wasn't bottled—a muted color, like sand. It was really long—down to her waist—and wispy, almost reminiscent of a hippie in the '60s.

It seemed like she was from another time or something. Her thin arms were toned. She was almost too skinny, apart from her voluptuous breasts. *Those eyes, though.* Her eyes were the lightest shade of green, and they glowed through the screen. It was as if I could see through them—I was sure as hell trying to. *Damn.* That violin preview photo definitely did not do her justice. This girl was a knockout.

When she finally stopped singing, comments lit up the screen, one after the other.

**LordByron114: Amazing!**

**SpyGuy86: Your voice is just as beautiful as you.**

**FranTheMan10: You are a fucking goddess, Montana.**

Most of them were respectful. Of course, there were some that weren't.

**Rocky99: Bravo. Now show us your tits.**

*Show us your tits?*
I spoke to the screen. "Fuck you, asshole."
This girl had just sung her heart out, and this dude was asking her to show her tits? Granted, that's what many of these guys were here for—maybe even me—but how fucking disrespectful at this point in time.

Everything on this site was tip-based. Users were paying Montana tokens to request different acts. There was a scrolling menu at the bottom of the screen that summarized the pricing: Fifty tokens and she sang a song. One hundred and she took her top off. Two hundred and she removed her panties. Three hundred and she masturbated on camera.

*Fuck.*

The thought of that made my dick stiffen.

Five hundred for a one-on-one, private "chat." Sure. I bet there'd be a lot of *chatting* going on in that scenario.

I really wanted to ask her why she'd chosen that old song. It nagged at me.

While it was free to watch her, if I wanted to interact, I had to register with the site.

After entering my email to sign up, I chose the username *ScreenGod90*, an ode to my movie-making roots and my birth year. Then I started typing.

**ScreenGod90: What made you choose "Blue Skies?"**

Montana was answering someone else's question, offering a guy advice on pleasing his woman. I wasn't sure if she'd even noticed my question. It was getting buried, lost in a bunch of scrolling sentences from various people.

I bet she would notice me if I tipped her. *Duh.* Money talks, Ryder. It took some time to get used to how all of this worked. Anytime someone gave her tokens, it made this *cha-ching* sound, and a notification lit up the screen.

I ventured over to the token bank and purchased 100 tokens. *What the hell?* I didn't gamble, so this was like my version of it.

I tipped her twenty to start and asked my question again.

**ScreenGod90: What made you sing "Blue Skies?"**

She glanced over and seemed to be reading the comments before looking directly into the camera—at me. "Hi, ScreenGod."

That made my body stir. I swallowed and felt my face heat up. Well, this was fucking weird. Seeing her looking right at me, talking to me through the screen was like taking a hit of a drug. I immediately wanted more, and it was only my first taste. All she'd done was say hello to me. In that moment, based on my reaction, a part of me knew it was very possible I could become addicted to this feeling... addicted to her.

"That's a great question. Why did I choose that song?" She closed her eyes as if to really concentrate on the answer, then said, "That song has always given me chills. It gives off an air of eternal optimism. The lyrics...they're so simple, yet they convey how great life can be when people are in love. Everything turns sunny and bright, even though you're living in the same world that might have seemed gray before you found the one you were meant to be with. Life is all a matter of perspective. I've experienced both the blue skies and the gray ones. But this song gives me hope, I guess, that blue skies will come again."

I fucking loved that answer.

Long after she'd moved on to someone else's question, I was still staring intently at her lips.

And from that night on, I was completely hooked.

## CHAPTER 2

# Ryder

I'd snagged an outdoor table at The Ivy. As usual, paparazzi were camped out across the street.

Even though this place was always crowded with people I knew or wanted to avoid, it reminded me of my childhood. My parents used to take me here when I was a kid. They'd preferred the indoor section to the patio. The antiques and colored furniture inside always made me think of my mom in a weird way because she had similar taste. My mother would always order the corn chowder here, so I did the same any time I came to The Ivy. Mom's spirit seemed to be around a lot lately.

Today I sat on the outdoor patio, surrounded by the signature white picket fence as I waited for my friend, Benjamin, otherwise known as Benny. He and I grew up together, and our fathers had once been business partners. Benny's dad was now retired but had also hoped to groom his son for a position at the studio. Benny wanted no part of making movies, though. Instead, he owned a marijuana dispensary in Venice Beach. As Benny liked to put it, he was all about "*weeding out* the bullshit" and enjoying life. Sometimes I wished I had his balls—to just say "Fuck it."

Benny finally showed up. He scratched his long beard as he sat down across from me and said, "You look like shit."

"I haven't been sleeping that well."

He opened a menu. "Something on your mind?"

"It's nothing."

"Dude, you know you can talk to me, right? Just cuz I may repeat it back to you doesn't mean I'm not listening."

Benny had a strange habit—something he'd done since childhood. He sometimes had to silently repeat the last part of whatever the person he was talking to said before he responded. You know how when you're watching a bad actor, you can see them silently mouthing their co-star's lines? That always reminds me of Benny.

I decided to come clean. "I've been thinking about Mallory a lot lately."

Benny mouthed what I'd just told him—*I've been thinking about Mallory a lot lately*. "I know," he said. "I heard."

*Heard?* I squinted. "You heard what?"

"She's getting married. That's what you're talking about, right?"

It felt like those words cut right through my chest. I was so confused. He did say *married*, didn't he?

"Married?"

"Yeah. I thought that's why you were upset. I saw it on her Facebook page. She posted a photo of her hand and the ring and the..." He seemed to realize from my face that this news was a shock to me. "Oh shit. You didn't know."

My appetite suddenly disappeared. "No." I stared off into space. "No, I didn't know."

My ex, Mallory, and I were together for four years. Even though our breakup had been almost two years ago, I hadn't really been able to shake her. She'd blocked me some time ago from seeing any of her posts on social media. Blocking me was the last straw in the destruction of our tumultuous but passionate relationship.

I had known she was seeing someone. I didn't realize how serious it was.

Benny was staring at me. "Are you alright, man?"

I'd told myself I'd accepted the breakup. But this was the first moment I truly realized I must have been holding out hope that we'd get back together someday. It was the first time I really understood that wasn't going to happen. It felt like a death in a way, perhaps one I needed to experience to fully get over her.

My chest felt raw. "Yeah. I'm good." When the waiter came back around, I said, "Can I have another Macallan?"

He nodded and went to fetch my drink.

Benny broke off a piece of bread and stuffed it into his mouth. "Hope you don't mind, I invited that girl Shera I'm seeing and her friend to join us for lunch."

My brow lifted. "Her *friend*?" That could only mean one thing.

"Yeah. She wanted to meet you. She's not an actress. I don't think she wants any favors like that. I think she just wants to fuck you, to be honest, so she can tell people she slept with Ryder McNamara."

"Great."

When I stared off, he slammed his hand down on the table, causing some of the silverware to go flying.

*Jesus.*

"You still down about the Mallory thing? Man, fuck her! Forget about it. She friggin' dumped you. It's been two years. Now she's with some...nobody. Move on from that shit."

I couldn't blame Benny for trying to rationalize with me. He'd never known the full story of what went down between Mal and me—why I took most of the blame for what happened between us, even though she was the one who ended it. I'd never shared the full story with anyone. He might have felt differently if he knew the truth.

The waiter brought my whiskey, and I downed it.

Two girls approached our table.

A tall redhead waved. "Hey. Sorry we're late."

Benny placed his hand around the redhead's waist. "Ryder, this is Shera. And this is her friend—what's your name again?"

She answered him but looked right at me. "Ainsley."

*Ainsley.*

As the third Macallan hit me, I suddenly felt very self-destructive.

*Ainsley, I think you're gonna get lucky today.*

I came home that night feeling like I needed a shower.

I'd ended up going to Ainsley's apartment and an-gry-fucking her while imagining she was Mallory. She had the same black hair, so it was easy to visualize. I was a sick fuck. I regretted it but couldn't take it back.

She didn't seem to mind a minute of it, though. We both came hard, and she had a huge smile on her face.

Then, per usual, I immediately just wanted to go home. Fucking-and-running had never felt good to me, but the sex only felt great in the moment. When it was over, the immediate need to flee always set in.

Fortunately, this girl had no expectations, so I didn't even have to pretend. Easy in, easy out. Still, the older I got, the crappier that scenario felt. At twenty-eight, I had started to want more than just a quick fuck. I just didn't think I was going to find the right person out here.

Anyway, my shower was a walk-in. It was more like a wet room with elaborate glass tile that changed colors depending on the level of heat. It was my favorite part of the house.

As the water poured down on me, I started to think again about the bomb Benny had dropped on me earlier today. My relationship with Mallory flashed before my eyes like a movie on fast forward. Then a tear fell from my eye.

*Fuck.*

Throughout the entire breakup, and everything that had gone on before, I'd never once cried—until now. In fact, I couldn't remember the last time I'd cried at all—probably my mother's funeral. Granted, this was only one tear, but it was one freaking tear too many.

I scrubbed over my face and vowed to let this be it—let this be the end of my guilt and the end of my dwelling on what happened with Mallory. It needed to end. I needed to move on as much as she needed her fresh start. She deserved that. I had to get over it.

Shutting off the water, I blew out a long breath before drying off.

Still wrapped only in my towel, I lay in bed and grabbed my laptop. A stream of water dripped down my abs.

I'd told myself I wasn't going to go back on that cam-girl site. But nevertheless, my fingers clicked away, and I somehow ended up in Montana Lane's chat room. I used the excuse that I was just going to see what she was up to.

There she was, looking as cheerful as ever. How she was able to sit in that room, talk to all these people, and look like she actually gave a shit was beyond me. She had these guys wrapped around her finger, though. I caught myself smiling at her and literally slapped my own face.

The bedroom behind Montana was always very cluttered, with various props lying around. Today I noticed her violin in the background, along with a feather boa and some dildos. She had white Christmas lights hanging on the walls and had made a canopy out of sheer curtains. She situated herself on the bed with her legs crossed. Her boobs bounced as she moved around.

The *cha-ching* sound of men throwing tokens into the pot rang out.

**Thirty tokens: James450 wants to see Montana Lane show her tits.**

They were all in cahoots, trying to throw in enough money together to get her to take her shirt off. The token sounds were on fire tonight.

*Cha-ching. Cha-ching. Cha-ching.*

It didn't take long to total the magic number.

She was mid-conversation when she must have noticed that the threshold had been hit. Montana lifted her shirt over her head, letting her beautiful, natural tits spring free. She'd handled that so casually, as if she'd done it hundreds of times before.

But this wasn't just any time for me. It was my first time seeing her topless. *Jesus.* More of a warning would have been nice. I swallowed hard, ill-prepared for how amazing her body was. Her breasts were like none I had ever seen, so full—with a slight drop but not droopy. Her nipples were a medium pink color and the size of half-dollars. This girl was the epitome of natural beauty.

I felt wrong gawking at her, like I was invading her privacy. That didn't keep me from staring. My dick swelled as I watched her rub her nipples with her fingertips. She started to slowly massage her breasts. My mouth watered.

*Et tu, Ryder?*

Yes. Fuck yes.

She lay down and continued rubbing her tits. Everything went quiet. Mesmerized, I tilted my head to get a better view. I refused to succumb to the urge to jerk off.

*Creeper.*

I chuckled at how pathetically entranced I was. *I bet she tastes as good as she looks.*

Some minutes later, Montana sat up and offered a teasing look at the camera before she pulled her shirt back over her head.

A mix of disappointment and relief hit me. On one hand, I was sorely bummed that my free peep show had ended. On the other hand, I wondered what right I had to be getting off on this anyway. Feeling protective, I was sort of happy she'd finished putting herself on display, even though I was certain she'd done far worse things than that.

I threw in more than the required tokens to request a song.

**ScreenGod90: I need to sleep tonight. Can you sing me a lullaby?**

She looked at the camera. "You again, ScreenGod?" It was like she was smiling right at me. "Any requests?"

There was that giddy feeling I got whenever she spoke directly to me. What was it about this girl? Or was it me? Was I just fucked-up in the head?

**ScreenGod90: I want you to choose.**

Montana closed her eyes for several seconds before she started singing a song I didn't recognize. It was beautiful, though.

When she finished, I typed.

**ScreenGod90: What's the name of that song?**

"It's called "Fly Away" by Poe. It's close to my heart. Did you like it?"

I wondered what she meant by that, why was it meaningful to her.

**ScreenGod90: I loved it. Thank you.**

I immediately knew I would be looking it up later.

As she moved on, interacting with the other men, I couldn't help wondering who this chick really was, how she'd ended up doing the webcam thing. Just based on her taste in music, I figured there was a lot more to her than this.

The *cha-ching* chimes kept sounding, and I saw that someone had put in enough tokens for a private chat. She apologized to all the other viewers for having to leave temporarily, and the screen went black as she disappeared.

*Well, ain't that a bitch.*

I put my laptop aside and scrolled through my phone as I waited for her to return. I looked up the lyrics of the song she'd sung. It seemed to be about loss. She'd said it was close to her heart. So that made me wonder more about Montana's story.

Fifteen minutes later, when she finally came back on, she seemed...different. I couldn't put my finger on what it was. She just didn't seem like her normal, smiling self.

"Alright, guys, I have to cut things short tonight," she said.

That's it? She came back to say she had to go? It seemed early.

Disappointment set in as I realized I wasn't ready to be alone with my thoughts tonight. I much preferred watching this beautiful woman and forgetting everything.

"I'll be back at the same time tomorrow night, around nine. Hope to see you all again." She blew a kiss to the camera.

It looked like she reached up to hit a button that was supposed to cancel her live video. But she was still there. Then she seemed to move away.

This was weird, something didn't seem right.

It didn't feel like she *knew* the camera was still on.

My pulse raced as I continued to watch her.

Montana curled up in a ball on the mattress and buried her face in her hands. I watched, horrified, as I realized she was crying. And then it hit me—she had no idea we could still see her. No freaking clue.

"You're on camera!" I stupidly shouted, as if she could hear me.

I decided to tip her some tokens, hoping the *cha-ching* sound would alert her to the fact that people were still watching.

It worked. She suddenly looked up and rushed over to the computer before everything went to black.

*Holy shit.*

I sat speechless. This girl had been smiling, laughing, playing around for hours, seemingly happy. But the second she thought the camera was off, all of that changed, like night and day.

It hurt me in a way I couldn't even describe, as if I was unknowingly contributing to her sadness.

*Fuck.*

Were we really so stupid we couldn't see it was all a show? I shut my laptop.

As I lay in bed, thoughts of Montana haunted me. What had happened during that private chat? Was that what had upset her?

I got up, reopened my laptop, and went to her page, even though I knew she wasn't active.

There was an email address where clients could contact her offline to arrange for private chats.

*What are you doing, Ryder?*

I logged into an email account I barely used, one that was not connected to my name in any way. I kept it to sign up for shit through sites I knew would spam me later. Despite feeling like it might not have been my place, I typed.

*Hey Montana,*

*It's ScreenGod90—the music nerd dude. I hope I'm not overstepping my bounds in writing to you like this. I debated whether to reach out. I just want to make sure you're alright. I know you accidentally left the camera on tonight after your show. I saw you crying, and you looked really upset. So, you've been on my mind. The purpose of this message is just to make sure you're okay.*

*Sincerely,*
*ScreenGod90*

I let out a breath, figuring the chances of her writing back were slim to none. But emailing her eased my conscience a bit, and my fatigue from the day eventually won out as I drifted off to sleep.

The next morning, bright sunshine streamed through my kitchen windows as I sat down at the table with my coffee and checked my phone.

It shocked me to find an email response from Montana Lane.

*Hi ScreenGod,*

*I really appreciate you reaching out to me. Yeah, that was unfortunate. I didn't realize I was still on. It was a moment. And it passed. I'd just been feeling really crappy all day, and so, I broke down. It had nothing to do with the chat. I don't want you to think that. Anyway, I obviously didn't mean for people to see me cry. I'm sorry for worrying you. I feel much better today.*

*P.S. I really love your musical requests. Thank you for wanting to hear me sing.*

*xoxo*
*Montana*

I sat there debating what to write back, if anything, for the longest time. I finally settled on:

*Dear Montana,*

*Really happy to hear you're feeling better. And as long as you keep singing, I'll keep request- ing. Your voice is as beautiful as you are.*

*Regards,*

*ScreenGod*

I immediately second-guessed my words. Really? *Your voice is as beautiful as you are?* With all of the men who hit on her on a daily basis, did I really think that was original? Even though that was how I felt, maybe I should've kept that to myself.

*Just be a good, quiet stalker, Ryder.*

I laughed to myself. This was some crazy shit—the lengths I would go to lately for a distraction.

It suddenly smelled like laundry detergent. Lorena, my housekeeper, walked into the kitchen with a bunch of clothes in a basket. She must have noticed my expression. "What's so funny?"

I shook my head. "You don't even want to know."

She kept squinting her eyes and looking at me as she folded. I decided to tell her the truth about my cam-girl obsession. Lorena could pretty much handle anything, even though she was fairly conservative. I loved shocking her.

After I spent about five minutes telling her the whole story, she said, "So she's, like, a nudie model?"

I chuckled. "Yes. A nudie model. She takes her clothes off from time to time. Even though you might not believe me, that's not why I watch her."

"Why are you bothering with that?"

I rubbed my eyes and chuckled. "I have no idea. Boredom, I guess?"

Lorena pointed at me. "That's the problem. You have all these *putas* throwing themselves at you all of the time. Nothing interests you anymore. Now you'll move to porn and hookers."

I lifted my index finger. "Hey, I'll have you know, I've never once gone to a hooker. Don't plan to, either. Not that there's anything wrong with that. But I don't have to pay for it, if you know what I mean."

23

"You're paying with this cam girl, aren't you?"

*Good point.*

"Yeah, but this is different...I guess. It's just innocent fun. And I only pay her to sing to me." I laughed, realizing how crazy that sounded—paying some chick to sing for me.

"She sings?"

"Among other special talents, yes. The first night I met her, she was singing "Blue Skies." Mom used to sing that song. So it freaked me out. That's how she initially got my attention."

"That and her big *tetas*."

I nearly spit out my coffee. "Yeah. Those are nice, too. *Really* nice." I cleared my throat. "Anyway, it was like I was meant to hear that song or something. And in the process of that...I discovered I like watching her."

She stopped folding for a moment. "*Mijo*, you need to go in the opposite direction of what you're doing. Stop going with the sluts and this porn and find someone who's a good person, who you can settle down with. Someone who is gonna take care of you—like one of my nieces."

*Oh boy. Here we go.*

I cringed. "No offense, but I'm pretty sure the last niece you wanted to set me up with had more facial hair than I do. Nice girl, but she legit had stubble."

Lorena was laughing, because she *knew* about that shit when she set me up with her.

"Okay, maybe not Adriana," she said. "But I have lots more. Twenty nieces. Lots to choose from. I know you like the pretty ones."

"Well, it helps if I don't have the urge to pull over on our date and buy a BiC razor to shave her face, yeah."

She laughed, even at the expense of her niece, because she knew it was true. The chick had whiskers.

"What about my other niece, Larisa? She's always asking for you ever since I brought you to church that one time. Such a pretty face on that one."

Larisa had tried to go down on me in a church hall coat closet within thirty minutes of meeting me. I hated to ruin Lorena's perfect image of her niece, so I'd never divulged that piece of information. I enjoyed aggressive women—but not *that* aggressive.

"She definitely gives good face," I joked, unsure if she'd get it.

She threw a dishtowel she was folding at me. "You know, I told your mother before she died that I would look out for you."

*Wow.*

"I never knew that, Lorena. She asked you to do that?"

"Well, no, but I told her I would, and that made her very happy. So, I feel a responsibility. You know?" She looked like she was tearing up.

Lorena had been my parents' housekeeper. She was always like part of the family. When I moved out on my own at eighteen, my mother sent her to come work for me, knowing Lorena would keep me in line. I wasn't happy about it at first; I didn't want to be under anyone's watchful eye. But as I'd gotten older, I'd come to appreciate having someone around who had my back, especially after my mom died.

At the same time, Lorena knew I had her back, too. She never asked me for help or for extra money, but there wasn't anything I wouldn't do for her. I truly considered her a second mother and was grateful that she looked out for me and cared about my well-being. My father, who meant well, had always been oblivious to what was happening in my life—and he became even more so after my mother's death. He'd ended up throwing himself more into work than ever. I couldn't say I blamed him.

So, while my father was blind, Lorena had seen it all. And she didn't judge me. She was there when I was a mess after the breakup with Mallory. Since then, she'd watched countless women do the walk of shame out of my bedroom. Despite her feelings about my actions, she always made sure my dirty sheets were cleaned. She never gave me shit unless I asked for her opinion.

Then, boy, would she give it to me.

## CHAPTER 3

*Ryder*

I told myself I wasn't going to go to Montana Lane's page again, but that was easier said than done. I'd find myself alone at night and would inevitably click over "just to see what she was doing." Virtually hanging out with her had become a familiar and comforting experience. I'd asked her to sing for me once or twice, but mostly I just watched her as a quiet spectator.

She'd never done more than show her breasts on camera during the public chats. But she'd disappear for chunks of time, and I always wondered what was happening during those private shows.

I'd visited her page five nights in a row. But this night was different. For the first time, I decided to take a chance on something.

I didn't even know what I was looking for, just that I wanted her to myself for a bit.

I threw down enough tokens and requested a private chat. Sweat permeated my forehead. *You're being stupid,*

I thought to myself, unable to believe I was actually nervous about interacting with her one-on-one.

She said goodbye to the audience and disappeared for a few seconds. Then I was granted access to the private chat room before she appeared on the screen again.

Montana waved. "Hey, ScreenGod. How are you? I thought you'd never ask."

I typed.

**ScreenGod90: Hey. How does this work exactly?**

"Well, you know you can talk to me in this room, or even activate your camera if you want me to see you. But you certainly don't have to show your face. Just turn your mic on so I can hear you. That way we can talk, and you don't have to type anymore. That's one of the benefits of the private room. If you prefer not to speak, you can keep typing, too. That's fine."

I hadn't realized I would actually be able to *talk* to her, or that I had the option to show her what I looked like. *Fuck.* That definitely wasn't going to be happening. I needed to keep myself in check. Showing her my face was risky. She couldn't find out who I was. The whole reason I was attracted to this scenario was the anonymity.

But letting her hear my voice was harmless. I found the button to activate my mic and clicked on it.

"Can you hear me?" I said.

She smiled. "Yes. Oh my God, yes. Hi." Montana seemed thoroughly amused.

"Hi." I grinned. "Okay...cool. I obviously haven't done this before."

"Your voice is much deeper than I imagined, Screen-God. Not what I was expecting."

*Hold up.*

*What the fuck?*

"What were you expecting?" I asked, deepening my voice even more.

"For some reason, I thought you were going to be this shy, soft-spoken man. Your voice is nice and deep. You have a *really* nice voice."

*Great.* She thought I was gonna sound like a girl. Nice work, Ryder.

"Thank you. So do you. I mean, not deep. But a nice voice."

"I know what you meant."

"Especially when you sing. Obviously you already know I love your voice," I said.

She adjusted her legs to sit with them crisscrossed, settling into the bed.

She seemed comfortable with me. "Yeah. I'm still baffled that all you want to do is listen to me sing. I assume you wanted this private time for *other* reasons, though. What would you like me to do for you?"

Umm...fuck. Was I that naïve? She'd assumed I called her into this chat room for some virtual sexual favors. Admittedly, I would have loved to experience something like that with her right now—I was horny as fuck—but I couldn't ask her to do anything. It just felt scummy.

"I just wanted to talk to you, actually." Technically, that was the truth.

Her eyes widened. "Really?"

"Yeah."

"Most people don't call me in here just to talk."

"Well, I'm not most people."

"I already figured that out in the short time I've known you, ScreenGod. You're definitely not like most of the guys who come to my page."

I looked over at the clock. "How much time do we have?"

"Twenty minutes." She glanced down to check her phone. "Well, fifteen now."

"Then what?"

"Well, typically, you can tip again if you want to extend the time, or I go back to the public chat."

"Okay."

Montana tilted her head and stared at me through the screen. "So, what did you want to talk about?" Even though she couldn't see me, it felt like she could.

"I'm kind of freezing up right now, to be honest. That doesn't usually happen to me."

"It's okay." She smiled. "There are no rules. You don't have to say anything compelling."

"I guess I just wanted you all to myself for a little bit, wanted your attention...or something. I think you're amazing. You fascinate me."

She looked genuinely perplexed by that statement. "Why?"

"I'm not referring to your looks. I'm talking about everything else."

"You're giving me a complex, ScreenGod."

"What?" That certainly wasn't my intention. "Why?"

"Compared to everyone else, you don't seem very interested in me physically."

That was laughable. "Are you kidding?"

"Well, you haven't once asked me to take my shirt off or anything. Either you find me unappealing, or you might be a halfway decent guy. Still trying to figure it out." She winked.

"Believe me, my thoughts when it comes to you are not entirely pure. It's just that...what attracted me to you initially wasn't just your looks. It was that you seemed different. Your violin preview photo was actually what sparked my curiosity in the first place."

She bent her head back. "Ah, I probably scare more people off with that than lure them in, yeah? Not sure why I chose it. I thought maybe it set me apart from the rest of the girls, but I bet it deters some people, too." She cackled. "Hey, here's a question. What do I have in common with my violin?"

"Uh...I don't know. What?"

"Our G-strings." She laughed, and her boobs bounced. I swear that was therapeutic for me.

"Nice." I chuckled. "Anyway, I think the violin thing is awesome. I was all about checking out the naked philharmonic. Where did you learn to play?"

She took a deep breath in. "My mother was a music teacher. She played a few instruments and taught me the violin."

"Ah. Interesting. Makes sense now. Is that the only instrument you know?"

"Yeah."

"Does your mother know you do this for a living? And that you're so creatively incorporating music into it?"

Her expression darkened. She paused then said, "No. She's gone. And she'd roll over in her grave if she knew about this."

*Well, okay. This conversation just took a depressing turn.* "Oh. Um...I'm sorry."

"It's okay. She died when I was twenty."

That definitely had an effect on me.

"My mother...she's dead, too," I told her. "She died a few years ago. So..."

"I'm sorry." We just stared at our screens, bonding in our common losses for a bit before she asked, "How old are you?"

"Twenty-eight."

"So, you were what? Twenty-five when she died? That's too young to lose your mom—like me. I can relate."

"How old are *you*?" I asked her.

"Twenty-four."

I hadn't invited her into this room to talk about heavy stuff. I wasn't sure if I could handle it right now. A change of subject was definitely needed.

"So, what's with all the props behind you? It's like a circus up in there. I haven't seen you use even half of them."

"It's like a cross between the circus and *Hoarders*, right?" She laughed. "It *is* crazy. They're all things people have requested over time. You never know when you're gonna need something. The only things that get used consistently are the dildos, though."

"Well, yeah, you never know when you're gonna need a feather boa or gigantic glasses in a pinch."

"Right?" She cracked up. "I suppose I should probably declutter. I've accumulated a lot."

"How long have you been doing this—the camming?"

"About a year and a half."

I settled into the bed, feeling more at ease by the second. "Do you remember your first night?"

She blew out a breath and laughed. "Oh my God. Yeah. I was so nervous. I kept checking the lighting, changing my clothes...thinking all that stuff mattered. But once I was live, I realized pretty quickly that no one gives a shit about those little details."

"So, you just...went on and winged it?"

She smiled. "Well, first I had a drink. A strong one."

"I can imagine."

"I remember looking at the room count, waiting for it to go up—it was really slow, at first. There were very few viewers. I almost just hung things up before it even started. I mean, there's so much competition out there. I wasn't sure if anyone would even show up. Once things got going, though, I got broken in real fast. I've heard and seen it all at this point."

"Not all of it good, I imagine."

She seemed to tense up. "No. Some of the things people say...it can be brutal."

My blood boiled as I thought about some of the losers I'd seen in the short amount of time I'd been visiting her chat room. I was seething just thinking about it.

"They're so fucking disrespectful. I can't tell you how many people I've wanted to virtually kill."

"Thank goodness the moderator usually removes those types pretty fast. The number-one rule is not to engage them. The beauty of this is that I make the rules. I don't have to entertain anyone I don't want to. And the *end chat* button is just one click away."

It made me happy to know she felt so in control.

I chuckled. "If only real life were like that—if there were a magic *end chat* button."

"Exactly." She smiled wide.

"I work in the entertainment industry," I said, deciding to open up a little. "It's very cutthroat, and I'm constantly dealing with people wanting to know me because of the opportunities they think are in it for them. I expect a certain amount of brownnosing, but sometimes it would be awesome if I could just pick and choose who to interact with like that."

"Or just log off and disappear mid-conversation." She laughed.

"Yes! That would be perfect."

"The best is when people expect that they can sweet talk me into stripping down for them without having to pay—as if I'm not here to make a living."

"You do a good job of making it seem like you *want* to be there, though. I have to give you that."

"Don't get me wrong...I don't hate it. But I wouldn't be doing it for free. You know?"

"Of course. This is your job."

"Most of my regulars understand that. I love my regulars—like you."

That was strange to hear. "I guess I am a regular at this point, aren't I?"

"Yes. But you don't show me your dick. Which I appreciate."

I snapped my fingers. "Damn. You just ruined my plans for tonight."

We were both laughing now.

"Sorry about that." She grinned.

"Note to self: keep dick in pants." I sighed. "Seriously? A lot of guys show you their dicks? I just assumed they were watching *you*."

"I wish that were the case, but I definitely do see my share of dicks."

"What do they want? Your approval?"

"Yeah, basically."

"I'm gonna send you a button you can press that plays 'That's the most beautiful dick I've ever seen' over and over. That way you won't have to say it."

Montana snorted. "I would love that, because that's exactly what they want. They want me to lie to them and tell them they're the biggest, the best." She rubbed her eyes. "Lord."

"Is that the scariest part of being a cam girl? Strange guys who show you their dicks?"

"No. Believe it or not, it isn't. I think the scariest part is when certain guys think I owe them because they send me unsolicited gifts or pay me a lot of money. They get mad or jealous when I'm not attentive to them, and sometimes they turn hateful. This site is pretty secure, and I actually have my home state blocked for privacy reasons... but you just never know."

Fuck. That gave me chills. I hated the thought of someone trying to hurt her.

"So, people who live in your state can't see you?"

"It's supposed to work that way, yeah."

Nodding, I said, "I guess I know you're not in California then, if I'm able to watch you."

She simply smiled. She wasn't about to divulge where she lived, and I couldn't blame her.

We continued talking for several minutes, and I totally lost track of time.

Montana let out a long breath. "Well, this is definitely the first time I've ever vented to a cam john."

"A what?"

"Cam john. That's what we call clients."

"Like a john who sees a prostitute?"

"Yes, I suppose that's where it comes from."

I looked down at myself. "Fuck, I'm creepier than I thought."

She burst into laughter again. "No, you're not creepy at all. I don't know how I know that about you, but I do."

"Well, thank you. I aspire not to be a creeper."

She looked over to the corner of her room and then back at me. "Shit."

"What?"

"Our time has been up for ten minutes. I didn't even notice. Another first for me."

I really didn't want her to leave.

"Hang on," I said.

Without even having to think about it, I purchased enough tokens for another chat.

When she noticed the sound, she said, "Are you sure? That's a lot of money to spend in one night."

If she only knew money was no object for me. I would have paid any amount to keep talking to her now.

"Yeah. I'm sure, if you're okay with hanging out with me some more."

"Honestly? Yeah. I'm really enjoying talking to you. It's different for some reason. It feels like we're just *talking*. It's not forced."

It was weird how comfortable I was with this girl. This was our first real one-on-one interaction, but it felt like we'd done this many times, like I'd known her forever, maybe even in a different lifetime.

"I know what you mean," I said. "I could talk to you all night. I don't normally feel that way around women."

"Are you shy?"

"No. I'm not an introvert or anything, and I should clarify. I don't have a *problem* getting women—just the opposite. I just can't connect with the majority of them."

"Interesting." Montana seemed to be pondering my words. "Do you visit any other rooms on the site?"

"What do you mean?"

"Any other girls?"

"Oh. No. You're actually my first."

She seemed shocked. "Are you kidding?"

"No. I didn't think this was my thing. And it really isn't. But you're different. Basically, you had me with "Blue Skies.""

"That's right. You seemed really interested in that song. You asked me why I'd chosen it. Does it mean something to you?"

My heart felt heavy all of a sudden. "My mother used to sing it to me, actually."

She nodded. "That's why you asked me about it."

"Yeah. It means a lot to me, and I couldn't believe you'd chosen it. Truthfully, if you hadn't been singing it, I might have just passed right by you. But now that I've gotten to know you, that seems pretty hard to imagine."

"I love the Frank Sinatra version," she said.

"Willie Nelson, you mean?"

"Well, he sang one, too. There are many versions of the song."

I felt dumb for correcting her. Of course, there were different versions. That song was old as hell. That's why I was so surprised she'd chosen it. But Montana seemed to have an old soul.

One thing was clear to me. She was way more relaxed around me than she seemed in front of the larger audience. I wondered if she was feeling half of what I was right now. It was a feeling I couldn't quite identify. But it felt damn good, whatever it was.

Montana curled into her mattress. "Well, I'd say maybe we were meant to meet, ScreenGod."

## CHAPTER 4

*Ryder*

Her real name was Eden.

I'd always suspected the name Montana Lane was as fake as ScreenGod.

For three weeks we'd been chatting in a private room for at least an hour every night. I never asked her to do anything more than talk to me.

I still hadn't turned the camera on myself, either, so Eden continued to have no idea what I looked like. I preferred to keep things that way for the time being. Was I ever gonna show her my face? Not sure. I was tempted to, so she'd know I wasn't a freak. But that would take things to a different level for me, one I wasn't sure I was ready for.

I would've booked her for the entire night every night if she would have let me. In fact, I tried. But she didn't think it was a good idea to disappear entirely from her public audience. She'd lose customers that way, and I understood that; I couldn't blame her. But damn if I didn't look forward to our time together after a long day.

Even though we opened up to each other about life and our days, there was a limit to what we shared. I still didn't know where she lived or any personal details like her last name. We'd agreed to keep it that way for the time being.

She knew my name was Ryder. She knew my favorite food was pizza and my favorite band was Pink Floyd. She knew a lot of things about me, but she didn't know what I looked like, where I worked, or my last name. Yet at the same time, it didn't feel like that lack of information mattered. I was starting to feel like we knew each other intimately. And that made me think—who we are in this world has nothing to do with our names, our jobs, our social status, or all the labels we place on one another. It was possible to know someone without any of those things.

I probably would never have thought that before meeting Eden. But she'd shown me that true relationships *can* be based on how two people connect, their shared ideals and tastes—their overall chemistry. And mine with Eden was off the charts.

There was no doubt that working at a movie studio could be invigorating. Employees and crew members mingled with celebrities coming and going. It was a constant rush of energy. But I'd gotten so used to being around famous people, it didn't faze me anymore.

I'd held lots of different roles at my father's company, McNamara Studios. Dad made me start at the ground and work up. In high school, I worked at the gate, granting talent and executives access to the lot and turning other people away. I also drove around in a golf cart and fetched food for cast and crew.

Eventually, after graduating from college, I moved to the production side of things, assisting in making sure scripts were finalized, coordinating the filmmaking process, and keeping things on budget. I ended up getting my master's degree in business from UCLA. My major was film production as an undergrad, but my father wanted me to garner the business knowledge that would be necessary to run the company someday.

As of late, I'd been spending more time off the lot, shadowing Dad in his office downtown. On this particular day, he was raring to go as he sat me down during a work break.

He kicked his feet up on his desk. "There's a major shift happening, son. It's requiring us to be more globally focused. And you're gonna play a big role in this."

I reached for one of the starlight peppermints in the jar on his desk and removed the wrapper. "Okay. Explain."

"Well, it used to be you produced a good movie in Hollywood, it played around in New York or L.A., and that was good enough. It was all very one-dimensional. It's not like that anymore. Everything's gone digital. You know this. I don't need to tell you. We have the world at our fingertips now. And that means being cognizant of the global market and all of the different platforms we have. Streaming is taking on a bigger role in how people view movies, but at the same time, it's allowing us the potential for a much bigger audience."

"Okay...this isn't really news. Explain my big role in all this."

"I want to have you traveling more, be our leader in the international marketplace. The person who leads this company into the future is going to need that kind of experience."

My brow furrowed. "You're shipping me away?"

"Only for small chunks of time. It's going to be imperative that you have international experience if you're going to be running this place."

"Where's my first stop?"

"I'm thinking India."

"India?" That was probably the last place I'd expected.

"Yes. Bollywood ticket sales are astronomical. We need to pay attention to this. I'd like to set up a branch in Mumbai, and I'd like you to spearhead it. That's going to mean you taking some trips out there. We have the potential and the budget to be better than Bollywood and reap the benefits of that hot market."

"Is this a done deal?"

"I've already set up some meetings for you. You leave in two weeks." He must have gotten a load of my face when he added, "You look like I just pissed in your Cheerios."

"It's just...I wasn't expecting this."

"I was hoping you'd be more excited."

"Maybe if it wasn't halfway around the world."

*Why aren't I excited?*

I hated to admit it, but I knew India was something like twelve hours ahead. I was really enjoying the nightly routine I'd gotten into lately and didn't want to disrupt it. But I couldn't tell my father I wasn't going to help him take over Bollywood because I'd miss my appointments with a cam girl.

So, I'd suck it up and go.

It didn't take long for the prospect of this India trip to get me all worked up.

I'd spent the afternoon on the phone with one of our contacts there to discuss the itinerary. It was going to be a lot of pressure in a completely foreign territory. I just wanted to forget about it for one night.

Once I was tucked into bed that evening, I logged into Eden's room and immediately threw down enough tokens for a private chat.

Her face always lit up when she noticed me online. She'd stare into the camera and give me a look that showed she knew I had joined. And of course, that did things to me.

"Hi, ScreenGod. I thought you'd never show." She waved to her audience as she prepared to log out. "I'll be back online soon, guys."

Eden couldn't open the private room soon enough for me.

When she finally appeared, she seemed concerned. "Hey, Ryder. Is everything okay?"

"How could you tell something is off?"

"I don't know. I could hear that your breathing was a bit heavier just now. Are you stressed?"

"I *am* actually, but I'm surprised you could pick up on it just from a couple of seconds of breathing."

"Well, it's all I have to go on. Since I can't see you with my eyes, I think I'm more in tune to my other senses. I'm more sensitive to other things—like the way you sound."

"Jeez. Because I can see you so clearly, I guess I forget I'm just a voice to you."

"That's because a certain someone doesn't want to show his face," she teased.

Eden probably thought I was afraid to show her what I looked like. It had nothing to do with that. There was just a certain comfort I felt in being able to interact with her like this. But it wasn't fair; I knew that. We were beyond just cam girl and cam john at this point. If this was to continue, I'd need to show her my face, eventually.

Eden reached for a fuzzy, fleece sweatshirt and threw it over her head. "It's freezing in here. You don't mind, do you?"

"Of course not."

"It's not like you ask me to do anything with them anyway." She winked, and it took me a few seconds to realize she was referring to her breasts.

She had no idea all of the things I dreamed about doing to those beautiful tits. In my imagination, I'd already devoured and fucked them every which way. But I'd chosen to keep those thoughts to myself.

"I appreciate that you don't expect those things, by the way," she said. "But if you ever wanted…you know you could ask me, right?"

I swallowed. "I'm good, Eden."

My dick hardened in protest. Her words alone—"*you know you could ask me, right?*"—had given me an instant erection. My balls tightened. *She has no idea.*

I changed the subject, choosing to focus on her frumpy clothes in an attempt to bring down my hard-on. "Is this the real Eden? Fuzzy sweats? I like it."

"You don't know the half of it. I'm the antithesis of sexy when I'm off the clock. You can find me in jeans, Chucks, and a hoodie most of the time." She laughed. "And I'm always cold—like, freezing no matter what temperature it is."

*I'd love to be able to warm you up right now.*

I relaxed into my pillow and took in her face for a while.

She tilted her head. "So...are you gonna tell me why you're in a bad mood tonight?"

"I'm not anymore. You always put me in a better mood."

"That's not an answer."

Letting out a deep breath, I said, "It's looking like I'm gonna have to travel to India for work. And I'm not really looking forward to it."

I'd recently told Eden my full name and where I worked. I was no longer hiding anything from her. A part of me wanted her to come find me. The full disclosure wasn't reciprocal, however. She still kept much of her life private.

"India? Oh my God, really? I would *love* to visit India. Actually, I'd love to go anywhere other than here."

"Why can't you?"

She hesitated then said, "My life is just not conducive to travel."

"Why not? Money?"

She ignored my question. "How long will you be gone?"

"A few weeks."

"Oh." Eden looked almost depressed.

"Hey—you gonna miss me or something?"

"Can you take me with you virtually?"

"Well, India is, like, thirteen hours ahead of West Coast time. So, it's likely that I'll be working when you're camming."

A worried look washed over her face. "We'll have to figure something out. I don't think I could go three weeks without talking to you."

Her words gave me pause. That's exactly how it was for me, too. I felt like I couldn't sleep at night without hearing her voice anymore.

*What is happening between us?*

She seemed to regret being so candid. "I shouldn't have said that. Do you think it's weird? In my line of business...I'm not supposed to be getting attached."

"What—do I think it's weird that you're bonding with a faceless voice?"

"Yeah." She laughed. "God...when you say it like that."

"No, I don't think it's weird. Maybe I *should* think it's weird, but I don't, because I feel the connection, too."

"I've grown so accustomed to talking to you. You're my outlet. It's what I look forward to at the end of each day. I feel like I can tell you things, and you won't judge me."

*Who the fuck am I to judge you?* "I have no right to judge anyone."

"Is there a specific reason you're saying that?" she asked.

I let out a laugh. "Plenty of reasons."

"Well, I like that you're not perfect. Makes me feel better about all the crazy shit I've done." She winked.

*Pretty sure falling hard for a cam girl is the craziest thing I've ever done.*

Eden sighed. "This time always goes by too fast."

"You know my offer still stands if you want to stay longer. I'll book you the whole night."

She almost looked like she was considering letting me do that. I could tell she didn't want to leave me and go back to those strangers. That was weird to say, since I was virtually a stranger, too.

Then she floored me when she said, "How about if we meet here in the private room after my shift ends at midnight? But I don't want you to pay."

"What do you mean? I can't let you do that."

"The camming site lets me override payment if I choose. I like your company, Ryder. I don't feel right making you pay when it's *me* who wants to talk to *you*. That makes me uncomfortable. So, I'm going to have to insist on not accepting payment for anything beyond the one private chat."

I let her words digest. This was a game changer. It was the first time I truly believed the feelings were reciprocal. She was asking me to come back after midnight because she wanted *me* there—not my money.

"Whatever you prefer," I said casually, even though inside I was freaking out a little—in a good way.

She blew a breath up into her forehead, seeming tense, as if she'd been nervous to tell me what she wanted. "Okay...so, see you later?"

It pained me to have to let her go back to those vultures. "Yeah. Alright. See you then."

I couldn't watch the public show anymore. I didn't want to see Eden taking her clothes off for those assholes, and

I couldn't deal with some of the disrespectful things guys said to her. If I'd known where some of them were located, I would've tried to hunt them down.

So instead, I took a hot shower, watched an episode of *Stranger Things*, and chilled until it was time for our private chat.

A couple of minutes before midnight, I logged into her room to catch the tail end of her shift so she could connect me to the private room.

She granted me access without my having to pay. Eden looked tired as she waved. "Hey."

"Fancy meeting you here."

"I know." She sighed. "I thought this night would never end."

"I'm still floored you would want to come back on with me after a long shift."

"Well, I don't have to put on an act around you, so it doesn't feel like a continuation of work."

"Your refusal to let me pay sort of blew me away. I guess this was the first night I really believed you liked talking to me as much as I like talking to you."

"I *love* talking to you," she said as she pulled a sweatshirt over her head and lay down on her mattress.

The white Christmas lights were still on, and all of her props were strewn about.

"I'm not gonna keep you up too long," she said. "I just wanted to hear your voice before bed."

On camera, she was always so giving of herself, but the person she showed me now was vulnerable, needy—maybe even a little lonely. I wondered how long it had been since someone offered to do something for *her*.

"What can I do for you, Eden?"

"What do you mean?"

My voice was more of a whisper. "Tell me what you need."

She seemed to ponder that, then said, "Tell me a bedtime story."

*A story.*

*Hmm...*

*Okay.*

She curled into her pillow and stared into the camera, blinking, waiting. In moments like this, it was always hard to believe she couldn't see me.

I thought about what kind of story to tell, then decided to wing it.

"Once upon a time, there was a little boy. He lived a very charmed life. He grew up in a huge mansion in California. His father worked all the time. His dad was never around, so he was a mama's boy. His mother tried her best to teach him values despite the excesses surrounding him. She sang songs to him sometimes and showered him in love. He was a lucky kid, took things for granted. And his life continued like this uninterrupted for many years."

I took a deep breath in and continued. "When he was in his twenties, he met a girl and fell in love—or so he thought. Everything in his life was perfect until his mother found out she had cancer. She fought for a good year before she died. Losing her crushed him. Then shortly after that, he fucked things up with his girlfriend, and she left him." Closing my eyes, I paused. "In a short amount of time, he lost the only two women who had ever loved him. This boy—now a man—who'd been lucky enough to never deal with tragedy until that point, was left devastated and lost for the first time in his life. For two years, nothing and no one could break him out of this perpetual state of emptiness. Everything in his life seemed superficial, from the women he slept with to the shallow, Hollywood types showing up at the many lavish parties he threw. It was a meaningless existence. But that all changed one night when he clicked on a photo of a girl playing the violin."

She lifted her head from the pillow as if to listen more closely to my story.

"And there she was, one of the most beautiful girls he had ever seen. She was singing. When he heard her voice, it brought back so many of the feelings and emotions he thought were dead. And he felt things he'd never experienced before. Even though he didn't fully understand why, night by night this girl replaced the emptiness in his life. A beautiful distraction. And for the first time in a long time... he was happy again."

*Holy shit.*

Eden had tears in her eyes. She placed her hand up against the camera as if to touch me. I placed my hand on the computer screen as if to touch her back. It was an incredible moment, one that made me ask something I hoped I wouldn't regret.

I forced the words out. "Do you want me to turn my camera on, Eden?"

She put her hand down and seemed taken aback. "Really? You want to?"

"Only if you want to see me. I don't want to make you uncomfortable."

She licked her lips, seeming a little freaked out. "I do. I *really* do. But I'm scared."

I laughed nervously. "Not as scared as I am."

"Not because I care what you look like," she was quick to clarify. "I'm just so used to things the way they are, and I feel like seeing you will take it to a different level. That's not necessarily a bad thing, just something I'll have to get used to."

"Yeah." *Okay. Bringing it up was a bad idea.* "I mean...I don't have to."

"No! I really want you to." She'd said it fast, probably before she could change her mind.

"You sure?"

Expelling a shaky breath, she nodded repeatedly. "Yes."

I sat frozen for a bit. *Think this through, Ryder.* There was no coming back from this.

*Okay. I'm gonna do it.*

Taking a deep breath, I placed my fingers on the mouse and clicked the camera icon.

## CHAPTER 5

*Eden*

Needing a few seconds to prepare, I closed my eyes the moment I knew he was about to turn on the camera.

I don't know why I was so afraid to see him. Maybe I was worried his looks would somehow change the way I viewed him. I hated that I'd even had that thought. I didn't want to be unattracted to him physically because I was so very drawn to him in every other way. Shouldn't those be the ways that mattered? I was scared I would somehow feel differently about him, and he deserved better than to be judged on his physical appearance.

"You can open your eyes," he said.

My heart felt like it was pounding out of my chest.

Here goes.

*One, two, three...*

When I saw him right in front of me, my mouth fell open.

*Oh.*

*Oh my.*

*Oh wow.*

Big, glowing eyes. Perfect nose. Stubbled, angular jaw. Full lips. Strong arms. I just kept blinking because I couldn't believe my eyes. He looked like a model or a movie star. A rush of insecurity hit me.

*Is this a joke?*

No, it wasn't.

It was really him.

Ryder.

*Oh my God.*

The lust consuming me made me feel almost guilty. But I was so damn relieved that he was truly as beautiful on the outside as I believed him to be on the inside. He was almost *too beautiful,* if there were such a thing.

He looked nothing like the vague image I'd formed in my head, which was sort of like a silhouette without a clear face but with a brown beard, kind of like a hipster. Not sure why I'd pictured him like that. It was kind of funny how off base I was. This was not what I'd been expecting. Because how could someone so thoughtful, attentive, creative, and considerate be so strikingly handsome that he made me speechless? And it was clear now that his sexy voice absolutely fit him.

"You're..." I hesitated.

"Oh shit." He laughed. "What are you thinking?"

"No. No, no, no. Nothing bad at all. I just don't even know how to articulate it. You're...beautiful, Ryder. Absolutely beautiful."

He let out a breath. "And you're...*handsome*, Eden. Very handsome." His impish grin was so sexy.

I chuckled. "I know beautiful is an odd term for a man, but you are. All this time you've been hiding from me when you're drop-dead gorgeous. Why?"

"You really did think I was ashamed of my looks, huh?"

"Well, I'd be lying if I said that didn't cross my mind. I wondered if there was something you were self-conscious about. That always made me a little sad. But it never mattered to me, because I've been connecting with you on a deeper level."

"I think that's exactly why I didn't want to change things," he said. "Why fix something if it ain't broken?" When I fell silent, he asked, "What are you thinking?"

A nervous energy overtook me. "Nothing. I'm...still just taking you in."

"Okay. Let me know when you're done so I can stop sucking in my abs."

He was surely joking because there wasn't an ounce of fat on his hard body. He was shirtless, his beautiful skin so tan and toned.

In a way, I felt like I didn't know how to act around him anymore. This new insecurity was the only thing I hated about knowing what Ryder looked like. I'd gone through the opposite scenario in my head and felt prepared for how I'd react if he were really unattractive. I knew I would still want him in my life no matter what, because he made me feel good. What I wasn't prepared for was *this* scenario. I hadn't once considered the possibility that I'd be *attracted* to him, that suddenly my desire for him would expand into the physical realm, that I would want to jump through the screen to touch this man.

I kept staring at him. Ryder's hair was a medium brown, cropped and framing his chiseled face perfectly.

His eyes were like light blue crystals. Mesmerizing. And now I'd gone from seeing nothing to feeling as though he could see right through me with them. His jaw was peppered with the perfect amount of scruff. I wanted to feel his stubble against my face and taste his lips.

*Jesus.*

*I may never get over you now, Ryder.*

"Are you alright?" He smiled. "Still with me?"

*His smile.* When he smiled, he had dimples.

"I'm just getting used to you in a new way." *Getting used to these butterflies. They're new.*

I had not felt like this in years. He was so right. Things were much less complicated before I knew what he looked like. I'd told myself nothing could happen between Ryder and me "in real life." Now my attraction to him made what once felt difficult feel impossible.

"Now it makes sense," I finally said.

"She speaks!" he joked. "What do you mean?"

"You mentioned once that you never have a problem getting women, that your problem is connecting with them. You could have any woman you want. I see that now. They must be falling at your feet."

"Ah, yes. So it *would* make perfect sense then that the one girl I'm into right now won't even tell me where she lives." He winked. "Yup, I've got it made. *So* made."

I probably should have laughed at that, but I didn't. It made me sad.

There were some days I wished I could tell him everything there was to know about my life. He knew so much already, just not the most important thing. I didn't know everything about him either, but I knew enough to realize our actual lives were so very different, and we could never work outside of this platform. But that didn't mean I wasn't yearning for more, especially now.

"So...is this the part where I dance?" he asked.

That made me burst into laughter.

"Dance?"

"Yeah, you know, now that you can see me, I can entertain you. We can finally have a fully mutually beneficial relationship."

"Entertain me, huh? Are you hiding any special talents up your sleeve?" God, everything sounded suggestive now. It was hard not to flirt with him.

"Well, none that I can demonstrate from here." He wriggled his brows.

See? He was totally picking up on it.

My cheeks felt hot. The dynamic between us was definitely different now. I was blatantly flirting with him and embarrassed at the same time. It was an awkward mix. In a matter of minutes, I'd developed a massive crush on this man. It felt like I was just meeting him for the first time and had forgotten how to speak.

"Actually, I do have one talent I can demonstrate," he said.

"What is it?"

He leaned in. "Listen closely, okay?"

I giggled in anticipation. "Okay."

Suddenly, I could hear...crickets. Not figurative ones, literal ones. Did he have bugs in his room?

"Crickets! Where are they coming from?"

He didn't answer as the sound continued. Then I saw his lips were moving—barely. It was so subtle that I hadn't noticed, never considering that it was Ryder making the sound.

"You're doing that? It sounds exactly like crickets!"

He stopped and burst out laughing.

"It's frighteningly accurate," I said, giggling into my hand. "That's a pretty cool special talent. How did you even figure out you could do it?"

"One night when I was a kid, I was listening to some crickets outside my bedroom window, and I started mimicking the sound. With practice, I perfected it. On the rare occasion that my father took time off, we'd go camping up in Big Bear, and the crickets would come out at night. I used to get my mother pretty good with it. She could never tell if it was me or them."

My cheeks hurt from smiling. "That's so cute."

"Uh-oh. Cute? That wasn't what I was going for. Maybe I shouldn't have admitted this."

"It *is*. So cute and innocent."

"I may be cute, but I'm definitely not innocent, Eden. Not in any way, shape, or form.

A chill ran down my spine. Now that I knew what he looked like, I knew that had to be true. He was more of a bad boy, which was ironic because he had inherently good parts.

A funny thought occurred to me. "You know what? Between your looks and your weird talent, you could totally be a cam dude. You would be so popular. Women would be emptying their pockets. Men, too."

"Yeah, but then I'd have to whip out my dick. So there's that."

I burst into laughter. "It would be the opposite of the problem I have."

He held out his hands. "Not that I would be ashamed to whip out my dick. I just want to clarify that."

"Of course. I'm sure it's the most beautiful dick I've ever seen," I teased, offering the line we'd previously joked about.

"Aw, shucks...bet you say that to all the guys."

After our laughter dissipated, I resumed staring at him, and he seemed to take notice.

"Hi." He smiled.

I nearly melted. "Hi."

"You want me to let you go to sleep?" he asked.

"I don't think I'm going to be able to sleep now. I'll be thinking of your face. It's gonna keep me up."

He grinned. "A nightmare? Or..."

"No. Far from it."

"Now you know how I feel. Every night. I go to sleep thinking of your face...and your voice. Sometimes other things. But mainly how you make me feel."

Feeling giddy, I was sure I was blushing. I needed to bow out tonight before I made a fool of myself. I needed to go splash some cold water on my face. Actually, make that an ice-cold shower.

"You're right. I'd better go," I said.

He lifted his brow. "Same time tomorrow?"

"Yes. Same time."

Neither one of us was willing to be the first to leave. We sat there staring at each other. Truly addicted, I really didn't want to let him go.

His breathing got heavier, and he looked like he wanted to ask me something. Finally, he released the question he'd been holding. "Are you with anyone, Eden? We haven't talked about it. I've always assumed you're single. Maybe it's none of my business, but I've been really wanting to ask you that question."

I told him the truth. "I'm not with anyone."

He smiled, seeming pleased by my answer, and that was painful for me, because I felt like I'd given him false hope. There was no way we could ever work, and I was starting to think Ryder might be angling for that.

Knowing my limitations didn't stop me from wanting him, though. And that certainly didn't stop my feelings of jealousy. The wheels in my mind had been turning ever since the story he told me earlier tonight.

"Who's the girl who broke your heart?"

Ryder seemed unprepared for my question. Then he let out a long breath. "Her name is Mallory."

"She must be beautiful."

"Not as beautiful as you," he whispered.

I swallowed. He had no idea how much I needed to hear that right now, even though it was foolish of me.

"What happened?" I asked.

He looked down for a bit, then said, "We were together for four years. And I screwed things up pretty badly. It's a long story."

I needed to know. "You cheated on her?"

"No. It was nothing like that."

A sigh of relief escaped me. I'd been really hoping he didn't cheat.

"Do you want to talk about it?"

"Honestly, not right now. I'll tell you what happened someday, though. Okay?"

"Okay."

He cracked a slight smile, and there we were, staring at each other again, both seeming to have forgotten we were supposed to say goodnight.

"Tell me something about you that I don't know, Eden." When I stayed silent, he said, "I know you want to keep certain things private. I get it. But I'm dying here. I need to know more about you."

There was so much he didn't know that I could have told him. But then what? His little fantasy would be over. That's what I was to him, wasn't I? And the fantasy is always better than the reality.

I decided to share something anyway. "I once had dreams of moving to New York. I wanted to work on Broadway. I was always in musicals in high school, and that's what I aspired to do. But when my mother died, I lost my way. It never happened for me."

He looked sad to hear me say that. "It's never too late to pursue your dreams. And you're still young. If there's something you really want, you should go after it."

"I'm not sure what I want anymore. A lot has changed since then. But part of why I love to sing when I'm camming is that it sort of satisfies that itch to perform in front of an audience. Which is ridiculous, I know, because clearly the kind of performing I *actually* do most of the time is nothing like Broadway. And no one is really there to hear me sing." I chuckled. "Well, except you."

His tone was serious. "It's *not* ridiculous. That makes a lot of sense, actually. Thank you for telling me." He paused. "Why do you do the camming? Is it solely money? Or do you like it?"

"It's mostly the money. It would be hard to give that up. It's more than I can make doing practically anything else without a degree."

I'd told him the truth before, that I worked at a restaurant during the day and did the camming at night. Being a cam girl was really exhausting, mentally and physically. While I had the option to do it full time, I couldn't imagine more than a few hours of it a night. So, I sacrificed money for sanity.

There was one thing I'd always wanted to confess to him. This seemed like the right time to do it.

"You were right, Ryder."

"About what?"

"The night you accidentally saw me crying on camera, when I forgot to shut it off after my show—something upsetting did happen in the private chat just before that."

He let out a long breath. "Fuck. I knew it."

I nodded. "The man who'd ordered it asked me to masturbate for him. Everything was normal at the beginning, and about halfway through, out of nowhere, he started spewing things at me, calling me 'dirty whore' and 'nasty slut'. It wasn't the first time something like that had happened to me, but the way he did it, coming on strong so suddenly—like Jekyll and Hyde—really freaked me out. I ended the chat, but it really shook me up."

"Fuck. I'm so sorry you had to go through that."

"I have to assume I'll run into a certain amount of assholes."

His face was red. "Doesn't fucking make it right."

"Anyway, your email coming in that night—it actually made me cry, but not in a bad way. It made me realize that there are good guys out there who won't shun me for what I do to make a living. You restored my faith in humanity, even though you didn't even realize it. I really needed that message."

Ryder looked like he didn't know whether to be happy or sad about what I'd just admitted. "Well, I'm glad I could do that for you. I was genuinely concerned, but I didn't even know you then. I didn't know you would become an important part of my days. I can't ever repay you for bringing me out of the funk I was in."

It felt like I should be thanking *him*. "I didn't do anything."

"You're a good human. You give of yourself to make others happy, whether you realize it or not. I know you're doing the camming for the money. But you put your heart and soul into it. You listen to people's worries. You give real advice that comes from within, and you fucking sing your heart out. You smile when you're not feeling great because you're a consummate professional." Ryder stared off. "I'm sure if I told any of my friends about you, they wouldn't get it. They'd tell me I was crazy. But if this is crazy, I don't want to be normal, because I can't remember a time when I've been happier."

It felt like his soul was speaking to mine in that moment, because I was happier than I'd been in a very long time, too. My life had been dark for a couple of years, and connecting with Ryder had given me something to look forward to each day, something just for me and no one else. He was truly my guilty pleasure.

I knew this was going to end badly. It was only a matter of time before he would become tired of the limitations

I'd set. His real life would interfere, and corresponding with me online would take a backseat to everything else. What we had would fade away. But even knowing that, I wasn't going to be the first to let go.

## CHAPTER 6

*Ryder*

They call it the New York of India. Mumbai was not only the home of Indian filmmaking, it was a mecca of shopping and commerce. Now that I was here, I couldn't believe I'd ever been dreading this trip.

"I'm so happy you had some time to call me," Eden said.

For the past few days, my schedule hadn't allowed for any chatting with my favorite cam girl. But I'd finally found a moment to video-call her.

"I missed you. I had to make time." It was so good to see her face. It was even more beautiful because I hadn't seen her for a while, so it was almost like seeing her for the first time all over again.

"It's been weird not talking to you. Tell me about India."

"India's a whirlwind, but I'm having a blast. This trip has definitely exceeded my expectations so far. I'm in Mumbai, which is the entertainment capital. It's hot as balls here. I have a tour guide, Rupert. On the first day, he came to pick me up on a motorcycle. So that's how I've been getting around—on the back of this little scrawny dude's bike."

"Wow. Be careful."

"Yeah, we got caught in a monsoon the other day. That wasn't really all that fun. The traffic flow is crazy here. I have never seen anything like it. It's gonna be a freaking miracle if I make it home alive."

She cringed. "Oh my God. Don't say that!"

"I'm joking—sort of."

"But you're having a good time?"

"More than I thought I would, yeah. It's been busy during the day, though, which is why I couldn't break away for the past few days to chat. It's been meeting after meeting. And at night, Rupert's been showing me around, taking me to all the hot spots. Yesterday he took me on a walk along the Arabian Sea. It was pretty damn amazing. I thought of you a lot on that walk."

"You did?"

"Yeah, I thought about how you remind me of the ocean, a vast mystery."

Eden was smiling, but it didn't seem genuine. Something was definitely bothering her.

"Everything okay?" I asked.

"Yeah. Everything is fine." She hesitated, then began to remove her hoodie. "Hang on. I'm just gonna take this off. I'm hot." She never complained of being hot. It was usually the opposite; she was always cold.

I watched as she lifted it over her head. Underneath was a T-shirt that I saw for a blink of an eye before she removed it, displaying the tank top underneath. But I'd seen the T-shirt just long enough to catch what was on the front: *Ellerby's Grille Since 1985.*

She'd yanked it off fast, almost as if she didn't want me to see it, but it was too late. I had. And that name would remain etched in my memory.

"When do you get home again?" she asked.

"On the 29th."

"Okay." Her expression still gave off a sullen vibe.

"You seem a little down. Are you sure you're alright?" I asked.

"Yeah. I'm just... It's been stressful the past couple of days. Nothing specific. And not getting to talk to you every night has been a bummer."

I'd missed talking to her, too.

"I know. I'm sorry."

"Don't be. It's not your fault." She adjusted her position on the bed and said, "Tell me more about India."

Even though I suspected she was pretending to be interested in order to change the subject, I entertained her question. "Well, you've heard of the Taj Mahal?"

"Yeah, that big palace?"

"Yup. That's here, too. But it's kind of far from where I am. I was thinking about maybe going to see it before I leave, though. If I do, I'll take some pictures and email them to you."

"I would love that." She grinned.

"Tomorrow Rupert is taking me to his cousin's wedding. Not sure I want to go, but he's being insistent. He says it's gonna be a good time."

"The Indian girls are going to be all over the hot American guy. Watch."

It probably wasn't the right time to admit I'd already been propositioned several times by Bollywood actresses I'd met.

"Does that make you jealous?"

She hesitated before she answered. "Yes."

"Is it wrong that that makes me happy?"

"Just don't fall for anyone while you're there." She didn't look like she was joking. This was the first time Eden had been this vulnerable with me. I was sort of digging it. It was a nice change from me being the jealous asshole because of her camming.

"Are you really worried about that?" I asked.

"I know I'm acting ridiculous." She muttered. "None of this makes any sense."

"Falling for someone half a world away in India makes just about as much sense as falling for a cam girl I'm never allowed to meet."

Despite the tense tone of our conversation, I managed to get one genuine smile out of her before we hung up.

This wedding was like nothing I'd ever seen in my life.

The groom arrived on a freaking chariot with two horses pulling him. The guests were all dancing in front of it as he was led to the bride.

Cars honked their horns, and people chanted.

At the reception, I had a little too much to drink and decided to tell Rupert everything about Eden. To my surprise, he didn't seem shocked in the least. I'd mistakenly taken him to be a little more conservative. But he was totally digging the story of how we met.

"There's an old Indian proverb that my grandmother used to say," he said. "I don't know exactly how it translates into English, but the gist is: if love is not crazy, it's not love."

*Love.* Damn. No, this couldn't be love.

"We're not at the love point. It's not like that." I chuckled. "We haven't even met."

*Right? It isn't love? Fuck if I know what I'm really feeling.*

"Are you sure about that? You just talked about her for a half hour straight, and your eyes lit up more than I've seen since you've been here."

That was a little unsettling to hear. "Really?"

"Yes."

"Well, I'd put it into the obsession category before I'd call it love."

"Whatever you call it, my point is love is *supposed* to feel like this—nonsensical, risky—even if the person makes the least sense logically. It was a crazy way you met her, but who cares? If it's meant to be, she'll come around. She's probably just scared. If the connection you say you have is real, there's not going to be anything either of you can do to stop it."

"You think so, huh?"

"I know so," he said. "But on the off-chance you don't think it's gonna work out, my cousin Saanvi wants to meet you." He pointed to the corner of the room. "She's over there."

When I looked in that direction, a beautiful, dark-haired girl with the hugest brown eyes stared right at me. Had she been looking over here the whole time? I hadn't even noticed.

Wearing a bright aqua-colored sari embellished in gold, she was probably the prettiest girl here and definitely stood out from the crowd. But despite that, I had no desire to talk to her, no desire for even a quick fling while I was in India. It felt like I'd somehow be cheating on Eden. That sucked because I didn't *have her* in the real sense.

During any other time in my life, I might have thought Saanvi was the most beautiful girl in the world. But now that title was reserved for a mystery girl all the way back in Nowhere, USA.

## CHAPTER 7

*Eden*

I'd been counting the days until Ryder got back. His return from India couldn't come soon enough. Tonight was the first night things would be back to "normal"—if you could call our relationship that.

I hated how emotional I'd been the entire time he was away. It was a reminder of how dependent on his company I'd become and how difficult it would be when things inevitably ended.

Every night I wondered if he was hooking up with someone or whether he was realizing there was so much more to life than being home every night and talking to me online. I didn't have the liberty to travel the world and live the way he did. He didn't realize that talking to him was the highlight of my days.

The fact that I was getting so attached to him was troubling. My job was supposed to be a means for survival. But I'd let things get out of control with Ryder and couldn't help myself. I was already so far gone.

During the few times we were able to make our schedules work while he was away, I did a lousy job of hiding my mood. Even though I tried, he'd constantly asked if I was okay. That's how I knew my efforts to hide my true feelings were futile. It amazed me that he was always able to see through them.

Tonight, things were going to work a little differently. We'd be connecting on Skype for the first time since he came home. When he went to India, because our time was limited, we decided to use Skype for our chats instead of the private room. Skype was going to be an easier way to communicate, in general, moving forward, because it allowed more flexibility. He'd sent me a Skype message to expect a call at eleven. I told him I'd decided to take a rare night off, that I needed a break.

My breather consisted of spending the evening listening to music while anticipating his call.

Waiting anxiously, I did my hair and messed with my phone until the computer started ringing.

His face lit up the screen. "Hey, beautiful. I'm back."

"Welcome home."

*Welcome home.* His smile had become like home to *me.* My blood pressure seemed to drop at the sight of him.

"I'm glad to be home. I can't believe you gave yourself a night off. You deserve it. I don't think you've taken a break since I met you."

"I think you're right. I hadn't."

Now that he was right in front of me again, in the same country, I felt so much better. "I missed you. I mean, I know we kept in touch, but it wasn't the same."

"I missed you, too. Like crazy, Eden."

*Like crazy.* That was how all of this felt sometimes.

"Are you still glad you went?"

"You know, I really am. I made a lot of good contacts and learned a shitload about the international market. It was definitely worth the trip."

"Good."

After a brief pause, he asked, "What's wrong? Something's bothering you. It's been that way since I went to India." He frowned. "Is this not working for you anymore?"

"No!" I was quick to say. "Just the opposite."

He seemed really confused. "Can you just be honest with me? Please? Tell me what you're feeling."

"I don't know what I'm feeling... I'm just scared."

"Why?"

*Because I'm not supposed to be falling for you.*

"I was miserable when you were away. I missed not being able to talk to you at night. And that really freaked me out."

"What's wrong with feeling that way?"

"We agreed that our relationship would stay the way it is—virtual—and I feel myself losing control of my feelings for you."

"Then let me come see you. Tell me where you live. I'll be on the next plane."

"I can't."

"Why not?"

"I'm too scared it will change things. I love the way things are now." A tear rolled down my cheek.

"You don't look like you love it. You're in fucking tears."

"This is the way it has to be."

He watched me wipe my eyes before he said, "I am aching for you, Eden. I have never wanted anything more in my entire life than to smell you, touch you, hold you... and a whole lot more than that. I understand that there's something you don't want to tell me, and I've accepted that up until now. But it's damn hard."

This was the first time he'd confessed to a physical need for me. He'd always been the quintessential gentleman—to a fault. I sometimes questioned his attraction to me.

"Why haven't you told me you want me in that way before—physically?" I asked.

"Isn't it obvious how badly I want you?"

"Well, you never...you know, *ask me* for anything. I keep waiting, wanting you to—"

"*Ask* you?" His tone bordered on angry. "Don't you have enough fucking men asking you for sexual favors?"

"But you're different. I—" I stopped myself, knowing full-well what I really wanted to say.

*I feel like I might love you...or something.*

That was the thought in my mind, which I knew was completely crazy.

"What, Eden? What?"

My voice cracked. "You're the only man in the world I *want* to want me."

"I *do* want you...so much." He ran his fingers through his hair, then pulled on it in frustration. "But I don't want to watch you fuck yourself with a dildo—do you get that? I've always been afraid you'd think that's what I want. You're so conditioned to believe that's what men want from you—this one-sided show. I want *you*—all of you, in the flesh. But I promised you a long time ago that I wouldn't push it unless you voluntarily chose to tell me who you are and where you live." He laughed angrily. "You think I don't fucking want you? Why do you think I only let you see me from the waist up?"

I responded with the first thing that came to mind. "I assumed it was because you had a tiny dick."

He burst out laughing. "Wiseass."

"Kidding. I hope you know that."

"I'm *always* hard for you, Eden. Always."

"Really?"

"Yeah. And I'm turning into a jealous prick, too."

"Jealous? I thought I was the jealous one."

"Seriously. Do you have any idea how hard it is to know you go into those private chat rooms every night? It's your job, and I respect that, but I honestly can't even think about it anymore. There have been times when I've considered sending you so much money that you'd never have to work again, but I know you wouldn't take it, because that's the kind of person you are. I can't tell you what to do."

It hurt me to know my job made him so uneasy. "I never realized the camming bothered you like that."

"Fuck yes, it bothers me. I can't stomach you spreading your legs, showing other men your pussy up close while they jerk off. It makes me want to throw up."

My heart started to race—not only from the shock of hearing him admit that, but because knowing my work made him jealous was invigorating. I'd yearned for his jealousy, to know he cared about me in a possessive way.

"Why didn't you say something?" I asked.

"Would it change anything? You should be able to do whatever you want to do with your life. That doesn't mean I have to like it. But I'm man enough to accept it."

"But your feelings *do* matter to me. If something bothers you, I want to know."

"Okay…it bothers me that I can't see you in person. How about that?"

I let out a frustrated breath. "Good one."

We both fell silent. This was probably the closest we'd come to an argument.

After a while, he gestured with his index finger. "Come here."

"Where?"

"Come closer," he whispered. "Press your lips against the screen."

I did as he said and watched as he moved his own face against the camera. He groaned as he kissed me once gently—or pretended to.

Ryder smiled. "I've been wanting to do that for a while."

It wasn't real, but it felt important to me. "Did we just have our first kiss?"

"I've got the smudge marks on the screen to prove it."

I licked my lips as if it were real. "It's not enough."

"It won't ever feel like enough, Eden."

"Then let's do more tonight," I said.

"I meant the whole virtual thing. *This* will never be enough."

"I know. But I want to do more with you *tonight*. You're the first man in a long time whom I've wanted to do things for—not just for you, but for me."

He looked at me so intensely. "Can I ask you a question?"

"Sure."

"When you're...performing, do you get wet? I mean, do you get genuinely excited when you know someone is getting off to your body, or do you fake it?"

"It's funny you ask that; I've actually been studying that very thing."

"Studying it? Is there still space in the class? Because I'd like to sign up."

That made me laugh. "What I mean is—okay, there's a difference between true arousal—enjoyment—versus activation. *Sexual non-concordance* is the term. It's when your body responds to a sexual cue, even if you're not truly liking it. It's a physiological reaction not based on enjoyment but rather on the *idea* of something sexual happening. It's a very detached way of getting aroused."

"So you're saying that because you're thinking about sex, from the mere act of, say, masturbating—even if you're not into it—your body might still react. But there's no actual desire."

"Exactly. It's just a primal, almost automatic reaction. So there's a difference between that and what I feel when I look at you, which is true attraction, true arousal."

"What does it feel like when you look at me?" he asked.

*How can I even describe it?*

"All of my nerve endings are on alert. I'm so incredibly aware of every movement you make, every expression. It's a mixture of excitement and comfort, because I trust you."

He leaned back in his bed. "Tell me more."

"My nipples are always hard when we talk, and sometimes I get wet just being in your presence, even when we're just talking."

"More," he said.

"I feel like the muscles between my legs contract at the sound of your voice. Even before I knew what you looked like, your voice used to make me wet."

He bent his head back and let out a shaky breath. "You're killing me. You know that?"

"Do you desire me?" I asked.

He lifted his head and looked me straight in the eyes. "Eden, from the first night I saw you, I've done nothing but desire you. And it's to the point where I can't be with anyone else in the flesh because I would rather come online and look at you, talk to you, think about you. And that is utterly fucked-up."

"That's how I feel, too. As much as it might seem like I'm loose with sex because of what I do for a living, when it comes to letting someone inside—pun intended—it's not easy for me. I would never be able to do this if those men were actually touching me."

"That's the only consolation for me," he said. "That they *can't* touch you."

My palms started to sweat. "Can I ask you something?"

"Of course," he said.

"You said you haven't wanted to be with anyone in the flesh...but *have* you? Have you had sex with anyone since we've been talking?"

He hesitated. "Not since we've been connecting, no. It's the longest I've ever gone without actual sex."

Relief poured over me, and then I just lost it. "I want you right now," I panted.

The look in his eyes told me he was losing the control he'd worked so hard to keep.

He lay back. "Show me how much."

I slowly lifted my shirt over my head. My breasts felt heavy as they fell out of the fabric. My body buzzed with anticipation at the prospect of getting to see more of him.

"Your nipples are so hard. Is that for me?"

"Yes," I breathed. "I want to see more of you, Ryder."

He gritted his teeth. "You want to see how much I want you? Is that what you've wanted all this time?"

My breathing was heavy. "Yes."

"All you had to do was ask, baby." He unzipped his jeans and repositioned his body so I could see his gloriously hard cock, which glistened with precum at the tip. He pumped slowly up and down as he gritted his teeth and said, "There's not a moment I'm not hard for you. You just can't normally see it."

My eyes were glued to his hand, moving up and down his silky hard shaft. "Now I can."

He began to jerk himself harder. "What do you think?"

Ryder was more well-endowed than most men I'd seen naked.

"That's the most beautiful dick I've ever seen, and I swear to God I'm not lying this time." I laughed.

"Despite the fact that you're laughing, I'll choose to believe you."

"You know it's true. You know you're a beautiful man." I slid my hands down to my waist. "Do you want me to take off my panties?"

"Yes. I want to see how wet you are."

I removed my shorts and took my lace thong off, putting it close to the camera so he could see my wet spot.

"Fuck," he groaned.

"That's *real* arousal."

He let out a guttural sound. "You're killing me right now. I wish I could smell the fabric, wish I could taste you."

I slid my hand down to my clit and rubbed it as I continued to watch him jerking off.

"Spread your legs for me, Eden."

I did as he said. "What else do you want?"

"I want you to do whatever you want. I just want to watch."

"Will you pretend your hand is my pussy?"

"Already there."

As we stopped talking and enjoyed the act of pleasuring ourselves together, I thought about how different this was. I felt much more vulnerable than I did when working because, plain and simple, every part of this was real, not mechanical.

He quickly lost control. There was nothing sexier than the sound of his breath quickening, watching his body shake as he climaxed. I loved watching him come and let myself go at the exact moment he did.

Ryder collapsed against his headboard. "You win."

My chest was rising and falling. "What do I win?"

"You've finally turned me into a perverted cam john whose main objective is my next orgasm—because I'm totally ready to fucking do that again."

"There's nothing wrong with that."

It was the first genuine orgasm I'd ever had on camera, because it didn't feel like I *was* on camera. It was a real sexual experience.

## CHAPTER 8

*Ryder*

It was bound to happen, I guess.

Living in the same town, there was no way I was going to get away with not running into Mallory and her new man at some point. It finally happened when I'd least expected it.

I was in the middle of The Grove, casually strolling with a gelato in hand. It had been a pretty relaxing day. My father was out of the office, and I'd left early to buy a few things after work. The sun was setting. It was one of the rare times I was just chilling by myself.

*Figures.*

My heart dropped. There she was, hand-in-hand with him as they gazed into the storefront window at Barney's.

My first inclination was to run in the opposite direction, but a part of me knew taking advantage of the opportunity fate had put right in front of me was the better option. This wasn't going to be any easier three months down the line. I needed to get it over with so the unknown wouldn't matter anymore. This was the last step to moving on, as far as I was concerned.

Mallory looked good. She had her long, black hair tied up in a ponytail and was wearing white capris and a fitted tank top. My eyes trailed down to the guy's hand on her ass. It made me uncomfortable but didn't upset me the way I thought it might.

I'd seen a photo of this guy, Aaron, before because my friend Benny, the ever-helpful bearer of good news, had screenshot it off of Facebook. I was secretly pleased to see that while he was a good-looking dude, he was much shorter than me in person.

I forced myself to walk right up to them and said, "Hey." It came out almost too enthusiastically.

Mallory flinched, realizing it was me standing before her. "Hi." She swallowed, looking extremely uncomfortable.

I immediately turned to the guy. "You must be Aaron."

He nodded. "Yeah."

I held my hand out. "I'm—"

"I know who you are," he said as he took my hand.

*Of course.* In Mallory's world, I was infamous—in the book of her life, probably the biggest antagonist. I was sure she'd filled him in on all of the details of our demise, a great example of all of the things *not* to do. Still, I'd loved her. I wanted her to have closure, and this was me giving it to her.

I sucked up my pride. "Hey, I hear congratulations are in order."

She cleared her throat. "Yeah. We...we got engaged." Rather than stick her hand out like most women might to display an engagement ring, she moved her hand behind her as if to hide it from me.

*Interesting.* Not sure if it meant anything, but I noticed.

It was weird. I'd always imagined this moment as worse than it actually was. As uncomfortable as it may have been to chat with Mallory and her fiancé, I did want her to be happy. My issues with how our relationship ended had more to do with my own guilt than anything.

"I want you to know I wish you the best. I'm really glad I ran into you today because I probably wouldn't have made a point to tell you that otherwise."

A part of me still loved her. I always would.

Her eyes seared into mine. "Thank you, Ryder. That does mean a lot to me."

I pursed my lips and nodded a few times before I said, "Well, I'll let you guys go."

Mallory's stare lingered on me, her eyes masking so many unsaid words. I knew if Aaron weren't standing right there, she might have unleashed some of them.

I wondered if this was how things would always be with us—just a blur of weird emotions and tension—or if someday we would be able to walk by each other and wave. Maybe someday the past would be in the past, but the look on her face gave me the impression that right now the past was still very much in the present.

I held my hand up. "Bye."

"Bye," she said. Aaron simply nodded.

As I walked away, I felt a sense of peace. Facing her had been the last step in ridding myself of the negative energy I'd been carrying around. Things may not have wrapped up neatly in a bow with us, but at least I faced her.

I knew, though, that a good portion of my peace really came from Eden, as fucked-up as that was. She'd come along at a time when I really needed a distraction. And what she'd given me was more than that. I'd thought I was dead inside until she helped awaken things again. She might not have wanted to fully reveal herself to me, but I was certain she cared. And that feeling of being truly cared for was something only a few people in my life had given me.

As the days went on, though, I'd begun to wonder more and more about who Eden really was, and what she was hiding from me. I didn't think I could last much longer like this.

The situation was slowly breaking me.

That night, I was more determined than ever to convince Eden to take our relationship to the next level. The conversation I planned to have with her kept playing in my head. I'd give her all the time she needed, as long she would agree that someday we could see each other. Maybe I needed to flat out give her an ultimatum, tell her I couldn't be celibate forever, that I needed release with an actual woman in the flesh. That wasn't exactly a lie. I had a little patience left in that area, but what if I made her believe I didn't? If she felt threatened, would she be more likely to agree to meet me?

When it was almost time for our private midnight chat, I still wasn't sure how I was going to approach things. I was revved up, so I would wing it.

Connecting into Skype, I noticed Eden was offline. *Hmm.*

That was strange. She normally logged on a little early, before her show had even ended.

As much as I tried to stay off the cam-girl site, I went over there now to see if she was still in the middle of a show. When I called up her page, it indicated that Montana Lane was offline. She was supposed to have been working.

A feeling of dread developed in the pit of my stomach. It was unlike her to be offline and not say anything to me.

Sweat beaded on my forehead. With each second that passed, I became more freaked out. This didn't feel right.

I dialed her over and over on Skype with no answer.

After that, I sent a message to her email account.

An hour went by with no response.

I then became certain something was wrong.

It was one thing if she had dumped me. That, I could probably get over—eventually. What I couldn't get over was the thought that something had happened to her. That idea was literally making me sick.

The wheels in my head were turning. What if one of those sick fucks found her and hurt her? What if a car hit her and she was dead? I would have no way of knowing.

When two hours had passed and there was still no response, my fear turned to full-fledged panic.

There was no way I was going to sleep tonight.

*Think. Think. Think.*

Suddenly, it came to me: the restaurant on her T-shirt.

When I was in India, she'd revealed something from her "real life." I never called her out on it, but I sure as hell had made a note of the name.

85

*Ellerby's Grille Since 1985.*

I knew she worked at a restaurant during the day—that was one of the few bits of information she'd given me—so logic told me there was a good chance Ellerby's was it.

With my heart pounding, I opened my laptop and typed the name into Google.

There was only one result with that exact name. A website for the restaurant popped up. I clicked on the *About Us* tab and took note of the address.

*St. George, Utah.*

The realization stopped me in my tracks. It felt like I was violating her trust.

Utah. That wasn't far. Maybe a six-hour drive?

*You're in Utah?*

I didn't know for sure. But it felt possible.

I scoured the website for any sign of her. It was a typical American bar and grill that served pub food and drinks. There were photos of platters—featuring close-ups of hamburgers, fries, and chicken fingers—and glasses of draft beer. My heart nearly skipped a beat when I came across photos of the staff in action. Some of them were wearing the same blue T-shirt I'd seen on Eden. Upon closer examination, none of them were her, though.

I'd gone through every page and found no sign of her. The only valuable information I had to go on was the location.

The question was...what was I going to do with it?

I managed to get about an hour of sleep. The first thing I did upon waking was check my email. There was still no response from her. I went to her camming page. Relief washed over me to see the preview photo was still there, even though it indicated she was offline. At least she hadn't deleted her account, hadn't disappeared off the face of the Earth altogether.

My ego taunted me, asking me why I couldn't figure out that I'd been dumped and move on. *Can't you take a hint?* But then I'd see her eyes in my head, the ones always filled with emotion when she looked at me. She'd led me to believe she cared for me. My gut told me Eden would never leave me high and dry, that she cared enough not to do something like that. And that's what made me worry. Because the only explanation in that case was that she was in some kind of trouble.

I didn't feel like I could breathe until I knew she was okay.

What if I went to Utah and that restaurant wasn't even her place of employment? Then what? Maybe she'd just visited there once. Jesus, what if her name wasn't really Eden? I had nothing to go on but a damn first name that might or might not have been real.

I paced in my bedroom, practically ripping the hair out of my head. A scream of frustration escaped me. It was a sound I didn't recognize.

A few seconds later, I heard footsteps.

"*Mijo*, is everything okay?"

Apparently, Lorena had heard my roar. She always arrived at the ass crack of dawn and had come storming up the stairs with a broom in her hand.

"Come in," I said.

"What's wrong?" she asked, opening the door.

Lorena was going to think I was fucking nuts. But that had never stopped me from unloading on her before. She was a straight shooter. In many ways, I needed her frank advice more than ever in this moment, because I was seriously considering jumping on a plane right now.

"I need to ask you something. And I need you to take it seriously, even though it involves something you have very strong preconceived notions about."

Her eyes widened. "Did you take drugs?"

I shook my head. "No. It has to do with the webcam girl I told you about before."

"The nudie model?"

I hated that she called her that. "Yes."

"Did you get her pregnant?"

"Uh...that's physically impossible. We've never met in person."

"That's true. What happened?"

"She's missing."

"Missing? How can she be missing if she's never here?"

"She still exists."

"Yeah. But you know what I mean. She's not with you. So how do you know she's missing?"

"She didn't show up last night for our chat, and I feel like something's wrong. That's the first time something like that has ever happened."

"Maybe she just needed a break from showing her *tetas* for one night."

I rolled my eyes. "Our relationship has evolved to much more than showing her *tetas*. It was never about that with us. I told you that. I can't even begin to explain it to you, Lorena. I know how nuts this all seems, but...a lot has happened in a short amount of time with her. I feel like I know her." My voice cracked. "Something isn't right."

She finally seemed to be getting that I was dead fucking serious because the expression on her face changed. There was no longer a hint of amusement. "Okay..." She leaned her broom against the wall and took a seat on my bed.

I let out a deep breath, relieved that she was taking me seriously. "We've chatted almost every night for weeks. She's cried in front of me. We've gotten to know each other very well, even if we've kept certain information private. We've gotten close—shared a lot of intimate things. And it's not like her to do something like this, to just *not* contact me. I'm worried sick that something bad happened to her."

"You don't know where she lives?"

I sighed. "No, I don't. But here's the thing, I accidentally figured out the place she might work. She told me she waitresses during the day. The name of this restaurant was on one of her T-shirts once. It's all I have to go on. I could go there and try to find her. But she might get freaked out, and then I could—"

She finished my sentence. "Lose her? You don't even *have* her."

That realization was eye opening. "That's true."

Lorena crossed her arms. "So, what are you asking me? If I think you should go?"

"Yeah, that's exactly what I'm asking."

"Are you gonna be able to sleep at night if you don't?"

I thought about it for a split second. "No."

"Then you don't need me to tell you what to do."

*Shit.*

A part of me had been hoping she would knock some sense into me.

*Am I really doing this?*

"I'm about to get on a plane to Utah, and I don't even know if she's there."

She scratched her chin. "Utah. Hmm..."

My brow furrowed. "Yeah. Utah. Why? What are you thinking?"

"Maybe she's a polygamist."

"What?"

"Have you ever watched *Big Love*? *Sister Wives*? There are a lot of polygamists in Utah. Maybe that's why she won't tell you who she is. Maybe she's married with sister wives. And doing this in secret."

That sounded ludicrous to me. "Oh, okay. I didn't realize everyone who lived in Utah was automatically a polygamist." I pulled my hair and shouted, "She's not a polygamist!"

*At least, not that I know of.*

*Jesus. How would I even know?*

*She said she wasn't married.*

*God, what the fuck do I REALLY know? Nothing!*

"Tell me the truth. Am I acting fucking crazy, Lorena?"

"No, *mijo*. You're love sick. Maybe obsessed—I don't know. And even though I don't approve of this whole situation, I can see how upset you are. It's the same look you had when that Mallory broke up with you. I haven't seen it since. You won't rest until you know. So, go and get your answer so you can move on with your life."

## CHAPTER 9

*Ryder*

With one connecting flight, St. George, Utah, was less than four hours of travel time from Los Angeles. I flew from L.A. to Vegas, and after a quick layover in Sin City, I landed at my destination. This part of Utah was also only a few miles from the Arizona border.

The Grand Canyon wasn't that far from here. If this were a recreational visit, I might have considered venturing out to see it. But this visit was far from recreational. What was it? Investigational? Even as I soaked in the dry heat outside of the airport, I was no more certain that I was making the right decision.

Wasn't this an invasion of her privacy?

After picking up my rented Audi, I punched the address for Ellerby's into my GPS and hit the road. It was approximately twenty minutes from the airport. I'd booked a hotel in town that I'd check in to later, depending on how things went.

Surrounded by canyons, I couldn't help but think a sky view of all the red rocks would be amazing.

I'd read up a little bit about the area while I was on the plane. Apparently, the sun shines here most days. The city was named for the nineteenth-century Latter-day Saints' church apostle George A. Smith. It wasn't all Mormons who inhabited the area, though. There was a mix of cultures. St. George connected three geographical regions: the Mojave Desert on the west-southwest side to California, the Colorado Plateau and its four national parks, and The Great Basin to the north. Seemed like a place I'd love to visit again sometime when I wasn't busy being a stalker.

Thirty minutes later, I finally pulled up to Ellerby's and found a parking spot across the street. It was four in the afternoon. I had no idea if Eden even worked at this place, let alone what her hours were. She did tell me she worked during the early part of the day, which would make it likely she wasn't even on shift.

After an hour of sitting across the street, observing people coming and going, I forced myself out of the car and entered the restaurant.

A man stood at the hostess station and grabbed a menu as he saw me approaching.

I forced my words out, trying to seem casual. "Is Eden here?"

"Eden doesn't work on Mondays. She's in tomorrow."

My heart thundered through my chest as I processed his response. Eden was her real name. Eden *did* work here. Eden wasn't dead—or at least they hadn't been notified of it.

"What time does she get here?"

"She does the lunch shift. So, like, eleven in the morning."

I swallowed. "Thank you."

Taking a deep breath, I made my way back outside.

*Alright. Calm down. You have until tomorrow to freak the fuck out.*

I got back in the Audi and headed to the hotel.

The first thing I did after checking in to my room was log in to my email to see if she'd responded. There was nothing. Then I ventured over to the camming website to make sure her profile was still there. It was, although it again showed her as offline.

Now that I knew she was expected in to work tomorrow, I felt more like she might have had a change of heart about continuing to interact with me. But then I reminded myself that she hadn't been online *at all*, not even for her show. So that told me something was wrong. The camming was her livelihood.

Tomorrow would be telling. I'd show up at the restaurant early so I could see whether she entered the building. And then I would wing it. Whether that meant going inside and confronting her or waiting for her to get off shift so I could follow her, I didn't know yet.

Maybe I would just make sure she was okay and leave. I was still so fucking confused. I really didn't want to bother her if she didn't want to see me, but the need to confirm that she was okay trumped all. Could I ensure she was okay without making my presence known? Would it be enough for me to just confirm she was alive? My gut told me I wouldn't be able to rest unless I knew more. And that meant confronting her.

I'd never been so damn nervous about anything in my entire life.

The next morning, I pulled up to Ellerby's at 9AM. I didn't know what time someone would show up for an 11AM shift, but I figured nine was early enough that I wouldn't miss her.

The street was pretty desolate, just a few brick buildings and the restaurant. There weren't a lot of other businesses around, and Ellerby's wasn't even open yet.

It was a long, slow morning, but nothing could have prepared me for the shock to the heart I felt when at approximately 10:45, I saw the silhouette of a woman approaching in the distance. As she got closer, I recognized her willowy body and long, wispy hair that was the color of sand.

*It was her.*

*My heart.* It was beating out of my chest.

From where I was parked, I couldn't make out her facial features. That wasn't necessary. It was Eden. There was no doubt anymore. It was her, and she was clearly fine.

The empty feeling in my stomach intensified after she disappeared into the restaurant.

*Now what?*

*Do I just go home?*

*Do I go in there and confront her?*

The sensible part of my brain told me to turn around and head straight for the airport. She was alive. Wasn't that good enough?

For shits and giggles, I decided to check my email from my phone. That's when I realized I had received a message earlier in the morning that would change the entire course of my day.

*Ryder,*

*I am so terribly sorry for not responding to your messages and for not being around the past couple of days. I had a family emergency and couldn't be online. My head wasn't on straight. I just saw your email and freaked out a little that you were worried about me. I am fine. I can't apologize enough for not reaching out. There is no excuse. I just lost my way for a bit Will you be online tonight? I really miss you.*

*Eden*

I just kept staring at it, now doubting my knee-jerk reaction in coming out here.

I could take this information and run back home with it as if nothing ever happened, or I could take a chance and let her know I was here.

By the way my heart was beating, I knew there was no way I was going home to L.A. without letting her see me. I just needed some time to figure out how I was going to approach this.

If I waited for her to get out of work, I could follow her and see if that provided me with any clues as to what she might be hiding from me. It felt like I needed more information before I just dropped this bomb on her.

I couldn't risk leaving even to grab lunch, because without the Ellerby's connection, I had no information to go on. I needed to be able to follow her home.

Four hours later, I was in the middle of a daydream when the sight of her exiting the building lit a fire under my ass.

Jumping up, I turned on the ignition and began driving slowly along the path she was walking.

There were no other cars in sight, and Eden was headed to her destination by foot. My biggest problem would be if she switched to public transportation. Were there buses or trains around here? I needed to keep her within my line of sight or I would lose her.

I followed her for nearly ten minutes. Damn, did she not have a car? Where was she going that she had to walk so far?

She turned a corner, and I continued to keep my distance so she wouldn't notice a car following her every move.

Eden suddenly stopped in front of a large, brick building. There were a few other people waiting outside.

I parked about a block away from her.

She looked down at her hands, seeming to be examining her fingernails as she casually waited.

*Who or what is she waiting for?*

My heart was racing now. I had to take off my jacket because I was burning up.

Even though I wanted more time to figure her life out, this seemed like my opportunity. Was it ever going to get easier to reveal myself, to let her know I'd come here without her permission? There she was, only feet away from me. Could I stand to spend the rest of the day watching her like a stalker, only to have to potentially face her later anyway? I'd end up in the same predicament I was in right now.

The answer seemed obvious: rip the Band-Aid off. The problem was finding the strength to *move* from point A to point B. It seemed like a simple step, but it somehow felt like Eden was miles away. I gave myself a mental kick in the ass and exited my car.

With one foot in front of the other, I moved toward where she was standing. Her back was to me.

As I inched closer, the voice in my head grew louder and louder.

*Turn around and go home.*

*This is a mistake.*

*Are you fucking insane?*

But I couldn't turn back now.

I stopped a few feet behind her. The handful of people around us were oblivious to my mental anguish. Her hair blew in the breeze, the sunshine bringing out specks of gold in her tresses. It felt surreal to see her in the flesh. She was everything I'd imagined. Eden had a graceful stance and was a bit shorter than I'd previously thought. Her hair had to be almost down to her ass. She was so close that I could smell her.

*Beautiful girl, please don't hate me for this.*

There wasn't going to be an easy way to do it. I took a deep breath and forced myself to call out her name.

"Eden."

Her body shook at the sound of my voice. She turned around, and I could see the transformation from shock to pure terror on her face.

Eden clutched her chest. Her face turned red as she took a few steps back and coughed out, "Ryder..."

A mix of emotions ran through me as I stood still: guilt for having put her in this position and an intense longing, because now that I'd seen her in person, right in front of me, what felt like a new fire had been ignited inside. It felt inextinguishable. How could I walk away now?

Her mouth was trembling. I wanted to kiss it so badly. This wasn't the kind of introduction I'd been hoping for with her. But it was to be expected.

She couldn't find the words. "What...how..."

"Can I explain?"

Eden nodded, seeming extremely nervous as she looked over at the door to the building.

"It's as simple as...you disappeared. I freaked out that something bad had happened to you. I used the one piece of information I had about your whereabouts to find you. It worked."

She licked her lips. "What was it?"

"The T-shirt you wore that one time with Ellerby's on it."

Eden nodded, like she already knew she'd fucked up by displaying that, albeit briefly.

"I made a mental note of the name," I continued. "I never intended to invade your privacy. I took a chance and came out here because I've grown to care a lot about you, and I needed to know you're okay. So please don't hate me for doing this."

"I don't hate you," she whispered. She closed her eyes. *Thank God.*

Eden looked defeated, like all of the work she'd done to hide whatever she was keeping from me had been in vain.

Her attention suddenly turned toward the front entrance to the building as we both fell silent. It became clear what was happening as I spotted a woman walking out, holding the hand of a boy who looked about ten or eleven. They walked straight toward Eden.

All of the puzzle pieces were coming together in my brain.

This was a school.

She was picking someone up.

Then it hit me.

*How could you be so stupid, Ryder?*

My heart felt heavy.

*This is her kid?*

*Is this what she's been hiding all along?*

The woman let go of the boy's hand and placed it in Eden's.

"He had a good day. The nurse checked in on him. I think you made a good choice in sending him in today."

Eden's voice was shaky. "Glad to hear that. Thank you."

"I hope you have a good night." The woman bent down. "Bye, Ollie."

*Ollie.*

The boy waved. "Bye." He had what looked like stitches on his forehead.

Eden looked at me as I stood there, dumbfounded.

Suddenly, the boy said, "Who's here?"

I noticed he wasn't looking at her as he spoke, just sort of staring blankly out toward the street. He wasn't looking at me, either.

She placed her hand on his shoulder. "You can sense someone, huh?"

"You're not moving, and I can smell someone else."

My stomach sank as I quietly observed him. A second later, I saw a sign I hadn't noticed before.

*St. George School for the Blind.*

## CHAPTER 10

# *Eden*

Ryder looked over at the sign on the front of the school. He was slowly putting two and two together.

I think I was still in shock. I couldn't even move. Poor Ollie was probably so confused. I'd forgotten I didn't have to say anything; he could tell just from my movement—or lack thereof—that something was off.

But I still couldn't move. Having Ryder here was almost too much to bear. Smelling his scent, recognizing the sheer power of his height, the penetration of his stare.

*Why did you have to come, Ryder?*

I cleared my throat. "Ollie, my friend is here. His name is Ryder." I looked into Ryder's beautiful baby blues. "This is my little brother Ollie."

The look of relief on Ryder's face was palpable. I knew he'd likely assumed Ollie was my son. Even though he was my sibling, he might as well have been my child. I'd had the full responsibility of raising him since our mother died in a car accident.

"Your brother?"

I placed my hand on Ollie's shoulder. "Yes, my little brother."

Ryder finally approached us, bending a bit with his hands resting on his thighs. "Hey, Ollie."

"Hi."

Ryder flashed a beautiful smile. "You smelled me before I could introduce myself. Do I smell bad or something?"

It was just the opposite. Ryder smelled so very good, like how California would smell if you bottled it up and sold it as a fragrance. It was a masculine scent, like sandalwood and leather with a hint of ocean—just how I'd imagined him to smell. Maybe even better.

"Not really," Ollie said.

"*Not really*. Okay, that leaves a little room for doubt. Good to know. Note to self—must take shower."

I couldn't help but smile. Ryder straightened up and met my eyes again.

It was hard to look at him, because doing so just felt... intense. I knew I had a lot of explaining to do. He would want to know why I never told him I had a brother, let alone one I cared for as if he were my own child. He might not understand my reasoning for keeping it from him.

Even though I felt like maybe I shouldn't give in to Ryder being here, I couldn't just go home and leave him standing here. He'd come all this way. Before I had a chance to say anything, Ollie broke the ice.

"Are we just gonna stand here, or are we gonna go home? I'm hungry. You comin,' Ryder?"

Ryder continued looking into my eyes. "That's up to your sister."

Here it was. This was the moment when I either coldly told him to go back to California, or I invited him home with us. One thing I was finding, it was far harder to resist this man in person than from afar.

"We only live a few blocks down the road," I said.

That wasn't exactly a direct invitation, but it was me agreeing to Ryder coming home with us.

He pointed back with this thumb. "My car's right there. I can drive us."

"Okay," I said, leading Ollie by the hand.

We walked over to Ryder's car. It was really nice for what I assumed to be a rental.

Before he started the engine, Ryder paused and looked at me. I could practically hear all of the silent questions in his head.

With Ollie here, I knew he wasn't going to get into it too much with me. That gave me some time to think about how I was going to explain everything.

As we drove along, I directed him. "You just take your first left up there. We're gonna be the last house on the right."

Ryder parked in our driveway, then followed me into the house as Ollie held my hand. I didn't always have to hold onto my brother. Despite the fact that he couldn't see, he knew his way into the house pretty well, but given his recent injury, I was being extra cautious. Even though the doctors had confirmed that nothing happened to his brain when he fell, I was still paranoid.

I watched as Ollie walked to his room. He was safe in there because I kept it pretty empty, nothing sharp or anything that could potentially harm him. He always got a little time after school to veg out before he had to do his homework.

When he was safely out of earshot, I just started talking so Ryder didn't have to initiate the conversation.

"I've been taking care of him ever since my mother died. We don't have the same father. Ollie's dad was a young tourist my mother had a fling with over a decade ago. He was her midlife crisis. The guy left to go back to Costa Rica before Mom found out she was pregnant. He didn't want anything to do with Ollie when she told him, so his dad has never been in his life."

Ryder took a few steps toward me. "Why didn't you tell me any of this? Did you think it would matter to me?"

"No," I insisted. "I'm not ashamed of my brother. I want to make that very clear. And it's not that I thought you would judge me for having to take care of him. But what good would telling you have done? It would have completely ruined whatever fantasy you had in your head about my ability to be what first attracted you to me—that carefree girl. My life is not that way, Ryder. Ollie is my *entire* life. The camming happens at night because that's when he's sleeping. He obviously doesn't know about it, doesn't know that's how I support us." I sucked in a breath. "And the past couple of days, you didn't hear from me because he fell and hit his head the one moment I wasn't paying attention to him. I took him to the emergency room. He needed stitches and some neurological testing. He's fine, but I freaked out a little because I thought it was going to be more serious than it was. I blamed myself. That type of thing is my reality. I can't ever travel or move to California or be the type of girl a man like you needs.

Ollie's school is here, as is the house he's familiar with. Everything he needs is here.

I took a deep breath. "But I couldn't come out and tell you what my life is really like because I didn't want to lose the fantasy we had either. Somehow it seemed *not* telling you would prolong everything."

Ryder looked down at the ground. He was clearly trying to process what I'd just thrown at him. His voice was low. "I get it. And I can't begin to imagine what your life is like."

"Those stitches on his head? That's my reality." I pointed over to the corner of my kitchen. "That sink full of dishes? That's my reality. That spot up there from the leaky ceiling? That's my reality—and it's not pretty, Ryder."

"No, it's not." He moved in and wrapped both of his hands around my cheeks. "It's beautiful," he whispered. "So beautiful. So different from anything I ever imagined. And I'd imagined some ominous things, Eden. Fucked-up things. But I still wanted to meet you. Nothing could take that need away."

He kept his hands around my face, and I shut my eyes to relish how good it felt to be touched by him. When I opened them, he was looking at me so intensely it gave me chills. His face had inched closer to mine when Ollie's voice interrupted, causing me to flinch.

"Can I have a Fruit Roll-Up, Eden?"

My breathing was heavy as I came down from the anticipation of a kiss that didn't happen.

"Hang on," I yelled over before walking to the closet to grab him a snack. Still so on edge, I fumbled with the box before opening the packaging and bringing the Roll-Up to his room.

When I came back, Ryder was still standing there, looking so tall and handsome with his hands in his pockets. I didn't know what to do with him. His presence was overpowering. It was so surreal to have him here in my little kitchen.

"How could I not have seen through it?" he said. "How could I not know that you're struggling? Am I that blind?" He looked down at his feet and swore under his breath. "Fuck. I didn't mean to use that term." He looked distraught.

I smiled. "It's okay. Ollie and I aren't sensitive."

He reached his hand out for mine.

I took it and looped my fingers through his. "I never feel like I'm struggling when I'm spending time with you. You've been my escape. You say you should've sensed something, but you couldn't have seen through anything because I'm so happy when I'm around you—albeit virtually." I squeezed his hand. "And I'm really sorry for worrying you when I was MIA. I just lost it when he got hurt and really fell into a depression."

"What caused his injury?"

I braced as I recalled it. "I'd fallen asleep on the couch. He didn't want to wake me. He knows I keep some of our food that I buy in bulk down in the basement. He tried to get his own snack and fell down the stairs. I've never been so scared in my life."

"I'm just glad you're both okay. My mind was all over the place thinking someone hurt you or you'd gone missing. All kinds of crazy shit went through my head."

"I'm a mess, but I'm alive and okay." I squeezed his hand, yearning for more. "God, I can't believe you're here. You're real."

As we stared at each other, I kept thinking he was going to kiss me, but he held back. Then he asked the strangest question.

"Do you like chicken pot pie?"

*What?* I chuckled. "I haven't had it in years, but yeah. I do. Why?"

"Because it's what I know how to cook, and I'm making it for you tonight while you relax with a glass of wine."

"You don't have to do that."

"I want to. Please let me cook for you and Ollie."

"I didn't know you could cook."

"I really can't."

"Then why make chicken pot pie?"

"My mother. It was all she ever knew how to cook. We always had a chef, so she rarely spent time in the kitchen. But when she did, she'd make that. One day when I was a little kid, I asked her to let me help her. And to this day, it's all I know how to make."

"That's so sweet."

"Do you think Ollie will like it?"

"He'll eat anything. Literally. He loves food."

"Okay. Good. So...you can freak out about all the stresses of life tomorrow. You can also freak out about what my being here means tomorrow. Tonight, it's chicken pot pie."

**CHAPTER 11**

## Ryder

Eden gave me directions to the nearest supermarket. It felt completely surreal to be here, picking out the ingredients to make her the only thing I could cook. My mind wasn't even focusing on what I needed to buy; it was too busy trying to absorb everything.

I looked out through the sliding glass doors of the market to the mountains in the distance. I was in freaking Utah, about to cook for Eden and her brother. *I am here with Eden.* What a difference a day makes.

My feelings could best be described as a mix of anxiety and relief. Relief that there was no sinister reason she was hiding her life from me. And anxiety because in a sense, she was right about everything. Eden had a ton of responsibility—too much for one twenty-four-year-old girl. And that was something I had to consider. There was no room for games. I had to tread lightly.

I pushed the cart around in a daze. This was the first time in a long time that I'd had no clue what the next hours would bring. But I wasn't ready to get back on a plane to California. My father was gonna have my head for taking time off from work when things were busy. But I just didn't care.

I took my phone out of my pocket and dialed my dad's cell.

He picked up after a few rings. "Son, where have you been? They told me you were taking a couple of days off, but no one seems to know where the hell you are."

I was glad to see Lorena had kept my secret. Not that I'd doubted she would. I didn't want anyone to know what I was up to. I decided to tell my father a version of the truth.

Leaning into my cart, I moved it along slowly while I talked. "Yeah. I know. I didn't exactly tell anyone."

"So, where are you? I need you here."

"Uh...I'm gonna be gone for probably about a week."

"A week? Are you in some kind of trouble?"

"No, no, nothing like that. I'm in Utah, actually."

"Utah? What the hell is in Utah?"

"I'm in St. George visiting a friend."

"A friend?"

"Yes."

"Who?"

I hesitated. "Her name is Eden."

My father blew a breath into the phone. "With the secretive way you've been acting, I thought you were going to tell me *his* name was Ed."

I couldn't help but laugh. "No. Still hetero as far as I know—not that there's anything wrong with the opposite. But I like women...a lot."

*Especially this woman.*

"Where did you meet this person that you're all the way in Utah?"

*How exactly do I explain?*

"Online," I said.

*Well, that's technically true.*

"I don't need to tell you to be careful. You're a smart guy. I'm sure you know there are a lot of opportunistic people out there who would love a piece of—"

"Dad, I know. She didn't even know what I did for a living when we first met. It's not about that, okay? When I told her your name once, she had never heard of you. I'm just enjoying her company right now. I'll let you know when I'm coming back."

"It better not be more than a week. I need you here."

I couldn't commit to anything because I had no clue how I was going to feel one moment to the next. "I'll keep you posted."

"Son...just watch yourself."

"Thanks for your concern. I'll be back soon," I said before hanging up.

Flanked by two cactus trees, Eden's house was one level and small. Inside it was cozy and warm—the total opposite of the huge, over-the-top mansions I was used to in L.A. This was the type of house that made you feel like you were home the moment you stepped into it. Well, maybe it was the people, not the house. I was used to stepping into echoey silence.

When I walked in the door, Ollie was sitting in the kitchen with his sister.

"Ryder's back," he said.

I put the paper bag down on the counter. "You smell me again or something?"

"No, it's your heavy foot. I could hear it. I bet you have giant feet."

That made me laugh. "Ah...so you sayin' I'm like Bigfoot?"

"Yeah." He giggled.

Eden smiled over at us as she unloaded the dishwasher. She looked down. "Come to think of it, Ryder does have big feet. You're very perceptive, Ollie." She winked at me, and I definitely felt it below the belt.

*Fuck.*

"You know what that means," Ollie said.

Eden and I both froze and turned to him at the same time.

Her brow lifted. "What exactly is that supposed to mean, Ollie?"

"It means he has really big socks, too."

The two of us collectively sighed.

"So...so far, I have big feet and I smell," I joked. "Way to keep making a good first impression."

"My sister told me you were coming back for dinner, so I was sort of expecting you anyway. It wasn't *just* your big feet."

"Ah, okay." I sat down across from him at the table and took some time to observe him. Ollie kept his eyes mostly closed. I had so many questions, ones that weren't exactly appropriate to ask. Like, could he see me at all, or was he totally blind?

Eden wiped down a plate. "Ollie, Ryder works in Hollywood with all of the movie stars."

Damn, that got his attention. The kid whipped his head in my direction. "Do you know Gilbert Gottfried?"

"No, actually, I don't."

"He was the voice of the parrot in *Aladdin* and the duck in the AFLAC commercial." Ollie mimicked the duck, "Aflac!"

"Sounds to me like he's pretty good at playing birds, then."

"He's so much more than a bird. He's really funny."

Eden looked over at me. "Ollie got in trouble for listening to one of his standup acts on the iPad that wasn't very age appropriate."

"Uh-oh." I laughed.

"Yeah. He's so funny, though. It was worth getting in trouble."

This kid definitely had a mischievous side. He reminded me a lot of myself when I was younger, always trying to get into things I wasn't supposed to.

Eden explained, "Because Ollie can't see, he's drawn to really strong voices, and I guess Gilbert fits the bill."

"I thought I knew all the cool people, too. But apparently not," I said.

Ollie shrugged. "Guess not."

My gaze wandered over to Eden, who was now leaning against the counter, crossing her arms. Our eyes locked, and it hit me that it was probably a good thing Ollie couldn't see me, because it was inevitable that I would get a hard-on for his sister at some point tonight.

I could get hard just looking at her. I couldn't remember ever having this kind of physical need for anyone before. The past several weeks had been like one long episode of foreplay. Now that I was near her, I couldn't help being so physically turned on, even though she wasn't doing anything specific to incite that. She didn't have to do anything except exist.

My brain was telling my dick to slow the fuck down, that we had to back up several miles now that we knew what was really happening here. But he wasn't quite getting the message.

I snapped myself out of my gawking. "Alright. Are you ready for me to take over the kitchen? Chicken pot pie-making is serious business. You need to steer clear, because I'm gonna need all this counter space."

Eden smiled. "Well, it's not every day we have someone cooking for us, so we will gladly steer clear. Right, Ollie?"

"Yeah, no one's cooked for us since Ethan."

*Ethan?*

*Who the fuck is Ethan?*

"Oh yeah?" Looking over at Eden, I crossed my arms over my chest. "Who's Ethan?"

Ollie laughed. "I bet you thought I said 'Eden' at first, right? Ethan sounds like Eden."

"Yeah...sure does," I said, still curious as to who the heck Ethan was.

"Ethan stopped coming around a long time ago," he said.

"Ethan is my ex-boyfriend," Eden admitted.

"I see." Not wanting to ask in front of Ollie, I didn't pry about what had happened to Ethan. If she wanted to tell me, she would. But right now, wherever *Ethan* was, I was glad he was gone.

I'd picked up a bottle of white while I was out. I remembered she'd once told me she loved pinot grigio. I poured Eden a glass so she could relax while I cooked.

Eden and Ollie sat at the table while I prepared the ingredients. I even made the crust from scratch, because that's how my mother taught me to do it. It took a little bit of time, but I always thought it was worth it.

We made small talk as I cooked. Eden and I stole glances at each other as Ollie told us stories from school.

About two hours later, we finally sat down to dinner, and when I say Ollie devoured half the entire pie, that's no exaggeration.

"Someone liked the pie," Eden teased.

"Not the kind of pie I'm used to, but really good," he said.

"Well, I'm very glad you liked it," I said.

Eden licked her lips. "It was really delicious, Ryder.

*Those lips look delicious.*

"Well, it's a good thing you like it, because like I said, it's all I know how to make."

Ollie stole my attention from Eden's lips when he said, "Wanna come hang out in my room?"

I paused, caught off guard by the request. But there was only one answer. "Oh yeah, sure."

"There's not a lot in there to see, but I can show you my iPad."

"Yeah. That sounds cool."

Eden tried to intervene. "Ollie, Ryder's probably tired from his trip."

"No. I'm good." I smiled. No way was I about to disappoint this kid.

She smiled back and mouthed, "Thank you."

I winked at her.

Ollie got up from his chair and led me to his bedroom. To say I felt like a fish out of water was an understatement. Not only did I have no real experience with kids, but I was terrified I'd say something fucking stupid without thinking, like I had when I used the term *blind* with Eden earlier.

Exhaling, I sat down on his mattress, which was on the floor. He sat on the other side of it.

"You seem nervous," he finally said.

"You think so? How can you tell?"

"Your breathing."

That reminded me of how Eden used to be able to sense the same thing back when she could only hear my voice. I chuckled because she'd probably thought about her brother when she said it.

Ollie's features were definitely darker than Eden's. His skin was tanned, and his hair was almost black. He had big brown eyes to her green. But they had different fathers, so that made sense.

He reached for his device and clicked on the YouTube icon, which actually sounded out the word *YouTube* in a robotic woman's voice as he pressed it. It must have been a special app that allowed him to hear what he was selecting.

"What do you like to listen to?" I asked.

"Comedy shows, mostly. Some podcasts."

"Nice."

He turned his body toward me. "So, who *are* you?"

His question amused me. He'd sat through an entire dinner with me, and he was only now asking this. But the truth was, no one had explained shit to him, other than to say I was Eden's friend.

"Who am I? That's a fair question."

"Like, where did you come from? How do you know my sister?"

I gave him the same line I gave my dad. "We met online."

"That's kind of creepy."

*Touché.*

"Yeah. The Internet is really only for adults, and even then, sometimes you have to be careful. But if you're lucky, you can meet some great people you never would have met otherwise."

"You came all the way here just to see her?"

"Yeah. Yeah, I did."

"Why?"

At his age, I suppose it made no sense. "I think she's very...nice. I wanted to meet her in person."

He looked almost troubled when he said, "You're not gonna take her away, are you?"

*Shit.* "Of course not."

"Because if she went away, I wouldn't have anyone to take care of me."

Damn. I could only imagine how scary it was for him to imagine that. She was all he had.

"I haven't known you very long, Ollie, but I can tell you with a hundred-percent certainty that your sister isn't going anywhere."

"How do you know? My mom died. How do you know nothing bad will happen to Eden?"

*Fuck.*

*How am I supposed to respond to this?*

"Okay, nothing is guaranteed in life. I know. But she would never willingly leave you. I promise you that."

I thought I had it bad when I lost my mother. It must have been scary to have lost your mother at such a young age and then to not be able to see on top of that. As he looked in my general direction, but not at me, I was really curious about whether he could see me even a little.

I hoped I wouldn't offend him when I asked, "Can you see anything at all?"

"I can see with my eyes like you see with your butt."

Once I processed his answer, I laughed. "I think I get it. Good analogy."

"What's that?"

"It means...good example."

"I can't see anything."

"Gotcha." Some awkward silence passed until I rubbed my hands together and asked, "So how are the kids at school? They treat you okay?"

He smiled. "The kids at school are pretty nice. They're all blind, too, so it's not like they can make fun of me or anything."

The mere thought of anyone messing with him angered me. "Why do you say that? Do *other* kids make fun of you?"

"Not really."

"Good."

"The only thing people really tease me about is my last name."

"Your last name? Why? What is it?"

He flashed a wicked grin. "Guess."

"Um...I'm gonna need at least a little clue."

"Can I touch you?" he asked.

His question made me pause. "Yeah."

He then reached for me and started to feel around my face and my shirt.

"You're wearing it. My last name."

"I am?"

Ollie snickered. "Yeah."

I wracked my brain. Colón...like cologne, maybe? I figured that was a good guess since his father was from Costa Rica.

"Colón?"

"No."

Then I remembered the father wasn't even in the picture, so why would Ollie have his last name? Duh.

"You're gonna make me totally guess, aren't you?"

"Yup." He giggled.

*I'm wearing it.*

"Pants?"

"Nope."

"Shirt?"

"No."

"Watch?"

He shook his head. "Uh-uh."

*Boxers?*

I snapped my fingers. "Boxer?"

He laughed. "No."

There really wasn't much else that I was wearing. *Jesus.* What could it be?"

"I'll give you a hint..."

"Alright..."

"You were close when you said 'shirt.'"

*Shirt. Shirt. Shirt.*

"I'm coming up empty, Ollie."

"It's the *kind* of shirt you're wearing."

"The kind of shirt...oh...black! You're last name is Black."

His giggle grew louder. "How would I know what color your shirt is if I can't see?"

*Damn it. Good one, Ryder. Fucking brilliant.*

Okay, it was something he could feel. I looked down at my shirt. "Cotton!"

"Nope."

I smacked my head. "You're killing me here. Put me out of my misery."

Ollie finally said, "It's Shortsleeve."

*Shortsleeve!*

*Shortsleeve?*

"You're last name is Shortsleeve?"

"Yup. Eden's, too."

*Eden Shortsleeve. No kidding.*

"Wow. That's a very unique name. I've never heard it before."

"Me neither...other than us. And Mom."

Eden peeked her head in. "Can I steal Ryder away, Ollie?"

He shrugged. "I guess."

"As you can see by his neutral reaction, I've been riveting company." I rustled his hair. "We'll hang out again soon."

"When are you going back to California?" he asked.

I looked over at Eden and said, "I don't know, buddy. I haven't figured it out yet."

## CHAPTER 12

*Ryder*

I looked around, noticing that Eden had cleaned up all of the dishes while I was with Ollie. The vague noise of Ollie's iPad in the background was the only sound that registered as I found myself alone with her for the first time in a while.

Our bodies were close as we stood before each other in her kitchen. Every inch of my skin was aware of her.

My lips ached to kiss hers. Even though I wanted that more than anything, I held back, unsure how she would feel. Hadn't I sprung enough on her today? Yes, she exhibited a certain level of comfort with me online, but this was the real deal. I couldn't just assume everything would be the same—she hadn't chosen this scenario. She hadn't invited me here. Until I could confirm her feelings, I wasn't going to assume it was okay to kiss her or touch her. And as of right now, she still seemed a little on edge around me.

"So, Ms. *Shortsleeve*, I can't believe you've been holding out on your last name."

"Yeah. That's me. Thanks a lot, Ollie." She smiled and just looked at me for a while before she shook her head. "I still can't believe you're here, that you found me."

"Are you happy I'm here?"

Eden nodded. "Yes. Please don't doubt that."

Relief ran through me. I reached for her hand, and she looped her fingers in with mine. Even that simple touch caused my dick to stiffen. If this was how it was gonna be, this would be one of the longest weeks of my life—or however long I was staying.

"I really don't want to...but I have to work tonight," she said.

Disappointment filled me. "You can't take the night off?"

"I've been off the last couple of nights, remember? I can't afford to disappear. It's making me nervous. I'll lose my clients."

Never had I understood her need to keep that job the way I did tonight. Now that I saw how much responsibility she had, it was clear why she needed that steady income. It was sure as hell a lot more money than she made waitressing.

"I totally get it, Eden. I'm sorry for not immediately understanding."

She looked pained. "Believe me, it's the last thing I want to do tonight."

It hurt me that she felt forced into it in any way.

"How about this? Why don't I go to the hotel and let you work. Then tomorrow night, in the early evening, I'll come back and take you and Ollie out to dinner before you have to start camming."

Her expression brightened. "That would be awesome."

"Is there any place in particular he likes to go? I don't know the area."

"Yes. There's this steakhouse that's cafeteria-style. You can pick what you want from a line-up of choices. He likes to be able to smell the different options before making a decision, since he can't see what they look like. He loves it. It's called York's."

"No-brainer then. That's where we'll go."

A long moment of silence passed as we looked into each other's eyes. Being here still felt so surreal. She looked like she wanted to tell me something.

"I know Ollie mentioned Ethan," she finally said. "He moved to New York."

"I see. You never mentioned him."

"I know." She paused. "He's one of the reasons I'm very reluctant to get attached to anyone. He got a job there and wanted me to move. I told him I wasn't willing to uproot Ollie. My brother loves his school, and it really is the right fit for him. Ethan had to decide whether to take the job or stay in Utah with us, and he chose the job. That's really all there is to that story."

I nodded. No wonder she was so hesitant about taking things further with me.

"You were with him for how long?"

"A couple of years. He walked into Ellerby's one day. That's how I met him."

"Have you dated anyone since?"

"No. Not a single person in the two years since we've broken up."

"So, you haven't *been with* anyone?"

"No, I haven't."

"That's a long time." I examined her face and could see the scars written all over it. "He really hurt you, didn't he?"

She took a deep breath. "The breakup with Ethan was my first real heartbreak. We were together for a year and a half. He made me feel protected, although I never expected him to want to take on everything that came along with me. You know? It just sucks when you care about someone, and they don't choose you. At the same time, I totally understand why he left."

I felt a tightening in my chest and couldn't figure out if it was jealousy or anger at him for hurting her and making her think he'd made the right choice by leaving.

"So, you weren't camming back then, when you were with him?"

"No. Not yet." She laughed. "He has no clue what I've gotten myself into. I haven't spoken to him in a long time. Sometimes I laugh, thinking about him accidentally finding me."

"That would serve the fucker right."

She laughed and looked over at the clock. "Crap. I need to get Ollie to bed and start getting ready. I'm sorry."

I didn't want to leave her, but I needed to let her work.

"Don't worry about me. I'm gonna catch up on some work emails and get some sleep. I haven't slept for shit the past couple of days."

"Because you were worried about me. That's my fault."

"It's not—and you know what? I wouldn't change a damn thing about what it took to get me here to see you."

Her mouth curved into a smile. "I wouldn't either."

I began walking toward the door. My heart pounded because I really wanted to kiss her goodnight. I hadn't felt this way since I was fourteen on my very first date, such anxious anticipation. But I wasn't sure whether it was okay to kiss her for a number of reasons. One, I didn't know if she wanted me to. Two, I suspected it would be like a drug—once I started, I wouldn't be able to stop and would want to do much more than kiss her. Three, I had to really think about whether whatever was happening with us extended into "real life." Suppose I kissed her...then what? We have a week of fucking around and then I leave? A kiss was a kiss...but with Eden, it would mean so much more. I needed to be careful.

She stood in the entrance as I stepped outside.

With my hands in my pockets, I said, "I'll come by around five tomorrow. Does that work?"

"That's perfect."

Eden leaned against the door, staring at me like she was still in awe of my being here. I reached for her hand and kissed it firmly, letting my lips linger on her skin longer than normal. That was my compromise.

After I got back to the hotel, I told myself I wasn't going to log in to her show. But curiosity got the best of me. I happened to catch it right at the point where she had taken her top off. It was just as hard to watch as I thought it might be. In fact, it was more difficult than ever.

Her nails were painted red. They hadn't been that color earlier. My heart started to palpitate as I fixated on her hands massaging her breasts and imagined her digging them into my skin...or someone else's. I hadn't watched her show in a while for this very reason—I couldn't handle the idea of other men ogling her anymore.

That was pretty damn ironic, considering how we'd met.

The next evening, the line to get into York's was long. While I preferred to sit down, order a meal, and not have to pick up my food like I was in a high school cafeteria, I could totally understand Ollie wanting to smell everything.

It had taken forever for five o'clock to roll around. I'd spent the day catching up on work emails and took out some of my nervous energy on the hotel gym equipment. I swam a few laps in the pool, too. Then my hand got a good workout in the shower as I rubbed one off to relieve the tension.

Now that I was with Eden again, it was clear that nothing I'd done today had worked to calm the adrenaline running through me. She looked stunning without even having to try—my gorgeous little hippie girl. She wore a long, flowy, white sundress. The material was so thin I could practically see through it. Her beautiful long, sandy brown hair was straighter than usual. She must have blown it out. And she was wearing a little eye makeup, even though normally she went au naturel.

She placed her hand on my arm. "I hope you like this place. I know it's likely not what you would've chosen."

"I bet it's gonna be great if Ollie loves it so much. If the line ever moves, I'll get to find out."

"It's always like this," Ollie said. "But the food is worth it."

"I trust your opinion, Ollie. After all, you loved my pie. You're a man of good taste."

Eden flashed me a huge smile, and as our eyes locked, we seemed to drift off into our own world.

*Fuck, I want her.*

Here we were in this busy restaurant line, and all I could think about was being inside of her. Ollie was playing with his iTouch, listening to something. It felt like Eden and I were the only two people in the room.

My heart raced. I knew in that moment that kissing her would be worth the risk. Unable to hold it in anymore, I placed my hand on her waist and pulled her closer to me, for the first time feeling her soft, supple breasts against my chest. I let out a shaky breath, because her body felt so damn good against mine.

She grabbed my shirt and dug her nails into my chest. There was something very erotic about that. It was like she read my mind—I'd fantasized about that very thing last night while watching her from the hotel.

The look in her eyes finally gave me the confirmation I needed. I slowly leaned in, and she pulled me closer. Her eyes turned hazy as she parted her lips, ready to receive my kiss.

The slight moan that escaped into my mouth made my dick harden. And there was no going back as I began to devour her mouth. Maybe this wasn't such a good idea. Her lips felt incredible as all of the sounds in the room faded away. I went all in, slipping my tongue out to fully taste her and circling it around hers.

Even though Ollie seemed to be into his game, I knew I had to stop before he noticed something or we got kicked out of this place.

Reluctantly pulling away, I looked at her and mouthed, "That felt so good."

"I know," she whispered.

I ran my thumb along her lips, so hungry for more.

"I heard you kiss," Ollie said nonchalantly.

Eden's face turned red as we both turned to him.

I cleared my throat. "You did, did you?"

"Yeah. Pretty gross," he said without turning his attention away from his device.

"Don't be rude, Ollie," Eden scolded.

"That's okay," I said. "He's entitled to his opinion. I used to think it was gross when my parents kissed. I get it."

Ollie scrunched his nose. "Why do people even do it?"

Eden responded, "It's a way of showing affection."

"Why don't you just hug? It's less slobbery."

"Because adults like to kiss. We don't have to explain why," she said.

I was a little stumped as to how to explain it to him, but I wanted to try. Then a thought popped into my head. "I can try to explain. Maybe when you're older, you'll get it. But a hug—it's like ice cream, right? Nice and sweet. Very good. But a kiss, with the right person, it's like the full sundae with warm chocolate sauce, whipped cream— the whole shebang. It makes you feel giddy. You know how when you're eating something and all of a sudden you start humming to yourself because it's so good? That's what kissing is like."

"Remind me not to get a sundae for dessert."

Eden and I looked at each other and laughed.

We finally got to the point in the line where we could grab a tray.

"Ollie, I'm gonna use you as my guide on what to eat here. I'm following the expert."

After adequately assessing the aromas, Ollie selected a salad with Thousand Island dressing, roasted chicken with garlic mashed potatoes, and green Jell-O with whipped cream for dessert.

I stuck to my word and put whatever he got on my tray as well.

After I paid for us, we found a booth and sat down.

Ollie had a great appreciation for food. He ate like there was no tomorrow. He'd been the same way with my chicken pot pie—ate every last morsel on his plate and then some. I theorized that maybe without being able to see, his sense of taste was amplified. Eating became that much more important and enjoyable.

While I definitely liked the food, my focus was on Eden: watching her enjoy her meal and feeling my dick twitch every time she licked her lips. That kiss was the best of my life, and I was dying to taste her again.

Desperately needing to get my mind off of sex, I asked, "So is Ollie short for anything?"

"Olivier. Our Mom was part French," Eden answered.

Probably why I like French fries so much," Ollie said.

"Could be." I chuckled. "Come to think of it, I love French fries, too, and I'm a quarter French. You're onto something. That explains it. Anyway, Olivier is a really cool name."

As I looked between the two of them, I noticed that he and Eden had the same nose. Other than that, they didn't really resemble each other.

When Eden caught me staring at her, she blushed. If she blushed like that from a single look, I wondered about her reaction if I did other things to her. We'd done stuff on camera, but there was a huge difference between virtual intimacy and the real thing. It was weird to think that while she'd seen me *come*, our bodies had hardly ever made contact.

She hadn't been with anyone in *two years*. Despite the sexual nature of her job, this shy girl in front of me was the real Eden. Everything she did in front of those cameras was an act; I could see that now.

Ollie interrupted my thoughts. "Can we take Ryder to the trampoline park?"

Eden seemed to think about it for a moment before she said, "No, I don't think that's a good idea with your stitches."

I rustled his hair. "Trampoline park, huh?"

Ollie drank some of his lemonade and nodded. "It's called Bounce. It's super cool. I went there once for a birthday party."

"Yes," she said. "But that was a small group of kids in a rented section. We can't just go on short notice when it's open to the public. It will be a free-for-all, and some kid will knock right into your head. You're still recovering."

Ollie looked disappointed, but he nodded in agreement. "You're right."

I wondered how many times Ollie had to give things up that typical kids took for granted because of his impairment. He was so mature. Most eleven year olds would be nagging their parents until they got their way. But Ollie only had to be told once before he came to the conclusion that Eden had his best interests in mind. He was a damn good kid. In the short time I'd known him, my admiration for this boy knew no bounds.

I scratched my chin. "You know what I like better than trampolines?"

"What?"

"Stand-up acts on YouTube. You want to go home and listen to some?"

He smiled. "Yeah."

Back at Eden's, after I'd hung out with her brother for a while, I joined her in the kitchen while Ollie stayed in his room.

I listened carefully for the sound of his device turning back on. That kid had the most sensitive hearing. When it was clear he was engaged in something that would allow us some privacy, I looked over at Eden. Her eyes were hazy, and I knew what she was thinking. I was thinking it, too.

Within seconds, my mouth was on hers. We took up exactly where we'd left off at the restaurant. It was as if our kiss had simply been on hold all night, as if I'd just released a pause button.

She tasted so incredibly good. I felt like a goddamn teenager—so horny, so hungry for her as my tongue explored her mouth. I didn't know what to do with my hands, because they wanted to go everywhere, touch everything at once. I settled for raking my fingers through her beautiful, long hair that smelled like flowers and coconut.

My hands traveled down her back and landed on her ass. I squeezed it hard and pushed her into me.

Lowering my mouth, I began to suck on her neck, stopping with each movement to notice how her skin was changing color from white to pink. *Fuck, that's such a turn-on.*

I really tried to stop myself, but I couldn't resist lowering my mouth and devouring her breast through the material of her dress. Her nipples were hard, poking through as I circled my tongue around her left one.

Her hands were on the back of my head as she guided me back up and pushed me deeper into her mouth. The sounds she made were killing me. I knew she could feel my erection against her. There was no denying how hard I was, and there was nothing more in the world I wanted right now than to fuck her on this counter. I would've given just about anything for that, to wrap her legs around me and empty all of my frustration into her.

But I knew my body was moving way ahead of my mind. Even though the prospect of sex with Eden felt like it was *right there*, the distance between the present situation and that scenario was like the length of a football field.

I stopped the kiss and buried my head in her neck. "I want you."

"I want you, too," she panted.

I looked into her eyes. "I don't think you understand how much."

Eden's breathing became heavier. "I'm scared."

"I know. That's why I stopped, even though I really didn't want to. I know you're not ready."

"I mean, you're leaving in what—a few days?"

"I'm leaving, but I'll be back."

"Then what?"

Answering honestly, I said, "I don't know."

"You're gonna keep flying back and forth, only to come to the conclusion a year down the line that it's not gonna work out between us?"

"Eden, I think you're jumping way ahead right now."

"Am I? There's no way this could work. No matter how strong our attraction to one another is, we're just in two different places in life. It's why I didn't want—"

"I know. You didn't want to meet me. I violated our agreement in coming to find you. I don't regret it for one second. I don't know what's going to happen tomorrow. I really don't. I only know what I feel today. And I feel *a lot*—more than I've ever felt in my entire life. But more than anything, I feel grateful. I'm grateful that you're okay." I pointed toward Ollie's room. "I'm grateful to have been blessed with that kid's presence. In one day of knowing him, he's inspired me so much—to slow down, to be a better person." I ran my thumb along her bottom lip. "I'm grateful that I got to kiss these lips. Because a part of me believed there was no chance in hell of that ever happening."

She looked like she wanted to cry. "Ryder, I'm feeling so much right now, too."

I kissed her hard before I said, "Give me today. Just give me today. But don't be surprised if I ask the same of you tomorrow and the next day. Will you take things day by day with me? Because I'm not anywhere ready to let you go. Not even close."

Her eyes watered as she pulled me close. "Okay. But just today. And don't be surprised if I say that tomorrow."

## CHAPTER 13

*Eden*

I was working the lunch-hour rush at Ellerby's when Camille came up behind me in the kitchen. "Eden?"

"Yeah?"

"Pretty much the most gorgeous man I've ever seen in my life is at the corner table requesting you. He has Paul Newman eyes. You know him?"

I smiled. *Ryder is here?*

"Yeah. I know him. That's the man who's gonna break my heart."

Excitement filled her eyes. "You'd better spill later."

After I dropped off a couple of plates at another table, I looked to the corner to find Ryder staring at his laptop. When he spotted me, a huge smile spread across his face.

"How can I help you, sir?"

"There are so many ways I could answer that question..." He stood up from the table.

"What are you in the mood for?" I asked.

"Again, so many ways I could answer that." He beamed and pointed to his cheek. "How about some sugar?"

133

I gave him a quick peck and asked, "What are the plans tonight?"

"I want to take you guys somewhere after Ollie gets out of school. I can come with you to get him, and we can go out straight from there, unless you have to take him home for any reason."

"That would be great. Where are we going?"

"It's a secret." He winked. "I want to take you guys out pretty much every day I'm here, if that's okay."

"Of course. Although, I was thinking that on your last night I'd like to make you dinner at the house—to pay you back for cooking for us. Have you decided when you're leaving yet?"

Ryder frowned. "My father set up a meeting he says he really needs me to attend on Monday morning. So I'd like to stay until Sunday and take the latest possible flight back." He took one look at my face and caressed my cheek. "I'll be back, Eden. Don't worry."

He'd read my mind.

I nodded. It wasn't that I didn't believe he'd be back. I just didn't understand how we were going to work long-term. My brother was a lifelong responsibility. Our lives were not conducive to the jet-setting lifestyle Ryder lived. He needed to see the big picture. Maybe he didn't want to think about that right now, but it's something I couldn't ignore.

He sat back down in the booth. "If you don't mind, I think I'm just gonna hang out here until your shift is over, get some work done."

"That's three more hours. Won't you be bored?"

"There's wireless here. Plus, I get to look at you. I don't get bored looking at you. Just the opposite—quite excited, actually."

Feeling my cheeks heating up, I shook my head. "What am I gonna do with you?"

He smirked. "Again, so many ways I could answer that question."

We picked Ollie up after school, and as we drove, Ryder refused to tell us where we were going. It made me wonder what he had up his sleeve, especially since he didn't know the area.

When we pulled up to the trampoline place, I didn't understand, because I'd specifically told Ollie in front of Ryder that we couldn't come here.

He whispered in my ear, "Before you get upset at me, I arranged for him to have his own space so he can't get hurt."

Squinting in confusion, I said, "His own space?"

"Technically I rented out the entire place for us."

My eyes widened. "What? How did you manage that?"

"Don't worry about it."

Ryder must have spent a fortune on this. I knew he was wealthy, but I didn't want him spending that kind of money on us.

"Where are we?" Ollie finally asked.

I blew out a breath, deciding to concede. Ollie was going to flip out. "Bounce," I said.

He squealed. "No way!"

Ryder turned around. "You said you wanted to come here, right?"

"Yeah, but I thought Eden said no."

"Well, I rented out the place, so you won't have to worry about anyone bumping into you."

"How?" he asked.

Ollie had no concept of what it was like to have money. We always had to save for nice things.

"I pulled a few strings."

When we entered, at least five people wearing the same neon orange shirts were lined up in a row, as if they were expecting us.

"Hello, Mr. McNamara," one of them said.

Ryder nodded. "Hey."

"The party room is set up for you. And you'll have access to any of the trampolines on either level. The whole place is yours. We just need an adult to sign a waiver for him. We also have these non-slip socks for everyone."

Ryder handed me the form to fill out. "Eden?"

Ollie was understandably confused. "Party room? It's not my birthday."

"The only way to rent out this place is for birthday parties," Ryder explained. "So, I just asked them to give us all the party stuff, too. We get pizza and cake for twenty people. If I had more time, I would've had you invite your friends, but I wanted to surprise you, and I also remembered that it's safer for you if no one else is around, so no one can knock into you. When's your birthday anyway?"

"It was a few months ago."

"See? I missed it. So, happy birthday."

It was nice to see the smile on my brother's face.

I signed the waiver, then began to remove Ollie's socks to put on the ones he was required to wear.

Ollie looked up at Ryder. "You'll jump with me, right?"

"Heck, yeah. Your sister's gonna jump, too." Ryder flashed me a smile that showed a glimpse of his inner child.

"Can we jump first, Ryder? Then eat?" Ollie asked.

"Whatever you want."

I handed Ryder a pair of the special socks. "We all have to wear these."

He examined them. "What do you know, Ollie? They make socks for Bigfoot-sized feet here."

Ollie laughed.

We made our way up the stairs to the biggest room in the joint. It was just a series of connected, flat, rectangular trampolines. The space was practically the size of a basketball court.

Ryder kept a close eye on Ollie, so I didn't have to do much except trail behind them as I admired the view. The way Ryder's jeans hugged his ass was absolutely divine. I wondered if he and I would have alone time later, because I really wanted to taste his lips again. It was all I could think about.

As I watched him jump with my brother, I realized Ryder was definitely a kid at heart. They counted to three to coordinate landing on their butts at the exact same time.

I decided to venture away from them for a bit, giving myself my own space on one of the trampolines at the other corner of the room. I jumped as high as I wanted, feeling happier and freer than I had in a long time. But I knew that likely had little to do with flying freely in the air and everything to do with the man jumping onto his ass like a fool in the other corner.

When I finally returned to them, Ryder's face lit up when he noticed me.

He patted his stomach as he turned to Ollie. "I don't know about you, but I'm starving. Wanna go eat?"

Ollie slowed down his jumping and came to a stop. "Yeah. I'm hungry, too."

We ventured downstairs to the party room. The table was set up with a couple of boxes of pizza, a pitcher of fruit punch, paper plates, and cups. On a table in the corner was a half-sheet cake that was supposed to be a trampoline. It had little people figures on the top.

After working up an appetite, we demolished an entire pizza and broke into the second. Ollie was working on his slice of cake when I took Ryder aside.

"I can't thank you enough for this afternoon. No one has ever done anything like this for him. But please don't feel like you need to do this kind of thing to make him happy. He would be just as happy with a pizza party at home."

"I wanted to. I wanted to do something fun for him that he doesn't normally have. It makes me even happier than it makes him. I promise, I won't pull this over-the-top shit all of the time."

"It seriously must have cost a fortune."

"What good is having money if you can't use it to make people happy? Do you know how much money I've spent over the years throwing parties for people I don't even know? This day brought me more joy than I've had in a long time."

I gripped the material of his shirt. "How can I ever thank you?"

"Again...so many ways I could answer that." He winked.

"I know just how I'm gonna do it."

He leaned in and kissed me on the cheek. "Oh yeah? Do tell."

"I'm taking tonight off."

He slid his hand down to my ass. "You don't have to do that."

"I want to. One more night of missed work is not going to kill me. I don't want to work when I could be spending this precious time with you."

"You're not gonna hear me complain about that, Eden."

Ryder brought my face to his and planted a long kiss on my mouth. He bit at my bottom lip. My panties were getting wetter by the second. This wasn't the appropriate place to be losing control. I could've kissed him endlessly but pulled away at the sound of my brother's voice.

"Ew...kissing," Ollie said.

I hadn't realized he would be able to hear it, since we'd been at the other corner of the room.

"Is there anything you don't hear?" I said to him.

We walked over to Ollie, hand in hand.

"I apologize," Ryder said. "But I *really* like kissing your sister."

My brother scrunched his nose. "You think?"

Ryder laughed, placing his hand on my knee and squeezing it. That simple act made my entire body weak.

He turned to Ollie. "After you finish your cake, you wanna go another round on the trampolines?"

"Can we?"

Ryder squeezed my leg again. "Yup. We got the whole place 'til six."

Ollie put his plastic fork down. "Then, yeah, let's go!"

This time, Ryder and I held hands as we jumped across from Ollie, giving him some space.

As I bounced hand in hand with this beautiful man next to me, I felt on top of the world.

After I put Ollie to sleep that night, I invited Ryder into my room. It was the first time he'd been inside the place where I worked.

He looked around. "So this is the infamous Montana Lane set."

"Yup." I sighed, kind of nervous for him to see everything. "This is it."

"It's smaller than it looks from afar."

I turned on the white Christmas lights. "Yeah..."

"It feels strange being in here, but in a good way," he said. "This room has been like a dream to me for so long."

He continued scoping out the space. His eyes landed on a bottle of lube sitting on my bureau. I knew what he was thinking, and I hated that it bothered him. I also couldn't help but notice the sizable bulge in his pants. He was very turned on right now.

This was the first time we'd ever been alone together while Ollie was asleep. I wanted Ryder so badly my body hurt. I wanted to feel his lips everywhere, wanted to feel his cock moving in and out of me. I knew beyond a shadow of a doubt that if he tried to have sex with me tonight,

I would give in. Resisting that would be impossible—not only because I hadn't had sex with anything other than a dildo in two years, but because I'd never wanted a man like I wanted him. Given that I couldn't resist him, a part of me hoped he didn't try. That would be best for me in the long run—especially if he got back to Los Angeles and came to his senses.

He then spotted my box of condoms.

*Shit.*

Would he think I was lying about my dry spell? The truth about those rubbers was almost too ridiculous to believe.

Ryder lifted the strip and raised his brow. "Just in case?"

"Actually, I have a client who...likes to watch me roll them onto bananas."

"Are you fucking serious?"

"Dead serious. And that's far from the weirdest thing people have asked me to do."

"What the fuck is wrong with people? A banana?" He wrapped his hands around me and pulled me into a hug. "At least go for an eggplant."

I laughed into his neck, relieved he was making light of it.

"My beautiful cam girl." He pulled back to look at me before enveloping my mouth in his.

My legs felt weak as I whispered over his lips, "I'm real."

"You're realer than I ever could have imagined."

My heart pounded through my chest.

He suddenly moved back and placed his palm between my breasts. "God, Eden. Your heart is beating so fast. Are you nervous?"

I decided to be honest with him. "A little."

"You think I'm gonna try to have sex with you right now? Is that what it is? Because we should really talk about that. I'm not gonna pressure you into anything. You're not ready. I know that."

"It's not that I don't want to—just the opposite. I'm just really scared to take that step...with you leaving."

"I get it. I think we'll both know when the time is right. So, take a deep breath and know that I just want to spend time with you. You don't have to worry about us doing something we may not be ready for tonight. I just want to be with you."

A mix of relief and disappointment ran through me as I took it upon myself to steal another kiss. There was no other feeling like his warm, supple lips on mine along with the prickle from the scruff on his chin.

Ryder wandered the room again and began picking up some of my props. We got a good laugh when he placed the feather boa around his neck. He flashed me a wicked grin, and I wanted to jump him.

The mood lightened significantly over the course of the next half hour.

He picked up my violin and handed it to me. I played for him as he sat with his eyes closed and took in every note of "Fanfare Minuet."

At one point, he found a pair of handcuffs I had laying around—another prop. Before I could stop him, he opened them and locked one of his hands to the bedpost.

"No!" I shouted, but it was too late.

"I'm just kidding around." He laughed.

"But I don't have the keys!"

His smile faded. "What?"

"I have no idea what I did with them."

"Are you serious?"

We laughed so hard we were crying.

"Well, I guess I'm stuck here for the night, then."

I lay down next to him. "Actually, I didn't want you to leave anyway."

"Is that right?" His tone was suggestive.

"I was hoping you'd stay the night."

"So this all worked out, my being tied to the bed. Is that what you're saying?"

"It did. Maybe later I'll go find a bobby pin and try to free you. But for now, I kind of like this situation."

He batted his lashes. "Feel free to take advantage of my vulnerability."

He even had beautiful eyelashes.

*God, losing you is not going to be easy.*

"Don't tempt me," I said before leaning in and taking another kiss.

Ryder lay down, his hand still locked in. I curled into him. Lying in his arms—or arm—was heaven.

We talked for a long while and laughed as he told me stories about some of the actors who'd starred in his father's movies. He spoke a little about his quirky friend, Benny, who sometimes repeats whatever the person he's talking to is saying before he answers.

I told him more about my mom, how it was just the two of us for so many years until she met Javier, a young guy from Costa Rica who'd traveled here to study abroad. After he went back home, my mother found out she was pregnant. Ollie came along, and life was never the same.

I also opened up to him about the day my mother was killed. Mom was hit head-on one night on the way home from work. Up until now, I'd never really divulged any of the specific details.

The fact that we'd both lost our mothers was definitely something that bonded us. But Ryder had a father in the picture, whereas mine had never been around. My mother had been a super-talented musician, artistic and beautiful, but when it came to men, her judgment definitely left something to be desired.

"There's something I don't think I ever mentioned about *my* mother," Ryder said. "I haven't been able to stop thinking about it ever since I met Ollie."

"Ollie? Why?"

"She died from ocular melanoma. It's a tumor that forms in the pigment cells that give color to your eyes. It's a very rare eye cancer. My mother actually went blind in one eye."

I covered my mouth. "Oh my God."

"Yeah. When I first met Ollie and found out he was blind, as you can imagine, I thought of my mother. And then I thought back to the song you were singing when we first met. That connection."

"That's eerie, Ryder. But beautiful at the same time."

"I know. I've always felt like I was meant to meet you, Eden. But never more than now." He stared into my eyes for a while. "Can I ask you to look for a bobby pin so I can free this hand? I really want to wrap both my arms around you."

I smacked my forehead. "Yes! Of course." I'd totally forgotten he was stuck to the bed.

After fifteen minutes of fiddling with the cuffs, I was finally able to get them off of him.

As I released him, I thought about the irony of letting him go; I really had to learn how *not* to get attached to this man.

*Ryder*

My last night in Utah came faster than I was ready for.

I'd managed not to screw up and lose control with Eden thus far. But this was the last time we'd be together for a while. It would be a miracle if I could maintain my resistance.

I knew she needed to see whether this could work before taking the next step with me. I couldn't blame her, nor could I guarantee her anything at this point. I didn't know exactly *how* we were going to make this work. I only knew I wanted to try.

I'd ditched the hotel since the night I accidentally handcuffed myself to Eden's bed. That next day, she decided to take the rest of the week off from camming until I left, which was a huge deal. I tried to convince her it was perfectly okay to continue working while I was here, but after we bonded in her bedroom that night, she vowed to focus on me until I had to go back to California. Even though I didn't want her business to suffer, that meant a lot.

We spent the entire Saturday, my last full day, with Ollie, taking him to this sound exhibit at the Science Museum and watching—or rather listening—to a movie. Then Eden made the most amazing lasagna, and she, Ollie, and I sat around at the table for a while after dinner.

The mood had definitely been somber while we ate. The plan was for the three of us to hang out tomorrow at the house and have a lazy Sunday morning before I had to catch my flight back to California. The thought of leaving made my chest hurt.

Eden and I had just tucked Ollie in and were settled into her room for the night. I'd poured two glasses of wine, and she put on some soft music. It might have been romantic, aside from the fact that all I could think about was sticking my head between her legs and giving her the best orgasm of her life. It was all I wanted to do. I'd been on my best behavior this entire trip, but man, in the eleventh hour when I knew I was leaving tomorrow, all I could think about was burying my face in her pussy. I really didn't want to be good anymore.

She sensed something as we were lying in bed. "What are you thinking?"

"I don't know if I should tell you. You might kick me out of here."

"Tell me."

"You sure?"

"Yes."

I rested my head in the crook of her neck and said, "Okay, then. I want to eat your pussy more than I want my next breath." I looked up to gauge her reaction.

Her entire face went flush, but I sensed it was in a good way as she bit her bottom lip and said, "Okay."

147

"Okay, as in, you're down for it?"

"Yes." She scratched her fingers along my chest. "On one condition."

"What's that?"

"I get to go down on you, too, while you're doing it."

Eden's face turned beet red. I knew she was no stranger to dirty talk because of her job, but man, I loved seeing her blush.

"I'm pretty sure I almost just came in my pants, Eden. You can't talk to me like that."

"Don't come. Don't waste it that way. I want you to come in my mouth." Her face turned even redder.

"Okay, that time I really almost lost it. You can't say stuff like that to me."

I pulled her to me and let out an exasperated breath in her mouth.

*Fuck it.*

I needed this.

We both needed this.

She started to pull her shorts down as we kissed. I don't think I'd ever unbuckled my pants so fast in my life. My inhibitions were dying with each second.

Our kiss deepened as she fumbled with my jeans to pull them off. My balls ached. I was so ready for this.

"Eden!" I heard from outside the door.

She jumped up. "Ollie?" She grabbed her shorts and put them on before running to the door.

*Shit.*

I quickly pulled up my pants and fastened my belt. Despite the interruption, my dick was painfully hard.

She opened the door, and Ollie was standing there holding his stomach.

"I don't feel so good."

Eden knelt down and placed her arms around him. "What's wrong?"

"My tummy."

"Do you feel like you're gonna throw up?"

"Yeah."

"Crap. Okay." She stepped right into action. "Let's go to the toilet."

Eden took him to the bathroom, and soon after I could hear the sounds of him hurling.

*Poor little guy.*

I walked over to the bathroom. "You need anything?"

"No. He'll be fine."

His head was halfway in the toilet bowl when he mumbled, "Hi, Ryder."

"Hey, buddy. I'm sorry you're sick."

He slowly got up, and Eden led him over to the sink to wash his hands.

"I normally sleep in his room when he's sick," she said.

"Of course. Do what you need to do."

"I'm sorry," she whispered.

"Don't be silly, Eden."

"Is Ryder staying the night?" Ollie asked.

"Yeah. I didn't feel like going back to the hotel."

"Can you sleep in my room with me instead of Eden?"

She tried to intervene. "We don't want Ryder to get sick."

"I'm not worried about that," I assured her. "I haven't thrown up since I was a kid. I really think I'm immune. I'd love to bunk with Ollie, keep an eye on him tonight."

"You don't have to," Eden insisted.

Trying my best to make eye contact with her in the dark, I said, "I *want* to."

She kept looking at me, as if she expected me to change my mind. "Are you sure?"

"Positive."

I stole one last kiss from her before I took Ollie's hand and followed him into his room. Despite not being able to see, he knew his way around the house really well. Eden had mentioned that being one of the reasons she couldn't move, because it would be so difficult for him to adjust to a new layout.

Eden followed us into his room with a large basin. "Keep this by the bed in case he vomits again."

"Got it," I said as Ollie and I both lay down on his mattress.

I reached for Eden's hand before she left and squeezed it. She bent down to where we were lying and kissed me. I would have much rather been doing what we started in her bedroom, but I knew I was needed in here more.

Things were quiet for a long while before I heard Ollie's voice. "I can't sleep."

I turned to him. "That's probably because you're thinking about it too much. Whenever I focus on not being able to sleep, I never can." I leaned my chin on my hand. "How are you feeling?"

"Still a little sick, but better after I threw up."

"Good."

Ollie let out some heavy breaths. I wondered if there was something more bothering him besides the insomnia.

"What's wrong, Ollie?"

After several seconds, he finally answered me. "Are you really coming back?"

It took me a moment to respond. "Yes. That I can promise, so long as your sister wants me to."

"I'm gonna miss you."

"I'm gonna miss you, too."

"Ethan said he'd be back to see me, but he never came back. I'm afraid I'll never see you again."

*Shit.* How could I argue with him when his personal experience backed up the theory of my never returning?

I let out a long breath and thought about how to best explain it. "Adult relationships are complicated, Ollie. I'm sure Ethan didn't mean to break his promise to you. But maybe it was hard for him to see you without having to see your sister. When adults break up, things can be weird between them. Sometimes, it might make them sad to see the other person again, so while he probably wants to see *you*, it's just too difficult with having to see Eden, too."

Despite my words, I didn't believe this Ethan guy had any excuse for blowing Ollie off. He could have come back to see Ollie if he wanted to. He could've grown a sack and sucked it up for the poor kid's sake. He could have found another way to keep in touch.

"Are you gonna break up with Eden?"

I wanted to assure him that wouldn't happen, but Eden and I were not even technically together, and things were most definitely complicated—fully up in the air at this point. Honesty was going to be the best policy.

"I don't know what the future holds for your sister and me. Everything is still kind of new. But I can tell you I really care about her—a lot. And I know I've only known you for a few days, but I care about you, too."

After the words exited my mouth, I wondered whether I should have said them. But they were the truth.

"I care about you, too, Ryder."

I smiled. "Thank you, buddy. I can't predict what's gonna happen. But I can choose to be honest with you always. I promise never to lie to you or tell you one thing and do another. And I can promise you this: you and I can always be friends, no matter what. I'm gonna give you my email and my phone number. You call me or write me whenever you want, okay?"

"Really?"

*Be careful, Ryder.*

"Yeah. Of course. No reason we can't keep in touch."

"Cool."

He was quiet for a while, but he was still fidgety. I started to move my lips, making my famous cricket sound.

*Cricket.*

*Cricket.*

*Cricket.*

Ollie jumped. "What's that?"

Trying not to laugh, I stopped just long enough to say, "I don't know," then kept going.

He sat up. "Sounds like there's a cricket in my room."

"It does."

"It stops every time you talk, though."

"It must not like my voice."

*Cricket.*

*Cricket.*

*Cricket.*

"How are you doing that, Ryder?"

It seemed I couldn't pull one over on him. Eden had been able to *see* my lips when I tried it on her, and it still took her longer to figure it out than Ollie.

"Who says I'm doing it?"

"Duh. It's obvious. But it's really good."

I laughed. "Thanks, man."

"You should try it on Eden. I bet she'll believe it."

"Already got her, dude."

He giggled. "Good."

We lay in silence for a bit. Then Ollie placed his hand on my chest, over my heart. It might have been a small gesture, but it felt significant. He was putting his trust in me.

I hoped I deserved it.

## CHAPTER 15

*Ryder*

Utah seemed like a dream now.

I'd hopped the latest possible flight back to L.A. on Sunday evening so I could spend as much time with them as possible.

Saying goodbye to Eden was hard as all hell, but I kept telling myself I'd return to St. George the next opportunity I had.

That Sunday night, it felt strange being back in my big, empty house—in my big, empty bed.

I longed for her even more now that I'd been in her presence. Eden and I never got a chance to explore anything sexually, and a part of me knew we were better off having waited, but I was dying inside, feeling like we had unfinished business I could hardly wait to get to.

But then that voice inside my head told me to hold my horses, reminding me that Eden had made her concerns clear. She didn't want to get involved with someone who would bail on her later. I still had a lot of thinking to do, so in many ways, it was a good thing I was back in L.A. for a while to clear my head.

Still, the six days I'd spent with them had changed me. Anytime I looked at something interesting, I'd think about the fact that Ollie couldn't see it. What once seemed like a necessity—sight—was actually a luxury. All of the superficial things we judge by looking at them were null and void in Ollie's world. I found myself closing my eyes just to listen to the sounds around me, appreciating them so much more.

Early Monday morning, I braced myself to face Lorena. I'd texted her from Utah to let her know everything was okay, that I'd found Eden alive and well. Since she was the only person who knew the true nature of my trip, I felt like I at least owed her that. I hadn't given her any details, though. It was just too much to get into, so I'd decided to tell her in person when I got back.

But how was I going to begin to explain everything to her? I was sure she had all kinds of crazy ideas floating around in her head about how my trip had gone. She'd probably envisioned me swinging from the ceiling, having salacious sex all damn week with my "nudie model."

Little did she know how far from the truth that was.

Lorena had just put some coffee on when I walked into the kitchen.

"*Mijo*, I've been dying to see you. This is all better than the *telenovelas* I watch. What happened with the girl?"

I took a deep breath.

Her eyes flitted back and forth over my face. "Wow."

"What?"

"You're, like, glowing or something."

"Glowing? I'm not a fucking pregnant woman. What do you mean *glowing*?"

"I mean glowing. I don't know how else to describe it. You seem like your face is lit up, like it's a different color than I've ever seen before. What did she do to you?"

I brushed my hand over my face in an attempt to wipe off this alleged glow. "Get your head out of the gutter. She did nothing. That's the thing. We did *nothing*."

"No monkey business after all that?"

"No. None. We just kissed."

"That's kind of a shame. What happened?"

Raking my fingers through my hair, I couldn't help but laugh when I answered her question. "I got my ass fed to me by life. That's what happened."

"What?"

Lorena listened intently as I told her the entire story of my trip—from Ethan to Ollie.

She shook her head. "This is the last thing I ever expected you to be telling me. Wow...a little boy."

"He's such a great kid, but he's seriously fearful of abandonment. That's why I gotta be careful. You can't play around with that shit. Eden's last boyfriend stuck around for two years and then took a job in New York. Never came back. Ollie had gotten attached to him. I think he takes it personally that the douche doesn't contact him anymore. That really sucks."

She gave me a warning look. "You don't want that to happen again."

"No, I don't."

"It sounds like Eden's got her plate full."

"Yeah. There's not a lot of room for anything else."

"I bet she'd *make* room for you." Lorena snickered.

"She doesn't think it could work, and I'm not sure I fully disagree."

"She doesn't think you would *want* to make it work. If there's a will, there's a way."

I let that sink in for a bit. "Look, I know how she makes me feel, but that's about all that makes sense in this scenario. My job is here. Her life is there. And then there's Ollie." I paused to reflect on the past week. "He's...so clever. I told him we could keep in touch no matter what happens."

"Sounds like you're already preparing him for the worst, as if you've already made up your mind."

"I don't know what to do. All I know is I'm not ready to let her go."

"So you've made a decision to have some fun with her and let her go later?"

The way she put that sounded so sucky. But was she right? Was I looking to have sex with Eden, have my fun, and then gently part ways when I finally got it through my thick skull that we couldn't last?

"My job requires me to be here. She's already given up one relationship because she couldn't move. How could this possibly work?"

"Well, it's certainly not gonna work if you believe it won't."

"When I'm here, it's like I can see things a little more clearly—how difficult it would be. But when I'm with her, I can't imagine being anywhere else."

"She wouldn't be willing to move?"

"I don't think so. Ollie really loves his school in St. George. It's a school for the blind."

Lorena flicked a rag at me. "You know what I think?"

"What?"

"I think it's too early for you to be worrying. You said you were honest with the boy. That's all you can do. You don't owe anyone a decision. Time will tell how you really feel. Just don't make anyone any promises you can't keep, and you'll be okay."

I let out a frustrated breath. "Yeah."

"If this girl is as amazing as you say, the right guy will come along for her and for that little boy. She's still so young."

Her words hit me in the gut, made me so freaking jealous. I wondered if that was intentional on her part. I didn't want anyone *else* to come along. I couldn't figure out how to make this work logistically, but I wasn't anywhere near ready to let the idea of her go.

All of a sudden, I put my hand on my stomach. It felt like my insides were twisting. At first, I thought maybe it was the stress of thinking about the situation with Eden. But as the rush of nausea tore through me, it quickly became clear that I was about to throw up.

I ran to the bathroom off the kitchen as fast as I could and hurled into the toilet.

Lorena followed. "Are you okay?"

With my hands on each side of the toilet, I looked up at her, dazed and confused.

"Is it stress?" she asked.

As I leaned over the bowl, I couldn't help but laugh. All these years, I'd figured I was immune to throwing up.

I just hadn't met the right eleven year old with the right stomach virus.

I might have returned to L.A., but Ollie was most definitely still with me.

Although still nauseous, somehow I managed to keep from vomiting at work.

My father had brought a consultant in for the meeting this morning. The guy went on and on about the state of the industry. I didn't appreciate having to come all the way home for this bullshit.

He just kept rambling. "Remember a time when people used to love going to the movies, and they would happily pay for it? The film business is sinking because, plain and simple, the movies suck. The only reason to take someone to the movies these days is if you're a dude trying to get laid. Something's got to change with the quality of movies being put out there, or the film industry is on its last leg."

I scrolled through my emails while he was talking and saw that something had come in from Ollie.

*A message from Ollie Shortsleeve using Voice-Text300:*

*Dear Ryder,*

*Testing. It's me, Ollie.*

That was all it said.

I chuckled to myself. That was freaking adorable. I discreetly typed a message back to him.

*Hey Ollie,*

*Guess what? Been thinking of you a lot. Not just because I miss you guys, but also because I caught your stomach bug. It's okay if you think that's funny. Now that I'm not hunched over a toilet, I'm laughing, too.*

*What are you up to this morning?*

*Ryder*

I returned to listening to the consultant, who continued to bore me. My father was pretending to be engaged, although I suspected he was regretting his decision to bring him in, since the guy had yet to offer any solutions to the problems he was so good at outlining.

A response from Ollie popped up in my inbox and once again stole my attention.

*A message from Ollie Shortsleeve using Voice-Text300:*

*Hi Ryder,*

*I'm listening to some videos and emailing you. Eden is making breakfast.*

*I'm glad you told me it's okay to laugh, because it's pretty funny that you threw up. I'm all better now. I hope you feel better soon.*

*P.S. I'm talking into my voice to text app to write this. That's why there are no spelling mistakes.*
*P.P.S. I miss you, too. So does Eden.*

I closed my eyes and pictured Eden in her kitchen, bending over the stove in her tight little leggings. Imagining the smell of her hair, I breathed in, once again cognizant of the fact that I was closing my eyes to experience feelings and sensations, something I was doing a lot more of lately.

After the meeting wrapped up, the consultant left the room, leaving me alone with my father.

"You seemed distracted," he said.

"Was I supposed to be paying attention to that garbage? He was full of nothing but hot air. You seemed unimpressed with him, too."

He changed the subject. "How was your trip?"

"It was really good."

"I hope you got whatever it was out of your system."

*Far from it.*

"*Its* name is Eden. And I did not get her out of my system. I'll be going back at some point."

He shook his head as if to totally disregard what I'd just said. "I really need you to focus. You can't be taking weeks away at a time to visit women in other states."

I didn't expect him to get it. "What good is vacation time if I can't use it? I never took time off up until last week. I've worked my ass off. Haven't I accrued a shit ton of vacation time by now?"

"McNamaras don't take time off. When I was your age, I wasn't taking vacations. All of my time was spent building my career. And that's exactly what you should be doing. You can relax when you're my age."

"That's ludicrous because you haven't slowed down one bit."

"Yeah, well, it's different now...without your mother. Things might be different if she were around to travel with me. But work's been good for me. I don't see that changing anytime soon. Someday when you're truly ready to take over my spot, I can scale back. That's why I'm working you so hard right now." He lifted his finger. "Speaking of which, I need to talk to you about the next leg of Operation Take Over the Global Market."

I braced myself. "What's the next step?"

"China."

"China?"

"China, yes. You sound almost as excited as when I told you that you were headed to India."

"Well, once again, you caught me off guard. What's the deal with China?"

"There are a few Chinese tech companies looking to invest in our studio. They're hunting for content right now. They've already collaborated with some big names. We need to get in on this. I've got you meeting with two different companies when you visit next month."

I knew there was no use trying to argue my way out of this trip, despite my recent disdain for international travel. My father seemed more determined than ever to expand my role here. I needed to suck it up and go with it. I'd figure out a way to work this China trip in with my plans to travel back to St. George.

No matter how hard I tried not to peek in on Eden's show, it was hard to resist when I was alone in my bed and had nothing better to do than to wait for our midnight Skype chat.

A few nights after I returned from St. George, I gave in to the urge to check out what was going on.

When I logged in, there she was, sitting with her legs crossed and chatting with some of her followers. I was immediately relieved not to have caught her with her shirt off or something.

She didn't seem to notice that I had joined. I preferred it when she didn't know I was watching. Eden admitted that my being there made her nervous now that she knew how much the camming bothered me.

I quickly became captivated, getting immersed in her world just as easily as I had in the beginning.

She was answering questions. Some guy was asking her what he should wear on a first date.

"You should wear whatever you're comfortable in," she said. "Whatever makes you feel confident. If you're a jeans and T-shirt kind of a guy, then rock that look, knowing you're showing her your authentic self. It's very important to be yourself."

I didn't know how she pulled all of this stuff out of her ass at the drop of a hat, but it was definitely a true talent, because she hardly even had to stop to think.

The token sounds went crazy all of a sudden. The viewers had collectively thrown in enough for her to take her top off.

I swallowed in anticipation, knowing it didn't normally take very long for her to give them what they wanted.

Sure enough, Eden placed her hands on the bottom of her shirt and lifted the material up over her head. She unclasped her bra from the back and let her voluptuous breasts spring free.

*Fuck.*

I missed her so badly. I hated this. I hated this so goddamn much.

Morbid curiosity led my eyes to the comments section.

**AdamAnton555: You have the most beautiful tits I have ever seen.**

**LouisGator1: I wish I could suck on them.**

**ElliotMichael33: I'd love to slide my dick in between those right now and come all over your creamy skin.**

I spoke to the screen. "I'd love to punch your fucking lights out."

Even though I knew this was part of the territory, hearing all of the things these fuckers wanted to do to her made me insane.

After she finished her little show and put her shirt back on, I impulsively purchased two thousand tokens and dropped them all in at once. When she looked down and saw my name, she turned fifty shades of red.

She got her act together, though, pretending I was just one of the guys.

"ScreenGod! It's been a while."

I decided to be a wiseass.

### ScreenGod90: Is that enough money for a private chat?

I knew full well it was more than enough and then some.

Eden played it cool and bid farewell to her viewers, promising to return at the end of our private time.

I braced myself, figuring she was going to be mad at me for interfering.

The reception I got was just the opposite.

"How did you know I needed to see you?"

"I didn't. I got jealous as fuck and lost it, but if you wanted an escape, then win-win."

"Two-thousand coins, Ryder? Are you crazy? I would've stopped for free if you just asked me."

"A private chat is worth much more than that to me."

"I didn't even see you log in. How long were you watching me?"

"Long enough to get pissed. I was stealthy, though. Snuck in when you were telling that lame dude how to dress himself."

She placed her hand on her forehead. "Oh my God. I know."

"If I ever have to ask you how to dress, do yourself a favor and dump my ass."

She laughed but then changed her tone. "Dump you? Do I even *have* you?"

Suddenly, the mood became tense. Her question was a serious one.

"You have me. You've had me from the moment you first looked me in the eyes and said my name. It's fucking insane how much you have me."

Her face contorted. "I miss you."

"It's painful being away from you again."

"I know," she said.

"I don't feel like sharing you tonight—or any night, really. I've never felt possessive like this over anyone in my entire life. I don't know what's going on with me. I feel so out of control of my emotions."

"What I do for a living is not exactly a normal situation for someone to have to deal with. I think you're reacting normally. I'm putting you in a tough spot."

"You're doing what you have to, and I admire you for that. More than you know."

"I'm not going back to work tonight. I'm just gonna stay on and talk to you. You paid me enough for a week."

"You do what *you* want, okay? Not what you think I want."

She pulled off her shirt before removing her shorts and underwear.

"What are you doing, Eden?"

"You said to do what I want."

She was panting, and her eyes were glassy. She looked horny as all hell. My dick was hard as steel as I watched her spread her legs apart, her glistening pussy taunting me.

"I want you to show me how much you want me. And I want to hear you groan and watch you come, Ryder."

*Well, fuck.* I thought I was already hard, but my dick stiffened even more.

"Lie back," I said.

Eden positioned herself so she could rub her clit while watching me masturbate. Even though we'd done this before, there was something so desperate about this time. I think we were both at the end of our ropes after being interrupted before I'd left her.

As I tugged at my cock, I said, "You're so hot, baby. I've never wanted to fuck anyone like I want to fuck you. I want you so bad right now. I can hardly think straight."

There was no bigger turn-on than the sound of her moaning while she touched herself to the sight of me jerking it.

I licked my hand to wet it so I could imagine it was her drenched pussy. I closed my eyes and imagined what her pheromones smelled like. We were both totally lost in the moment.

When I opened my eyes, she was squeezing her tit with one hand while she massaged her clit with the other.

*Holy shit, that's hot.*

Her legs started to tremble before she moaned in pleasure. I loved that she didn't give a fuck whether or not I was ready. She just let herself go.

"Eden...Eden...Eden..." I let out the longest breath, which I hadn't even realized I was holding, as my cum spurted out in buckets.

She watched every second of it. I kept milking myself to squeeze out the last few drops.

I collapsed against the headboard, momentarily sated but knowing that feeling of satisfaction would be short-lived.

We lay there for a while in silence. Eventually, she got up and put her shirt back on.

"So, Ollie told me you've been emailing each other," she finally said.

"Yeah. He's so cute." I wondered if she was mad about that. "I hope that's okay with you. I told him we could keep in touch."

"I know what you told him—that you'd be there for him no matter what."

My tone was insistent. "I'm not trying to overstep my bounds. I just don't see a reason why he and I couldn't keep in touch, even if..."

"Even if things don't work out with us," she said defensively.

I paused. "Yeah."

"You *do* know Ethan told him the same thing, right?"

*Fuck Ethan.*

"Yes. But I'm not Ethan. I'm not an asshole. I would never do anything to hurt him."

"Not intentionally. But life happens. Shit happens. He and I, we're not used to people who stick around. Sadly, that's the norm for us. Ethan, my father, Ollie's father—no men in our lives ever stick around. My brother and I have no one but each other, so we're not exactly conditioned to believe people when they say they're going to be there.

That hurt to hear. "I know. I get it." Leaning in, I said, "You've never mentioned your father before, only that he was never around."

"Yeah, well, there's not much to mention. My mother really knew how to pick them. Both men she got knocked up by were passing through town at the time."

"Is he alive?"

"My father is a drifter. He never stayed in one place more than a year or two. The last I heard he was somewhere in North Dakota."

"Were you born in Utah?"

"No. I was born in Montana. My mom was from there. She was a struggling student when she met him. They were around the same age. He took off after he found out she was pregnant. He came around one time when I was five. But at the time, I didn't know it was him. My mother introduced him as her friend Lane. She only told me years later who it really was."

*Montana.*

*Lane.*

*Montana Lane.*

*Fuck.*

"Wow," I said.

Even though Eden was downplaying her feelings, the fact that she'd chosen her father's name for her screen name spoke volumes. She was hurt by her dad's abandonment far more than she was letting on.

Another reason I needed to tread very carefully.

A week later, it was Friday afternoon when the China itinerary landed in my inbox. My father had scheduled two full weeks of meetings there for me. I'd be leaving in a month.

I hadn't booked a ticket back to St. George yet. Even though I wanted to see Eden badly, work had been so freaking busy. Maybe she was right. Maybe this couldn't work, no matter how much I wanted it to.

As I stared at my inbox, a new message came in. It was from Ollie.

*A message from Ollie Shortsleeve using Voice-Text300:*

*Ryder,*

*Last night I heard crickets outside. I thought maybe you came back. But when I went to the window, I called your name and you weren't there. It was just crickets.*

*Ollie*

*P.S. Are you coming back?*

That squeezed at my heart. My fingers lingered at the keyboard for a while, but I didn't know what to tell him. So I held off on responding, vowing to send him a message later.

It was 5:30, and I decided I'd had it for the day, so I got in my car and took off.

My original plan was to head home and catch up on the sleep I hadn't been getting.

When I got to my exit, though, I passed right by, staying on the freeway.

I told myself I might have accidentally missed the exit, but I knew damn well it was intentional.

I was headed straight for the airport.

## CHAPTER 16

*Eden*

Ollie was finishing off a glass of warm milk, something I often gave him close to bedtime.

"I emailed Ryder today," he announced. "But he didn't write back like he normally does."

My heart sank.

"Well, I'm sure he was just busy. Maybe he didn't get it yet."

"Yeah, maybe."

Ollie now anticipated Ryder's emails every day. As much as I hadn't wanted Ryder to engage with my brother because I didn't believe he could keep it up forever, it was so sweet to see Ollie's face light up whenever he told me about the messages. You'd think it was Gilbert Gottfried himself emailing or something.

Ollie's app had a button he could press that read aloud any emails he received. It always amused me to hear the robotic voice sounding out Ryder's words.

The problem was Ollie could be a bit obsessive. He didn't realize how busy Ryder was back in L.A., and Ryder had now trained Ollie to expect an email every day. It wasn't realistic to expect that to continue infinitely. Though I could certainly relate to unrealistic hopes.

"It's getting late," I said. "We'd better get you to bed."

"But I want to wait to see if he writes back."

"You can't wait all night. Maybe if you go to sleep, you'll wake up to an email." As much as I hated getting his hopes up like that, I couldn't have Ollie staying up too much past his bedtime because I needed to start my show. I always waited until I knew he was asleep, so some nights I started late as it was. I was lucky my brother wasn't a light sleeper. The few times he had woken up during my show and knocked on my door, I'd paused it to attend to him. But overall, he slept through almost anything.

Suddenly, my doorbell rang. That was odd for this time of night. Even though I probably should have peeked out the window first, I opened the door and immediately regretted it when I found a man I didn't recognize standing there.

My heartbeat sped up, and I instinctively shut the door a tad so only my head was peeking out. "Can I help you?"

He smiled, displaying prominent dimples. "I didn't mean to startle you. I'm Christian. I just moved across the street. It looks like I got a piece of your mail. I wanted to return it."

When he handed it to me, I was mortified. The packaging was open. It was a dildo I'd ordered.

*Mortified.*

"I'm sorry," he said. "I opened it before I saw that the name on the package wasn't my grandmother's."

I looked down at the hot pink silicone rod, noting the words on the box: *Ribbed for your pleasure.*

"Well, this is embarrassing."

Christian's face turned a little red. "Don't be embarrassed. Please."

Upon closer look, I could see he was only a little older than me. He had beautiful, big brown eyes and a nice smile. He was actually pretty cute.

"Where exactly across the street do you live?"

He pointed. "The gray house right there."

"That's Mary Hannigan's house. Did something happen to her?" Mary was a woman in her nineties who'd lived across the street for more than sixty years. She and my mother had been close.

"Oh, no. I'm sorry to scare you. I'm her grandson. I live a few hours north of here, but I work remotely, so I can spend my time wherever I like. I moved in with her temporarily to keep an eye on her. She's been slowing down lately."

"I see. Well, it's good to hear nothing happened."

He lingered in the doorway. I felt like maybe I was being rude by not inviting him in, but I didn't have too much time before my show. Although, Ollie wasn't anywhere near sleepy, so he'd probably be up for a bit, and I'd have to start late.

*What the hell...*

"Did you want to come in?"

"Sure. I'd love to." Christian followed me into the house.

"Can I get you some tea or coffee?" I asked.

"Coffee would be excellent, if it's not too much trouble."

"Not at all. I have a Keurig, so it's easy."

I placed my hand on Ollie's head. "This is Ollie, my little brother. Ollie, this is Christian, Mary's grandson. He's going to be living across the street for a while."

"Hi." Ollie waved. "I'm blind."

Occasionally, when I introduced Ollie to new people, he felt the need to start out with "I'm blind." I guess it made him feel better to get it out of the way.

Christian smiled. "Well, thank you for the heads up. It's really nice to meet you, Ollie."

"You would have figured it out, but..."

"I appreciate you telling me."

"I have to go to bed. I'm not leaving because you're boring or anything."

"I won't take it personally." He chuckled.

I excused myself to help get Ollie settled into bed before returning to the kitchen where Christian had taken a seat at the table.

After I fixed Christian's coffee and handed it to him, he said, "Wow. You have your hands full, huh?"

"Yeah. I'm his caretaker since our mother died."

"I hope you don't mind, but my grandmother filled me in on everything. She was telling me about your mother, so I already knew about Ollie. And she thinks you're amazing. Now I can see why."

I felt a little flush at the compliment. "Thank you. She's pretty awesome herself."

Christian reminded me of someone, and then I realized it was the actor Henry Cavill. If I wasn't so taken with a certain ScreenGod, I might have developed a crush on him. But at the moment, I only had eyes for Ryder McNamara.

"My grandmother also told me that back when you had a car, you used to take her shopping. Thank you for that."

"Yeah. My car shit the bed a while ago, and I haven't gotten around to replacing it. I walk everywhere now. Probably why I'm so skinny."

"You're perfect."

*Okay. He's most definitely flirting with me.*

His eyes lingered on mine before he suddenly looked down. "I'm sorry. That kind of just slipped out."

"No worries. Thank you for the compliment."

He took a sip of his coffee. "Well, I have a car, so if you ever need a ride anywhere, you let me know, okay?"

"Thanks. I appreciate that."

Over the next several minutes, Christian told me a little about his job as a web developer. He was easy to talk to, and I enjoyed not being the only adult around for a change. I looked at the clock and figured I had about ten more minutes before I had to kick him out so I could work.

The doorbell rang, and I jumped a bit. Two people showing up at the door in one night was definitely a rarity. With Christian here, I felt confident getting up to answer it.

When I opened the door, my heart felt like it was going to explode. Before I could even process it, Ryder had pulled me into his arms and kissed me so passionately, it felt like he was devouring my soul.

I was in shock. Total shock. So much so that when he finally released me, I was dizzy. I'd practically forgotten there was another man in my house.

Ryder's eyes suddenly darted to the area behind me where I turned to see Christian now standing.

Ryder swallowed, looking like he'd been punched in the gut. His mood completely darkened. "Who's this?"

I coughed. "This is Christian. I just met him, actually. He's my neighbor's grandson. He came over to drop off my mail that got delivered there by accident."

Ryder entered the house, and his eyes wandered over to the two mugs of coffee on the kitchen table. He was silent.

"Christian, this is Ryder, my..."

When I hesitated, Ryder said, "Boyfriend."

*Okay, then.*

Christian blew out a breath. "Nice to meet you."

Rather than offering a hand, Ryder crossed his arms. "Same."

Ryder's eyes then landed on the dildo sticking out of the open package on the kitchen counter.

"What's this?" he asked, lifting it.

"Oh..." I laughed nervously. "That's what Christian delivered, unfortunately. It was sent to his grandmother, Mary, instead. Quite embarrassing."

He was just staring at me now. "I see."

Things could not have been more awkward. I felt horrible. I could only imagine how this looked to him.

Christian clapped his hands together. "Well, I'd better go and let you two have some privacy." His gaze traveled back to me. "It was really great meeting you, Eden."

"Likewise."

He looked over at Ryder. "It was a pleasure."

Ryder sucked in his jaw and nodded but didn't say anything as Christian exited the house.

God, why had I invited Christian in? I never would have chosen to hurt Ryder like this.

I turned toward him. "Why didn't you tell me you were coming?"

"I wanted to surprise you. Unfortunately, I was the one who got the surprise."

I knew if there was ever a time to put aside my pride, it was now. This man had come all the way from California to surprise me, only to find me having coffee with another guy. Even if it meant nothing, he had *every* right to be upset.

I placed my hands around his face. "Listen to me. I know what that looked like. But there was absolutely nothing happening there. You have to trust me. I've spent this entire week miserable, missing you like crazy. Then, when Ollie said he hadn't heard back from you today like he normally does... I'm not gonna lie—I got a little paranoid. Now I know it's because you were on a plane. I am so fucking crazy about you, Ryder."

He stared into my eyes for a long time. I hoped he could see the truth pouring out of them.

His shoulders relaxed. "I felt like I'd been going crazy as it was, and then to see you with him. I just..."

I ran my fingers through his hair, and he closed his eyes. "I would've felt the same if I'd traveled all that way only to walk in on you having coffee with a woman. I get it. But that doesn't change the fact that what you saw was meaningless."

"I overreacted, but the truth is—this is the kind of shit that will happen when I'm not around. There will always be some other guy trying to nab you. You're such a fucking catch, Eden. I don't think you realize it, because you're humble."

I rolled my eyes. "Oh yeah...with my baggage and my crazy-ass job? I'm *such* a catch."

"Your brother isn't baggage. He's the fucking bomb. And your job is how I met you, so as much as I hate it sometimes, I'm damn thankful for it. You're beautiful and smart. And that guy was making a play for you, whether you realize it or not. I can't fucking blame him, but I still want to kill him."

I lifted my brow. "*Boyfriend*, huh?"

"I know we haven't really talked about that, but I wasn't about to lose an opportunity to stake my claim." He looked over at my kitchen clock. "You're late for work."

"I can't work with you here."

"Yes, you can. And you will. I want to watch you."

That took me by surprise. "What? I thought it bothered you."

His voice was gruff. "It does...but I want to watch anyway."

"After what you've told me about how you feel about my job, how could you want to witness...*everything*?"

"Morbid curiosity?" He tucked a piece of hair behind my ear. "I want to see it all, no holds barred. I want to watch you get ready. And then I want to watch your show, every second of it."

Even though it was against my better judgment, I wasn't going to deny him anything tonight.

"Okay," I said.

The tension in the air was thick as Ryder followed me into my bedroom. I could feel the heat emanating from his body, and the hairs on my back stiffened. His cologne wafted in the air, his smell alone turning me on. I didn't want to work tonight. I wanted to just lie in bed with him.

He sat in the chair in the corner of my room. Even though he looked exhausted from his flight, he was still sexy as all hell as he leaned back and stared over at me. His hair was perfectly tousled, and he wore a collared shirt. He was dressed exactly the way I imagined he did when he wheeled and dealed in Hollywood. *Fuck hot.* He must have hopped on the plane straight from work.

A few buttons were opened at the top of his shirt, and his sleeves were rolled up. The watch he was wearing had to have cost thousands.

He relaxed farther into the chair. "Show me everything. Tell me what you do to get ready."

His sexy glare made me a little nervous and turned me on at the same time.

"First, I take off all of my clothes, and I change into a fresh thong." I took a pile of panties out of my drawer and placed them on his lap. "Do you have a preference?"

He ran his fingers along them and wrapped a royal blue lace one around his hand. "This one. Definitely."

His eyes followed as I removed my cotton panties and tossed them aside before sliding the thong up my legs and over my crotch.

He swallowed as I lifted my shirt over my head and unsnapped my bra. Ryder's breathing quickened. He licked his lips as my breasts sprang free.

"You're so fucking beautiful," he muttered.

He continued to watch me intently as I put a camisole on and brushed my hair at the vanity. Through the mirror, I could see him behind my reflection. When our eyes met, he flashed me the sexiest smile that gave me goosebumps. I still didn't know what was happening between us, but I was damn happy he'd come back.

I turned around to face him. "Okay, I'm just about ready. You sure you wanna watch?"

He gestured with his index finger. "Come here first."

My nipples stiffened as I approached him. He pulled me onto his lap so I straddled him on the chair. His cock was bursting through his pants, as hard as you could possibly imagine. I tensed my muscles over him and could feel my wetness seeping through the material of my thong.

He moved my body over him, grinding into me. He pulled my face to his but stopped just short of kissing me, instead whispering, "I want you to think about me every second you're on tonight. Think about how hard I am for you, and know that I'll be right here waiting when you're done."

## CHAPTER 17

*Ryder*

It took a while for her to relax into her normal cam-girl persona. My being here was making her nervous. After about thirty minutes, though, she started to get her groove back.

She'd glance over at me from time to time and we'd exchange smiles. I even managed to stop myself from intervening after she'd taken off her shirt for five minutes. But with each passing second, my desire for her grew stronger. The need to touch her grew stronger. The need to steal her away from these strangers grew stronger.

The ultimate test of my resistance happened when some guy requested a private chat.

Eden left her audience long enough to whisper to me, "Are you sure you want to watch this?"

I wouldn't have dreamed of leaving her now. As hard as I knew it would be, I was all in. "Yes," I said.

"Okay." Her breathing was rapid. "But just remember that I'm thinking about you every step of this, okay?"

She returned to the bed and clicked on whatever it was she used to transition to the private chat room.

She sat with her legs crossed and smiled when she seemed to notice him on the screen. "Hi, Greg."

*Fuck you, Greg.*

*"Hey, Montana. You're looking beautiful as always tonight,"* I heard him say.

I couldn't see his face because the computer was turned away from me.

"Thank you. How was your day?"

*"Really stressful."*

They went back and forth talking for a while, and it was actually boring me a little. I was tuning out until I heard him say, *"I would love to look at your ass tonight."*

That definitely got my attention. It felt like all the blood in my body suddenly rushed to my face. Fuck. I was wrong. I really couldn't handle this.

Eden stared straight at me as she slowly slid her panties down her legs. Then she got on all fours and stuck her ass in the air. I'd never seen it from this angle. Since I couldn't see the man on the screen, I tried to forget he was there for a moment as I fixated on her.

Then came his voice again. *"Make yourself come while I jerk off to your ass."*

My body stiffened. It took everything in me not to explode from the combination of jealousy and arousal. This was a test of endurance—one I wasn't sure I was going to pass. She'd told me to remember she was thinking of me, but it was damn hard. I refused to touch myself, to willingly get off on the fact that another man was getting off on her—even though I was hard as fuck.

Staring at her ass, I was ready to explode.

Then there just came a point when enough was enough. I couldn't take it any more, and no man in his right mind in my position should have been expected to handle this.

I wanted to give that man the surprise of his fucking life, show him who this girl really belonged to.

So, I did.

She turned her head and noticed me approaching the bed. I'd done it slowly enough so she could have stopped me if she'd wanted to. She didn't move, though.

The next thing I knew, my mouth was on her butt, devouring the skin of her ass cheeks and gently biting her.

"*Holy shit,*" I heard the man say.

I laughed inwardly. *You weren't expecting me, were you, fool?*

Refusing to look at him, I flipped Eden over and buried my face between her legs. I flicked my tongue along her tender skin before pressing it against her beautiful mound, licking her up and down from her clit to her asshole as she wriggled beneath my mouth.

She grabbed a fistful of my hair and pulled on it, guiding my face into her.

*Fuck yes.*

I began to fuck her with my mouth, desperately staking my claim with my tongue. Her breathing quickened. That told me she loved it, so I kept at it, so engrossed that I'd practically forgotten that this dude was watching me eat her out. Eden certainly seemed oblivious to anything but me.

"Hope you enjoyed the show." I came up just long enough to shut off the computer without ever getting a look at him.

*She's done for tonight. I'm calling it.*

Eden seemed unfazed by my sudden cancellation of her show.

*We interrupt this regularly scheduled programming...*

Her eyes were hungry as she began to unbutton my shirt.

Skin to skin, we were kissing so hard, barely coming up for breath as she worked to remove my pants.

She wrapped her legs around my back and pulled on my hair, never breaking our kiss.

Eden dug her fingers into my shoulders as she said, "Fuck me, Ryder. Please..."

"You sure about this?" I asked, hoping to God she said yes. It was the only time I would question her.

"Yes. And I'm on the pill. It's okay as long as you're—"

"I'm clean." I pulled back to look into her eyes as I finished her sentence.

*Fuck yes.*

Any doubts I might have had about whether she was ready were buried beneath the intense need to be inside of her right now. The world could have been crumbling around me, and I wouldn't have been able to stop this.

I slid my boxers down and let my engorged dick spring free. "I need you, Eden. You ready for me?" I breathed the words into her mouth.

She answered by wrapping her hand around my cock, the tip wet from my arousal. She led me into her entrance. The opening of her tight, wet pussy felt better than anything I could remember ever feeling.

She winced a little.

I'd only made it a couple of inches in when I asked, "Am I hurting you?"

"No. You're just...big."

*I've definitely heard worse things in my life.*

"Do you want me to stop?"

"No. Please don't. Just go slow. I need you inside of me."

"I can do that."

Eden was extremely wet, which told me she was excited and not hesitant. That gave me the confidence to continue moving in and out slowly until I was fully inside. And then it just felt like pure ecstasy. Her pussy clamped hard around my cock as I took her with reckless abandon.

"You feel so good."

Closing my eyes, I let all of the worries of the world fade away as I dove into her. When she let out a loud gasp, I covered her mouth with my palm so she wouldn't wake her brother. When I removed my hand, she dug her teeth into my shoulder to muffle her sounds of pleasure.

With every thrust, my need to completely claim her grew. I took weeks of frustration and jealousy out on her body. I needed release but wasn't anywhere near ready for this to end.

"Tell me this pussy is mine, Eden."

"It's all yours." She looked me in the eyes as she said it, and that totally did me in.

Swallowing her moans with my kiss, I began to fuck her harder. She moved her hips in circles to take every inch of me. A part of me wished I could have gently made love to her our first time, but that wasn't an option. The wait had been too long.

Eden gripped me tighter as I continued to pound into her. I could feel her feet flexing at my back. She seemed close to losing control.

"I need to come inside of you."

She dug her nails into my back. "Please..."

"Look at me, Eden," I demanded, wanting to see what she looked like when I gave her everything I had.

Her name exited my mouth on repeat as I emptied my cum into her, seeing stars from the intensity of the feeling.

**CHAPTER 18**

*Eden*

I'd somehow nodded off and woke to the sight of Ryder looking down at me.

Glancing over at the clock, I noticed it was only midnight. Normally I'd be logging in to chat with him at this time, but instead he was here and had given me the best sex of my life.

My voice was groggy as I asked, "Can't sleep?"

"No. Way too wired," he said. "In a good way."

No matter what happened between us, I would never regret this night. The muscles between my legs were sore in the best possible way, the aftermath of his girth. The delicious smell of him was all over my skin. It was worth the risk.

I looked up at him and smiled as he ran his hand through my hair, massaging my head. It had been a long time since I'd felt this satisfied, content, and safe.

Despite that, something had been nagging at me, something Ryder had promised to tell me about when he was ready. Since we were both unable to sleep, I wondered if he would open up to me about it.

"Will you tell me what happened with your ex-girlfriend?"

He seemed caught off guard by my sudden question. He stopped moving his hand through my hair and scooted up. I did the same.

He nodded and exhaled.

"A few years ago, I was probably at my worst in terms of my state of mind. My mother had just died, and I was depressed. Mallory and I had a really good relationship for the first few years. She was there for me throughout my mother's last days, and I loved her. You know? I really did."

I tried to curb my jealousy. "You said you met her in school?"

"Yeah. We met during my first year of grad school at UCLA. We were both business majors, but she was in her final year. Mallory is two years older than me, actually."

"Did you live with her?"

"We moved in together the last couple of years. She moved into my house."

I took a deep breath in, readying to hear something that might upset me, although I had absolutely zero clue what it might be.

He swallowed. "Soon after my mother died, Mallory got pregnant."

And there it was. My stomach felt like it had been stabbed.

"Oh my God." I reached for his hand and squeezed it.

"I know." He let out a long, slow breath. "So, when she told me...I wasn't happy about it. It was just too much at the time. I *wanted* to be happy about it, but I couldn't. I didn't feel ready to be a father, and my depression made everything worse."

I braced myself for the rest of the story. *Does he have a child out there somewhere? Was the baby put up for adoption?* Different theories kept running through my mind.

"I made no secret of the fact that I wasn't ready for a baby, that I was freaked out. I couldn't hide that, as much as I *tried* to want it."

"Was *she* happy about it?"

"That's the thing—she was. Mallory always wanted to be a mother. So even though it wasn't the right time, she accepted it and was pretty excited about it." He stared off for a moment. "I wanted to share that excitement. I told myself I would grow to accept it, but I was cold and distant. I was scared. It sucked because I couldn't be the person she deserved. I started going out more, drinking—anything to avoid the fact that I was going to have this huge responsibility. I was an ass. I look back at that time now, the person I was, and I hate myself."

Unable to wait any longer, I asked, "What happened with the baby?"

He hesitated. "She was fourteen weeks along when we lost it."

My heart sank. "Oh my God. I'm so sorry."

"You'd think I would've felt relief after all the stressing out I'd done, but it was just the opposite. I felt devastated, and so guilty, like my unhappiness had somehow caused the miscarriage."

I squeezed his hand with both of mine. "No, Ryder. Please don't tell me you blamed yourself."

"I absolutely did." He shook his head. "I felt like I had wished it away."

I knew the pain was still fresh, and that made me really sad for him. "It's completely normal for you to have reacted the way you did. Believe me, I indirectly understand, because I remember how I felt after my mother died, when it first hit me that Ollie was my responsibility. Having a child is a huge life change. You would've eventually gotten used to the idea. But it takes time, a lot more than a few months."

"I guess I understand that a little more now, but at the time I just saw myself as a bad person—and so did Mallory. We fell into a bad place after that, one we couldn't come back from."

I couldn't believe what I was hearing. "She blamed you?"

"Not entirely, but she'd say things like 'Are you happy now?' or 'Admit it, you're relieved'. That killed me. That killed me so much. I never would've wished for the miscarriage."

I closed my eyes to fend off tears. "I'm so sorry."

He'd been carrying so much guilt over this.

"The thing is, I wasn't relieved. I'd committed to giving fatherhood a hundred-percent effort. I just never had a chance to prove myself." He paused. "She had to have a D and C, and they somehow were able to determine that it had been a boy. That was fucking painful to know. But she wanted to know the gender."

My heart broke as I imagined the little boy who never was, one who looked just like Ryder, with his eyes and smile. That choked my heart.

"So, you couldn't come back from it—the loss. You and she..."

"No. We couldn't. She resented me—hated me at times. And I distanced myself even more after that. We eventually broke up."

"You never fell out of love with her, though." I braced myself for his answer.

"Not immediately, no."

"So, you *don't* love her anymore?"

He looked like he was struggling with how to answer that. "A part of me will always love her, but not in the same way I once did. I'm gonna be honest with you and tell you that before you came along, I wasn't fully over her. But that changed when I met you."

I wasn't sure how I felt about that, knowing he'd still had feelings for her right before we met.

"Do you have a photo of her?" I asked.

He stopped to think. "Yeah...somewhere on my phone. Why? You want to see a picture?"

"Yes."

Ryder gave me a look like he thought my curiosity was cute, then reached over for his phone and began scrolling through his photos. I didn't feel like I was being cute at all. I felt like a jealous bitch, but my curiosity would have killed me.

He handed me the phone. "This was taken probably a month before we broke up."

Now I regretted asking. She was beautiful—tall with long, thick black hair. Her eyes were almond-shaped, and she had plump lips that I suspected were natural and not injected.

I cleared my throat. "You said she's engaged now?"

"Yeah. Actually, I never told you this, but right before I first came out to Utah, I ran into her and her fiancé. It was the first time that had happened, and it was easier than I'd expected it to be. I wished them well."

*That's closure, right?* "Thank you for sharing all of this with me. I'd always wondered what happened with you and her. Although I never imagined it was something like this."

"It's pretty crazy to think I'd have a toddler now. I try not to think about that, but sometimes it crosses my mind."

I brought his face to mine and kissed him on the lips. "Just seeing how you are with Ollie, I know you would have been an amazing father."

"Once I got my head out of my ass, maybe." He sighed. "I've changed a lot since then, matured a lot. But it doesn't change what happened and the pain associated with it. It's something I'll always have to live with."

I placed my hand on his stubbled face and turned his head toward me. "Look at me. You did *not* cause that miscarriage. Do you understand? No matter how you felt at the time, your feelings had nothing to do with her losing the baby. *Nothing.*"

"Rationally, I know that..."

"But you have to *believe* it. It's okay to feel guilty about feeling the way you did, but please don't ever blame yourself for what happened. Let go of that idea right now, Ryder. It's not true. You can't terminate a pregnancy with thoughts."

His eyes softened. "I'll try to believe that."

"Now that I know about this, please don't hesitate to talk to me if you need to. Sometimes guilt over the past can creep up when you're stressed about other things."

"Okay. Thank you for listening. I haven't told many people what happened. Only a few people even knew she was pregnant. It's good for me to talk about it with someone I trust."

The hurt in his eyes was still fresh. What happened was most definitely still having an impact on his life. Maybe you never really get over a loss like that. But I wanted to help him work through it.

"What about you, Eden? Anything you need to get off your chest?" he asked. "Anything you haven't told me?"

I tried to think on that, but there wasn't anything significant to confess. My independent life had been cut short before I had a chance to make too many mistakes.

"No, not really."

He searched my eyes. "I feel like I had this idea of you before we met, and then when I met you, while I still recognize your soul, there's so much I don't know about your life, who you were before these responsibilities fell into your lap."

"I'm not sure *I* remember who I was."

He rubbed my thigh. "That makes me sad."

I attempted to answer his question. "I was a girl who loved music, who was a little boy crazy but hadn't fallen in love yet. I loved my life. It was simple. My mother was my best friend. I could tell her anything. Ollie was an unexpected gift, the sibling I never thought I'd have. At twenty, I hadn't figured out what I wanted to do with my life yet, but that was okay. I had a good life. I still do—just different now. A lot different."

"So you don't feel like you ever had the chance to discover yourself."

"Right. I feel like I'm still a work in progress. Right now, I'm doing what I have to in order to get by, and that takes precedence over self-discovery."

"What do you think you'd be doing if you weren't taking care of Ollie? You mentioned once that you dreamed of moving to New York to perform on Broadway. Do you think you would have gone through with it?"

"That was mostly a pipe dream. I can't be sure if I would have bitten the bullet, but I definitely don't think I would have stayed here these past four years. I think I would have traveled, but I don't know if it would have been to New York."

After all, I'm the daughter of a drifter. It's in my blood. I didn't know my father, but there were parts of me that I suspected came from him—namely that feeling inside of me that there was always something more, something bigger I was missing out on. I knew I wouldn't have stayed in one place all these years. That's why I was so envious of Ryder's trip to India.

"I would've liked to see the world a little bit before I got tied down," I told him. "It's hard to imagine what I *would've* done, though. That's sort of a pointless thing to focus on."

"I know you lost a lot when your mother died—opportunities that may or may not have arisen. But I'm grateful I found you. You went through a lot of shit to get to where you were the night I met you. But I'm happy the stars aligned. Life is funny sometimes."

I caressed his stubble with the back of my finger. "That's the thing. Life takes you in unexpected directions.

There's good, and there's bad to that. Sometimes on a detour, you find what you need in the least likely of places. And then you wonder if that was the direction you were always meant to go."

He winked. "You mean like falling for a cam john?"

"Exactly. I'm glad you were one of the detours on my journey, Ryder."

He was definitely a detour. But was he a temporary stop or the final destination?

## CHAPTER 19

*Ryder*

The following morning, Ollie took a really long time to wake up.

Eden and I kept waiting for him to hear my voice and walk into the kitchen, surprised as hell to find me. She said he almost never overslept, so it figured he'd do it the one morning I was here and wanted to surprise him. We'd also been waiting to make pancakes. Eden had the batter all mixed with chocolate chips and ready to go.

Telling Eden about what had happened with Mallory was a huge weight off my shoulders. I hadn't been sure how she was going to feel about it. Here she was doing the best she could to raise a child she didn't anticipate. And I'd admitted I hadn't felt myself capable of the same thing.

But her words had comforted me, and I was grateful for that.

I massaged Eden's shoulders as she sipped her coffee. "Should I go wake him?"

"Might as well. At this rate, we'll be waiting all day."

Eden stayed close behind me as I ventured to Ollie's room and opened the door. His legs and arms were splayed across the mattress. He was totally out.

I placed my index finger against my mouth to let Eden know I didn't want her to say anything. Instead, I curled my lips, unleashing my infamous cricket sound.

Ollie stirred, then jumped up. Eden tried hard to hold her laughter in as we watched him move his head around in confusion before calling out, "Ryder?"

I stopped making the sound. "Yeah, buddy. It's me."

"You came back!"

Hugging him, I said, "I told you I would."

"You didn't write me back yesterday. I thought maybe..." His words trailed off.

"No. Whatever you were thinking was wrong. I was on a plane to come see you."

The sun streamed through Ollie's window. He was happy to see me. This was a good day.

"Why don't I let you two hang out while I make pancakes for all of us?" Eden suggested. "I'll holler when they're ready."

After she retreated to the kitchen, Ollie turned toward me.

"It's weird that you're here. I dreamed about you last night."

"Really? What was I doing in your dream?"

"Nothing, really. You were just there."

"Well, I guess your dream was more like a premonition then."

"A what?"

"A premonition is a thought that ends up coming true. Because I'm here now."

"Oh yeah. That's freaky."

"I know. Hey—what do you see in your mind when you dream?"

"I don't see anything. I hear things and feel them, just like I do when I'm awake."

"Wow. That's fascinating."

I guess it was silly to think he could see things in his dreams if he'd never seen them in real life. I'd never thought about the dreams of people born blind before.

There were so many questions I wanted to ask Ollie, but I was always afraid to offend him somehow.

As if he could read my mind, he asked, "You want to ask me something?"

*Damn.* "How did you know that?" I grinned.

"The way you said 'wow' and then you just stopped talking, like you were thinking about what I said."

He was so perceptive.

I laughed. "You got me. There's a lot I'm curious about when it comes to your blindness. I just don't want to bore you with my questions."

"Nobody ever wants to talk to me about it. The kids from school who are like me don't have to ask me questions because they know the answers. But adults, like, people we know or people in the street? It's like they're afraid." He shrugged. "You can ask me."

"I think people are afraid to be rude sometimes. It's not really any of their business, even if they're curious. But since you gave me permission to be nosy, maybe I'll ask you some questions I've been wondering about."

"Okay."

"One thing I wonder is if you try to imagine what everything you encounter looks like."

He thought about it for a moment before he said, "Sometimes, but it kind of freaks me out. I don't know if I would want to know. Sometimes I think seeing things would be strange. I can't imagine what that would be like."

He was born blind, so that made sense. Not being able to see was all he knew. The concept of sight was probably overwhelming—all the lights and strange-ass people.

Still, I had to know. "If given a choice, would you *want* to see?"

He blinked several times. "Probably. I guess if I didn't like it, I could just close my eyes. My eyes are closed half the time now anyway because I don't need them."

"You got a good point there, little dude. I never thought of it that way." The questions kept popping into my head. "How come you don't have a guide dog?"

"I could have one, but I don't really go anywhere far away. Eden is with me, and if I'm not gonna be with her, I can use a pointer stick to feel things out."

My dirty mind heard *pointer stick* and *Eden* and wandered to last night—feeling her out with my pointer stick. Last night was incredible.

I shook my head to bring myself back to the present. "So, you don't need a dog then."

I was ready to go buy him one.

"Eden says someday I might need one when I'm a little older and go more places without her."

"Cool. I just wondered if there was a reason you didn't have one."

Ollie flashed an impish grin. "You want to see what I think you look like?"

"Uh...sure."

"I drew you."

"You did?"

"Yeah. Let me get it." He walked over to his desk and brought over a piece of construction paper. The drawing was unidentifiable. Actually, it looked sort of like a big cock with hair and eyes.

"This is how you envision me?" I chuckled.

"Yeah. I don't know why. I don't really know what you look like, but I have this idea. It's weird. I don't think I can even explain it."

*I can: I look like a big fucking dick to you.*

"What does my drawing look like?" he asked.

"Um…I think if I squint my eyes enough, I can see myself in it. But it's sort of like a…cylinder with eyes and hair. A great guess." I handed him back the paper. "It's fascinating to see what your imagination comes up with."

"I understand shapes, but I don't know colors. I don't know the difference between white or black, blue or red, or anything else. They're all just names to me."

It hit me that in Ollie's world, there was no such thing as judging someone by the color of their skin. If only everyone could live that way without having to lose their sight.

"You make movies, right?" he asked.

His question amused me. "I try. Yeah."

"Action movies are great for people who can see and all, but someone like me? I need to hear things, listen to people talk. If a movie is mostly stuff you're supposed to be watching and not hearing, I can't enjoy it. You should make more movies I can listen to."

Letting that sink in, I had a light-bulb moment. "I don't think that's something we consider enough. You're right."

Eden yelled from across the house, "Pancakes are ready!"

We joined her for breakfast in the kitchen, but I couldn't stop thinking about Ollie's words.

After we ate, I excused myself to step outside. I needed to call my father. I needed to tell him about my realization.

He picked up. "Son, where are you? Lorena said you were out of town for the weekend. You're not back in Utah, are you?"

"Yes, I am." I scratched my head. "Listen, I need to talk to you about something."

"Alright..."

"Have you ever considered what it might be like for someone to experience one of our movies if they couldn't see?"

After a pause, he said, "Well, movies are visual, so I suppose I haven't really thought about that, no."

Pacing along the sidewalk, I said, "That's an incorrect perception. Movies aren't just visual. They're comprised of sounds and good dialogue, and we're making a mistake when we start to undermine how important those other things are. Think about it. If you close your eyes in the middle of a scene where there's nothing but visual elements, what's there? Nothing! Someone should be able to enjoy a movie even with their eyes closed. How could we not be taking this into consideration? For every compelling image in a movie, we need to match that with equally compelling dialogue and sounds."

"Where is this coming from?"

Over the next few minutes, I told Dad about Ollie, about how I'd grown close to him and how he'd caused me to look at the world differently.

My father listened to every word. He was always very set in his ways, but surprisingly, he seemed open to my suggestion. "Interesting. Well, you know, when your mother was losing her sight due to the cancer, this never even dawned on me. Perhaps it should've."

"Yeah. Just something we need to keep in mind."

"I've never heard you so passionate about anything. I can see you've really grown attached to this kid—and his sister."

"I don't know what's gonna happen, Dad. I'm just taking it one day at a time. But yeah, I really like being here with them."

He let out a long sigh into the phone. "You're a good man, Ryder. I don't tell you that enough. I know I can be hard on you, and I see how hard you try to please me. I'm proud of you, son."

*Wow.* Well, I definitely wasn't expecting that to come out of this phone call. But it was nice.

"Thank you, Dad."

"Now, figure out a way to get this girl out to L.A."

I chuckled. "Not that simple."

"Alright, well, keep me posted on when to expect you home. And I will take what you said today into consideration. Maybe I'll even task you with creating a team to assess how much we balance the use of visual and non-visual elements in our films."

"I would love to take that on."

"Very good, then. Have a good rest of the weekend."

"You, too, Dad. Try to take a break."

"Love you, son."

"Love you, too."

When I walked back into the house, Eden was alone in the kitchen. Ollie must have returned to his room.

My mood was apparently obvious to her. "Why are you smiling?" she asked.

"I just had a nice conversation with my father. And that's pretty rare." Grinning from ear to ear, I said, "It actually had a lot to do with Ollie."

"Aw, really?"

"Yeah, some stuff he helped me realize about movies. I'll fill you in later. Right now, I just want to kiss you."

After devouring Eden's mouth for a few minutes, I grabbed her and spun her around. I was feeling content, just so happy to be here in Utah with her.

"You trying to dance with me, Mr. McNamara?"

"Why not? I think we're overdue for a dance, Ms. Shortsleeve."

I wrapped my arm behind her back, and Eden placed her hand in mine as we swayed to the non-existent music. We didn't seem to miss it or need it.

Later that night, the three of us sat down and watched a movie I'd chosen from an online list of films that were deemed to be heavy on narration—"blind-friendly." Ollie had seen most of the movies on the list, except for *Forrest Gump*, so that's what we watched.

The fact that *Forrest Gump* had also been my mother's favorite movie wasn't lost on me.

## CHAPTER 20

### Eden

That Sunday morning started as normally as any day did with Ryder here.

He and I had stayed up late into the night having amazing sex. I'd skipped camming to spend the full evening with him.

We woke up before Ollie to have some private time over coffee, and Ryder had decided to stay for a long weekend until Monday. He couldn't take much more time off of work right now, but I was happy for any time we got with him, even if it was just a few days.

He was pouring cream into his mug when he looked down at his phone.

Picking it up and staring at the screen, he said, "Hmm. That's odd."

"What?"

"I missed a few calls from Lorena while we were sleeping. My ringer was off. And now she just texted me to call her."

"Lorena is your housekeeper, right?"

"Yeah." He looked concerned. "Hang on. I'm just gonna see if everything is okay."

I watched as he dialed her.

"Lorena, hey. I just got your message." After a bit of a pause, he said, "Why do you want me to sit down?"

My heart beat faster as Ryder slowly sank into one of the kitchen chairs.

The next few minutes were a blur. His breathing became labored as he listened to the call.

Ryder's voice was shaky. "What? How could– how could this be?" Suddenly, his lip trembled. "No," he whispered, then shut his eyes tightly.

*Oh my God.*

*What is happening?*

Panicking, I rushed over to him and placed my hands around his shoulders. I didn't know what was going on, but I knew he needed my support.

"Are you sure?" he asked her.

Several minutes passed as he silently listened. Then he hung up the phone and tossed it aside. He placed both hands around his head and looked at me. It seemed to take forever for the words to come out. And when they did, it was like a sucker punch.

"My father died."

I put my hand on my heart.

*Oh no.*

*No.*

Tears filled my eyes. Not knowing what else to do, I held him. "Oh, Ryder."

He looked up at me in a daze, like he couldn't believe he was saying the words. "Heart attack. His housekeeper found him this morning. She called Lorena to get in touch with me. It happened in his sleep."

"Oh my God," I whispered. "I'm so sorry."

The right words completely escaped me. I knew better than anyone that life could change in an instant. I knew how devastating it was to lose someone so suddenly. Ryder was an only child. His mother had already passed. His father was his entire world. I couldn't even begin to imagine the pain he felt.

He held on to me for dear life. "I don't know what the fuck I'm gonna do, Eden."

I wished I knew how to respond. His pain was palpable—so much so that my own body physically ached.

"I have to get on the next plane," he muttered.

He got up and ventured into my bedroom.

Feeling totally helpless, I asked, "Are you okay to drive to the airport? I'll wake Ollie, and we can drive you there in your rental."

"No. Don't do that. I don't want to upset him. I'll be okay."

"Are you sure?"

He exhaled. "Physically, anyway. Yeah."

The hurt in my chest was almost too much to bear. "I'd do anything to make this go away right now. Please tell me what I can do for you."

Ryder hadn't brought anything with him, since his trip out here was impulsive. He'd gone to the store yesterday to buy a few items of clothing for the rest of the weekend, along with a small duffel bag.

I followed him around the room like a lost puppy as he grabbed his things.

We walked to the door together in silence. I knew I would never forget this moment. It was utterly heart-breaking.

Not wanting to let him go, I kissed him harder than I ever had. The words *I love you* were at the tip of my tongue. I wanted so badly to say them, but I was afraid to make this moment about me or anything else. I also didn't want him to associate the first time I said it with his father's death. This was neither the time nor place to introduce those words.

He opened the front door, then lingered at the threshold as he rested his forehead against mine.

"Please keep in touch with me," I said. "Call or text me if you don't feel like talking. Just let me know you're okay."

Tears fell down my cheeks and onto his. He wiped them with his thumb before kissing me one last time. It felt like a tornado of sadness was spinning inside of me.

And then he was gone.

I was staring at Ryder's full cup of now-cold coffee still sitting on my table when Ollie finally woke up and walked into the kitchen.

"I don't hear Ryder," he said.

A part of me wanted to keep what had happened from him, because I was afraid it would hit too close to home. There was really no way I could do that, though. I needed to tell him.

"Come here, Ollie."

"What happened? Did you fight with him?"

"No. Come here. Sit on my lap. I have to tell you something."

He could tell by the tone of my voice that something was wrong. "What happened?"

I just came out with it. "Ryder's dad died."

His breath hitched. "What? Oh no."

"I know. It was sudden. Just happened last night."

"How?"

"He had a heart attack."

He took a few moments to process before he asked, "Is Ryder sad?"

"Yes. I think he's still in shock."

"Was he crying?" he asked.

"No," I whispered.

Ollie's eyes opened. He kept them closed a lot, but sometimes when he was stressed, he would open them. "What can we do, Eden?"

"We just have to let him know we care and that we'll be here for him if he needs us."

He paused before wiping his eye quickly. He didn't want me to notice he was crying.

"It's okay to cry," I said. "I know how much you care about Ryder."

Rubbing his back, I let him process his thoughts.

He finally turned to face me. "He doesn't have anyone. We lost Mom, but I have you, and you have me. Ryder doesn't have anyone."

Ollie's genuine concern both broke my heart and warmed it. I knew Ryder had spoken to my brother about them both losing their mothers.

"We're not his family, but we can be here for him. He'll

be okay, Ollie. It will just take time. A lot of time. It's gonna be really hard for him for a while."

So much of Ryder's life revolved around his father. I knew in my heart he was never going to be the same.

Ryder texted me to let me know he'd returned to Los Angeles safely. Other than that, I hadn't heard from him and didn't expect to for a while. I'd sent him a lengthy email to let him know I was thinking of him. I knew I needed to give him space while he dealt with everything back home.

The following day at Ellerby's, I was barely able to complete basic tasks. Unable to stop thinking about Ryder, I eventually broke down in the kitchen.

Camille happened to notice me wiping my tears.

"Eden, what's going on? Is everything okay with Ollie?"

"Yes. Everything is fine with him."

"What, then?"

I sniffled and grabbed a tissue. "You remember Ryder?"

"Yes. Young Paul Newman with the gorgeous eyes? How could I forget? He hurt you? I'll kill him."

"No. Nothing like that." I took a deep breath and said, "His father died suddenly."

Camille frowned. "Oh man, I'm so sorry."

"He got the call yesterday while he was visiting for the weekend. He's an only child and already lost his mom to cancer. I'm so devastated for him that I can't think straight, can't even do my job today."

She covered her mouth with her hand. "Oh honey."

"It's killing me that I can't be there for him."

"Why can't you?"

I looked at her like she was crazy for even asking. "I can't just fly to L.A. on a whim."

"Why not?"

"Lots of reasons. Ollie's never been on a plane. He's scared to fly. And even if I drove, I can't drag him around a strange city, can't take him to a funeral."

"There's got to be a way." She pursed her lips and seemed to be thinking. "How about if I stay at your house for a couple days, watch Ollie for you?"

"I can't ask you to do that."

"Yes, you can. Are you forgetting that I looked after him once before? He survived, didn't he?"

I actually *had* forgotten that. Ethan had surprised me with an overnight trip to Arizona during the first year we were dating. He'd spoken to Camille about how best to surprise me, and she'd offered to watch Ollie for the night. It had been the first time I'd ever left my brother with anyone, and I remember being super nervous about it. It had all worked out in the end, though. We came home, and Ollie was still in one piece.

"Yes, I remember you watched him that one night… But I'd probably need to be gone for a couple of days if I went all the way out there. I wouldn't want to show up, then bolt on him."

"Look, I have some vacation time. I'm sure Bobby will let me take it on short notice if we explain the situation." She glared at me. "Eden, when was the last time you did something for yourself? Seriously. I know you're doing this to support Ryder, but it's clear to me that *you* need to be with him right now."

My voice trembled. "I want to go to him so badly."

She gripped my shoulders. "Then go. I've got you. I will take great care of your boy for a few days so you can take care of your man."

*My man.*

Ryder and I weren't even officially exclusive, but it didn't matter. Right now, aside from Ollie, he was the most important person in my life. And he needed me.

I knew what I wanted. "Are you sure?"

"Positive. Let me do this for you."

"Okay." I just kept nodding, wondering if there were any reasons I should reconsider. "Okay. Thank you so much. I owe you big time."

*Apparently, I have a flight to book.*

**CHAPTER 21**

## Ryder

It had only been a couple of days, but it felt like an eternity. People had been coming and going through my house. It was one big blur of *"I'm so sorry"* and *"Please let me know if there's anything I can do."*

There was *nothing* anyone could do. My father was gone, my life turned upside down.

Trays of catered food were everywhere, along with an explosion of flowers. And I was completely in a fog.

Lorena took a seat across from me at the kitchen table. With a splitting headache, I'd been sitting here with my head in my hands and no motivation to move.

*"Mijo*, have you eaten anything?"

I shook my head. "I'm not hungry."

She placed her hand on my shoulder. "You want me to tell people to stop coming?"

"No. It's okay. It's nice to know they care. I'm just so numb that nothing is affecting me."

"You let me know if you want me to kick them out. It's what I do best. I'll break out the cowbell."

I cracked a slight smile, my first since before my father died. "I will."

The doorbell rang, and when the next person walked in, I immediately regretted not telling Lorena to stop the visitors.

It was one of my father's board members from the studio, Sam Shields. As much as I didn't want to think about what Dad's death meant for the state of the business, I knew there were hundreds of investors panicking right now. My father would want me to deal with it, and so I'd have to do just that.

I never left my spot at the table as Sam approached, holding a large basket of wine and cheese. He placed it on the center island.

"Ryder, I'm so very sorry," he said, taking a seat across from me. "We're all so devastated."

"Thank you."

"I wanted to let you know we're here to support you. I know you're probably not ready to think about the next step at McNamara Studios, but it's something we need to decide very soon, and I wanted to offer my help."

"What kind of help?" I asked.

*Can you let me bury my father before we discuss this?*

"Well, did your father ever explain to you what would happen with the studio in the event of his death?"

"We never went into it in too much detail, because this wasn't something we expected. My father was too young to die. But I know he left me with enough voting rights that I can basically vote myself into his job."

"That's right. Technically, you could, but that's not what I would recommend, given your lack of experience for the position. I know your father's intention was that you would run the studio someday, but I think you would agree, he was counting on several more years to groom you."

"Yes. I know that."

"Anyway, I know it's not the best time to discuss this right now. So I'd like to propose we set up a meeting next week."

"Fine."

"I'll give you some privacy. You take care of yourself, Ryder. Let Laura and me know if there's anything we can do."

*Leave. That's what you can do.* "Thanks. I appreciate it." *Now go.*

Thankfully, he did. I couldn't deal with thinking about the state of the company on top of everything else right now. I knew what was going to happen: Sam would round up a bunch of his cronies, and they would work to convince me to make the decision that was in *their* best interests. They would try to get me to appoint one of *them* to my father's position.

Once my head cleared, I would need to decide what Dad would have wanted. That wasn't going to happen in a week, no matter how impatient they were. In all of the preparation my father had done with me, we'd never once discussed what would happen if he died prematurely. No one had expected him to drop dead at the age of fifty-eight. Certainly not me.

The house emptied out, and I found myself alone with my thoughts for the first time in a while. There were a couple of hours until the wake tonight. Then tomorrow would be the funeral and burial.

I still couldn't wrap my head around everything. Looking up, I spoke to my dad, wherever he was.

"I can't believe you're gone. If you thought I was in any way ready to survive without you in this world, you thought wrong. I might have put up a tough front and resisted a lot of what you had to say, but man, I'm not ready for this." I shook my fists toward the ceiling. "You need to help me figure it out from wherever you are. Because I don't know how to live without you."

I quietly pleaded with my father for guidance before opening a box of items that had been brought over from his house.

Sifting through some of the old photos Dad's housekeeper had found, I came across one of my parents and me when I was about seven years old. It was taken on the day of my First Communion. Sundays were always the one day my father took off from work. We would go to church and have family time. I hadn't a care in the world back then, never imagining life without both of my parents before I'd even reached thirty.

I looked down at my phone, which I hadn't bothered with in hours. Eden had sent several texts this morning to check on me. I quickly wrote back that I was okay and getting ready for tonight but that I would call her after the wake. It was hard for me to talk to anyone right now—even Eden.

There was a knock at the door. I guess my reprieve from visitors was short-lived. I really needed to shower and get ready for the wake, so I hoped whomever it was didn't plan on staying long.

When I opened the door, I found the last person I'd expected to see. She looked as heartbroken as I was.

"Mallory."

She started to tear up. "How come you didn't call me?"

*Does she even have to ask?* "Given that we're not together anymore, it didn't made sense to call you."

"You and your dad are like family to me—always will be, no matter what happens between us. I'm so sorry, Ryder. So sorry." She took a few steps closer. "Can I come in?"

I didn't realize I hadn't budged from the doorway. "Sure."

It shouldn't have surprised me that she showed up. As much as we'd been through, she knew my dad well and truly understood what this loss meant to me. Dad was always very fond of her and had been disappointed when we broke up. He looked at her like a daughter. Given that Mallory had daddy issues—her father had taken off on her and her mother when she was young—she'd always respected my father for being loyal to his family.

Mallory suddenly threw her arms around me. My body stiffened. I took a deep breath, though, and let myself be consoled by her without judgment for a few seconds. Mallory had been the most important person in my life at one time. She was important to my father. I told myself it was okay to take comfort in familiarity at a time like this.

"I'd been thinking about you a lot lately as it was, and then when I heard the news, it just shattered me. God, Ryder, I have so much in my heart right now." She placed her hand on mine. "Will you let me be here for you today?"

While I could understand her wanting to support me at a time like this, it still felt a little out of left field.

"How will Aaron feel about that?" I asked.

She looked down at her feet and paused. "I wasn't going to bring this up because it's not the right time."

"Why? What's going on, Mal?"

She met my eyes. "I broke off the engagement."

*What?* "What happened?"

"I don't want to get into it now, if that's okay. My being here isn't about me."

Well, that was definitely interesting fucking news. An unsettled feeling came over me. But regardless, she was right. Now was not the time to discuss it. I couldn't handle anything that was going to stress me out before having to see my father's body.

I would allow Mallory to be a friend to me tonight and not overthink it any more than that.

## CHAPTER 22

*Eden*

Part of the road had been blocked off to help control traffic. My Uber driver couldn't get anywhere near the funeral parlor, so he had to drop me off down the street.

There was a line all the way down the sidewalk to get into Sterling McNamara's services. I knew Ryder's father had been a bigwig in this town, but I guess I never really *got it* until now.

I'd decided not to tell Ryder I was coming to Los Angeles. I didn't want him to feel like he had to make accommodations for me or worry about me in any way. He had enough on his plate. But now I was sort of regretting not mentioning anything to him, because I had to stand in line with everyone else, and I worried I might not make it in before the viewing hours ended. It was going to be at least an hour before I got inside the place.

I thought about texting him, but I didn't want to be disruptive. He was likely receiving guests, shaking hands with people and wouldn't be able to leave to come let me in. I remembered how it was when my mother passed away. Even though she didn't have a crowd of people at her wake, the responsibility of the entire event fell on me. I was sure it was no different for Ryder.

So, I resigned myself to waiting with everyone else. I could wait. This wasn't about me; this was about showing my support for him.

Looking around at all of the fancy people in their expensive clothes, I felt out of my league. The woman in front of me was holding a handbag I knew cost more than my mortgage. Meanwhile, I'd put on the only black dress I owned, the same simple sheath I'd worn four years ago to my mother's funeral. There'd been no time to go shopping prior to coming out here. I'd just brought one carry-on bag of things thrown hastily together.

I looked around at all of the exotic cars and inhaled the cloud of expensive fragrance. This was Ryder's world, so very different from mine. Those differences were clearer than ever right now.

After almost a full hour, I finally made it to the entrance. A sea of people dressed in black blocked my view of the casket, and of Ryder—or at least of where I assumed he'd be standing.

When I finally spotted him, he nearly took my breath away. Ryder from a distance, so tall in his perfectly tailored dark suit, was a sight to behold. His hair was gelled a bit differently, but he looked incredible all dressed up. He was shaking hands and leaning into the embraces of people, one by one. He looked a little out of it, like he was just going through the motions. I remembered all too well how that felt. I wanted to hug him, be there for him, protect him from all of these people. I couldn't get to him fast enough.

My eyes then moved to the woman standing next to him. I'd already been nervous to make my presence known to Ryder, but the sight of her caused my stomach to full-on drop. Because she wasn't just any woman. If my memory served me correctly, that was Mallory.

*Isn't it?*

I squinted to get a better look.

*Definitely Mallory.*

Her eyes were unmistakable, and her long, black hair fell to just below her breasts—medium-sized ones, smaller than mine. She was much taller than I was but shorter than Ryder. She had her hands crossed in front of her and seemed to be watching every interaction he had as if she were some sort of gatekeeper.

I'd wanted to be the one to protect him, to be by his side tonight, but apparently she had the same idea.

My heart beat so fast.

*What the hell is she doing here?*

*They broke up.*

My mind raced, filled with some crazy scenarios. What if they'd never really broken up at all? Or maybe she'd come to comfort him the past couple of days, and they'd gotten back together. Maybe that's why he'd been distant.

The line in front of me kept getting shorter, and I was running out of time to decide how I was going to deal with this. It was only a matter of seconds before Ryder would spot me.

Should I just act like she wasn't there? I couldn't confront him about her at a time like this.

*Breathe, Eden.*

The moment his eyes met mine, I wanted to burst into tears. I felt so many conflicting emotions. Then a smile spread across his face, and his eyes never left mine even as he greeted the last few people before me.

When Ryder finally embraced me, it was like I fell into his arms and evaporated into his body. Mallory no longer seemed to exist. His heart beat so fast against my chest.

He held me tightly as he whispered in my ear, "I can't believe you're here."

I closed my eyes and breathed him in. His body was warm against my skin, which had been riddled with goosebumps moments ago. It felt so incredible to be in his arms—I'd done nothing but long for that for forty-eight hours straight.

"How did you manage to get away?" he asked.

"A friend is watching Ollie."

He shook his head slowly as he squeezed my hands. "I'm so happy you're here. So happy."

Our attention seemed to turn to Mallory at the same time. She stood there frozen, looking as surprised to see me as I'd been when I first noticed her. The sudden look of concern on Ryder's face told me he knew I recognized her from the photo.

"Mallory, this is my girlfriend, Eden."

Relief poured through me. *His girlfriend.* He'd still called me his girlfriend.

Mallory looked like she'd been smacked in the face. She cleared her throat. "Girlfriend... Oh, I didn't realize."

"Hello," I said.

"Hi." She nodded. "Excuse me for a moment."

I watched as she rushed through the crowd and disappeared into a hallway.

I turned my attention back to Ryder. "I'd better move. I'm holding up the line."

He grabbed my arm. "Don't go. I want you to stand with me."

"Really?"

"Yes, if you don't mind."

I was honored that he wanted me next to him. My bladder felt like it was going to burst, though. I had rushed here from the airport and hadn't used the bathroom since Utah.

"Let me just find a bathroom. I need to go badly. And I'll come right back."

He nodded. "Okay."

I found a lavatory across the hall and relieved myself. As I was washing my hands, it became clear where Mallory had disappeared to as she was suddenly staring at my reflection in the mirror. We were totally alone.

"I'm sorry for walking away rudely," she said.

I shut off the water and shook my hands. "Oh, I didn't take it that way."

Her eyes were red. They weren't that way before.

*She's been crying.*

"It's just... I was a little taken aback," she said. "I didn't think Ryder was with anyone." She exhaled as she turned on the water. "I needed a moment to breathe."

Not knowing what else to say, I blurted out, "You're his ex-girlfriend."

"Yes. I'm sure he's mentioned me?"

"Yeah. He has."

A look of sadness washed over her face. "I'm so devastated for him."

"Me, too."

"I love him," she confessed. She started to wash her hands and repeated, "I still love him."

All of the muscles in my body seemed to tighten at once as I swallowed. "Okay..."

"I'm sorry. I know you probably don't want to hear that."

*Yeah. No shit, I don't.*

When I didn't respond, she asked, "How long have you guys been together?"

"A few months..."

She grabbed a paper towel and began wiping her hands. "Is it serious?"

"I care about him very much."

*I love him, too, but I haven't told him that. So I'm sure as hell not telling you.*

She looked like she was almost ready to cry.

"Look, I don't know what's going on here," I told her. "I thought you were engaged to someone else."

"Aaron." She shook her head. "I broke it off with him."

*Ugh. Of course.*

I pretended to be calm as I panicked inside. "What happened?"

"To make a long story short, we ran into Ryder one night, and I didn't do a very good job of hiding my feelings after we got home. Aaron kept pushing, trying to get me to admit I still had feelings for him." She inhaled then exhaled slowly. "In the weeks after that, I started to realize I'd been in denial. I'd rushed into the relationship to hide from my sadness over the way things ended with Ryder. I realized ending things with him was the biggest mistake I've made in my life."

I felt like I was gearing up for war. "What are you saying?"

"I'm saying I'm still in love with him. He's the love of my life, and I think he's still in love with me, too."

I felt nauseous. "Have you told him all this?"

"We only saw each other for the first time in a long time earlier today. I told him my engagement was over, but I didn't tell him how I feel. He knows nothing about my feelings."

"Why are you telling *me* all of this right now?"

"Because I think you should know I do plan to tell him. Not today. Not tomorrow. Not during this difficult time. That wouldn't be appropriate. He needs time to heal. But I'm going to tell him soon."

When someone walked in, her head turned toward the door. "Please don't mention we had this conversation. It will stress him out, and I don't want that right now."

A woman came between us to wash her hands. After she left, Mallory said, "Did you know Ryder's dad?"

"No."

"His father was his entire world. It's going to be a long time before Ryder can deal with anything else. So again, please don't mention we had this conversation."

Before I could respond, she walked out. It took me a few minutes to regain my bearings enough to return to the main room where Ryder was waiting.

"I was starting to worry you weren't coming back," he said. "I thought maybe I'd hallucinated you coming in the first place."

"Sorry. There was a wait."

"No worries. I still can't believe you're here."

Mallory had given us space, choosing to sit with the others who'd already made it through the line and given their condolences.

My feelings were very revealing. I'd always told myself I was going to lose Ryder, that our lives were too different for things to work out. Yet at this moment, I felt completely sideswiped, devastated, like all of the hope had been sucked out of me—hope I didn't even realize I'd been hanging on to. So maybe I had thought things might work out with us.

*Until now.* Now I was terrified of losing him, and my hands were tied. Bringing it up with him would have been an asshole move, given the circumstances.

"Have I told you how happy I am you're here?" Ryder whispered in my ear before greeting yet another person in line.

I stood by his side for a while. At one point, Mallory approached us and hugged Ryder goodbye. Every second of that hug was painful for me.

Then she left, and I felt like I could breathe—for the time being.

The funeral director came by and told Ryder he'd closed the door to stop anyone else from coming in.

A half-hour later, the line finally came to an end.

Ryder grabbed me by the hand and led me out a side entrance, where a driver was waiting for us. It felt like we were jumping into a getaway car.

The second the car door closed, Ryder buried his face in my chest and started sobbing. It was the first time I'd seen him cry all night. He'd apparently been holding it in and waiting for this moment—when people were no longer watching him—to let it all out. My own tears fell as I held him, his shoulders shaking in my arms.

His crying eventually wound down into heavy breaths. He whispered over my skin, "Nothing and no one can make me feel better, but when you walked in, it was the first time I felt alive again." Ryder softly kissed my neck. "How long can you stay?"

"I'll be here for the funeral tomorrow. My flight is the next day."

"So, who exactly is taking care of Ollie? You said a friend?"

"My friend Camille. She offered. She works with me at Ellerby's."

"Is she responsible?"

I smiled at his concern. "Yes. She watched him once before."

"Whoever she is, remind me to give her a big kiss for allowing you to come to L.A. I could never repay her for letting me have you right now."

"I'm so glad you wanted me here."

He once again brought me closer to him. "How could I *not* want you here?"

"I just wasn't sure if it would be...too much."

"There's only one thing I need tonight, Eden."

"What's that?"

"I want to take a hot shower with you, bury myself inside of you, and forget about everything else. *You're* all I need."

For the time being, hearing that was all *I* needed.

"We can do that." I held him tighter. "Are you okay?"

Seemed like a dumb question, considering the circumstances, but it escaped my lips before I thought better of it.

"No," he answered. "It's gonna be a while before I am. It still hasn't sunk in."

"I know."

"But I'm the best I could possibly be right now with you here." He straightened up to look at me. "I know you're probably wondering why Mallory was with me when you arrived."

*You don't know the half of it.*

"You don't have to explain."

"Fuck yes, I owe you an explanation." His tone was insistent. "She showed up at my house out of the blue this afternoon before the wake. She was close to my dad. I hadn't even told her about his death. I figured she'd find out because it was all over the media. She said she wanted to support me tonight. Honestly, I didn't have the energy to question anything." He paused. "She also told me she broke off her engagement, but we didn't have any time to talk about it. To be honest, having her here was really stressing me out. Then you showed up, and I stopped thinking about it."

I was happy he was being honest. And I was tempted to confess what she'd told me in the bathroom, but opted not to. I'd be damned if I spent the short time I had with him talking about his ex-girlfriend, who apparently wanted-ed him back. If he knew she still loved him, would he feel differently about her? That question would silently haunt me. My stomach was in knots pondering that, but I'd come all this way to be with him. I wasn't going to let anyone take this time away from us.

The driver interrupted my thoughts. "Here we are."

We exited the car, and I looked up at the massive structure that was apparently Ryder's house.

All I could think was: *holy shit*.

**CHAPTER 23**

# Eden

It was a place like I'd only seen in the movies.

Surrounded by lush, landscaped grounds and a large, wrought-iron gate, Ryder's house was breathtaking.

After we entered the tall, dramatic front doors, my shoes echoed as I walked along the marble floors in the entryway.

*I'm not in Utah anymore.*

"Welcome to my humble abode," he said sarcastically.

"Ryder, I never imagined..."

"I know you didn't, because you're not materialistic. How I live is not something you think about. I know that." He grabbed a remote control and flicked on the fireplace in the living room. "You know what, though?"

"What?"

"I'd take your cozy little house in St. George any day over this cold, empty place. I sit here at night and think about how much more comfortable I am there."

"That's a little crazy."

"Alright." He cracked a slight smile. "We can agree to disagree."

Ryder showed me around a bit. Just outside of a set of French doors was a gorgeous in-ground pool and patio area, illuminated in blue lights. There was a state-of-the-art theater with plush, velvet seats, a wine cellar, and a home gym.

In the grand kitchen, huge bouquets of flowers covered the granite island. Ryder stared as if the sight of them had once again slapped him back to reality.

He turned to me and whispered, "I just want to forget."

I reached out my hand. "Let's go forget then."

Ryder took it and led me down a hallway, then up a spiral staircase.

The smell of his cologne saturated the air in his bedroom. With dark wood and lots of black accents, Ryder's room was sexy and masculine. A padded, slate gray headboard I knew I'd seen before took up most of the wall behind his bed. He pressed a button, and his shades began to close.

"So this is where you'd watch me from, huh? I recognize the headboard."

"This is it. Scene of the crime."

He undid his belt before turning me around and unzipping my dress. It fell to the floor, and I stepped out of it. Ryder continued to undress me until I was stark naked. He stood behind me as he showered my back with slow but firm kisses, sending chills through my core. I loved how eager and desperate he seemed for me. His erection pressed against my ass, so hot and hard through the fabric of his suit pants.

He kissed the back of my neck. "My beautiful Eden. I'll never forget that you came to be with me." He turned me around and took me in for several seconds.

So many emotions ran through me as I unbuttoned his shirt. The most striking was fear. I didn't want to lose him. I knew that more clearly than ever tonight, and yet I'd never been more scared of it.

He stepped out of his pants. Wearing only his boxer briefs, he pulled me into his rock-hard chest and wrapped me in his arms as he rested his mouth in my hair.

He rocked me gently back and forth. Closing my eyes, I relished the feeling. He'd never told me he loved me, but if this wasn't what love felt like, I would never know. It hit me that no one had ever held me like this in my entire life—certainly no man. I liked to consider myself a pretty tough person, someone who didn't need to be cradled or coddled. But damn, it felt good to be held like this. He'd been through so much today, yet here he was rocking *me*.

I wanted to scream, *"Please don't leave me. She's going to come back for you. You might be confused and not know what to do. But I love you, Ryder. Please trust in that."*

But of course, I remained silent, vowing to bring my mind back to the present and not dwell on the uncertain future, which had always plagued our relationship.

Ryder led me into a humungous bathroom just off the master suite.

Holy mother of all showers—it was like a room in and of itself with the most beautiful glass tile.

We stepped into it, and then he slipped out of his boxers and turned a handle. We were both completely naked now. I'd never seen him like this before, and I realized how perfect he was as the water cascaded down his body like a waterfall over carved stone. The V at the base of his abs aligned with a thin trail of hair leading down to his cock—his beautiful, thick cock that was so perfectly intimidating, but that I knew I could take.

Ryder pulled me close as the water sprayed out of three gargantuan showerheads. He placed his forehead against mine as the water rained down over us.

Once he started kissing me, that was it. We were in our own world under this water. Nothing else mattered, and I sure as hell wasn't going to let all my scary thoughts ruin this sacred moment. All I wanted to do was make love to him, comfort him, and have him feel nothing but me for a while.

I placed my hands around his face and drew him closer as he kissed me, his tongue exploring my mouth as if he needed my breaths to survive, as if he couldn't kiss me hard enough. This moment felt different from any other I'd experienced with him.

He leaned his weight into me, then lifted me up over him as if I weighed nothing. I wrapped my legs around him as he held me against the tile wall.

I immediately felt his crown at my opening.

He started to enter me without warning. "I'm sorry. I can't help it," he muttered.

"Don't stop. It's okay."

It didn't take any more convincing. In a second flat, Ryder had pushed all the way inside of me. His eyes rolled back as his body rocked against mine while he fucked me. His hand gripped the back of my neck, and the sound of our wet skin slapping together resonated throughout the bathroom, along with the echoes of our pleasure. It was wild and primal, and for the first time in my life, I wasn't worried about my own choreography during sex. He was in the driver's seat, and he was doing a damn good job driving. I just let go, closing my eyes and feeling the sheer force of his body pummeling through me.

I couldn't remember the last time I'd had the liberty to moan as loudly as I wanted. And there was nothing hotter than the guttural sounds Ryder made as he fucked me.

His arms wrapped around me tightly as he continued to pound into me, his frantic breaths in sync with his thrusts. Everything else in the universe faded away.

"Am I hurting you?" he asked, breaking me out of my trance. He slowed down for a moment, and that small break felt like torture.

I shook my head no, then arched by back and bucked my hips, grinding harder against his body to show him. When I tightened my muscles around his cock, his breaths became even more ragged. He gently bit my neck as he continued to fuck me into oblivion.

"So fucking good," he rasped. "I feel like a fucking animal with you...can't get enough."

Despite how rough this was, I felt one-hundred-percent safe. I had fully surrendered, and that had most definitely never happened to me before.

My eyelids were heavy as I bent my head back. He placed his hand around my chin and stuck his thumb in my mouth. I sucked on it as he watched intently.

My orgasm suddenly rolled through me. As I cried out, his body began to shake. He groaned in ecstasy, and I felt a rush of heat as he came hard, balls-deep inside of me.

Ryder moved in and out of me slowly long after we'd both climaxed. I could feel myself revving up all over again, wanting more.

After a few minutes of holding me against the wall while his breathing calmed, he finally pulled out and put me down. "That was...wow."

Still breathing heavily, I nodded, unable to find words.

Ryder grabbed a sponge and squirted some shower gel into it. He began to wash me gently. As he placed it between my legs, I could feel his semen spilling out of me, gathering between my thighs.

Teasing me with the sponge, he whispered in my ear, "I love seeing my cum drip out of you."

His words made my nipples stiffen. I was most definitely ready for a second round.

He squeezed out the sponge a few times before reapplying the soap and handing it to me. "Will you wash me?"

"I would love to."

From top to bottom, I ran the sponge over his gorgeous body, appreciating every muscle, every groove on this beautiful man. I pumped some shampoo into my palm and rubbed my hands into his head. He closed his eyes to enjoy the feeling. When I'd finished, he opened them and put shampoo on his own hand to return the favor.

Ryder massaged the suds over my scalp with his large hands. I could have let him do that all night; it felt so good. After he rinsed all of the soap from my hair, he held me under the water again, kissing my head over and over. I'd never felt so cherished in my entire life, and I found myself in tears.

"Are you okay?" he asked.

"Yes, I'm just really emotional right now."

"Can I tell you something?" he asked, taking my face in his hands.

"Yes."

"My mind has been going in circles the past couple of days, thinking about a lot of shit—things I'd do differently with my father, other random thoughts. As I found myself lamenting my loss, I thought about you—how your father was never in your life, how we're both in the same position now, not having either of our parents around. I was fortunate to have my father as long as I did. But you live with the loss of a man who's still walking the Earth. And even though you don't talk about it, I know that hurts you. The moment I realized the meaning behind your stage name, I figured that out. You're just strong and don't show your vulnerable side."

He caressed my cheek. "Anyway, I do have a point to all this." He kissed me softly. "My point is, wherever he is, your father has no idea what a beautiful, kind, precious human he created. And that's a damn shame for him. Because you are undoubtedly his biggest accomplishment, and he doesn't even realize it."

The water rained down on us, washing away my tears as he continued.

"You've brought me so much happiness, and you coming here to L.A. is literally what's keeping me sane right now. You're precious to me, Eden. I hope you know that."

He'd rendered me speechless. He was right. As much as I'd never let my father's abandonment define my self-worth, there was a shadow of hurt that never really went away.

The urge to tell Ryder I loved him was strong, but I wasn't going to be the first to say it, even though I wanted to.

I settled on, "You're precious to me, too."

## CHAPTER 24

*Eden*

The funeral was even harder than I'd anticipated. The strength Ryder had shown the day before seemed nonexistent now. The finality of it all seemed to hit him today.

He bawled when they lowered the casket into the ground, and that was really hard to watch. All I could do was rub his back, but no words would comfort him.

After the burial, Ryder had organized a lunch at a fancy restaurant in downtown L.A. for family, friends, and the closest business associates. He didn't have a lot of relatives because his father was also an only child. Some cousins from his mother's side were there, along with some of his good friends, including Mallory, who'd stuck around for the meal, much to my dismay. Aside from whispering a couple of things to Ryder here and there, she'd kept her distance. But her eyes were always firmly planted on him. I could tell it was killing her not to be the woman by his side.

The thought of having to leave him tomorrow while so many things were up in the air was painful.

The restaurant was super high end—the type of place where the waiter pours a little bit of wine and swirls it around before discarding it to clean any residual taste from the glass. I'd chosen braised medallions of pork on a bed of mushroom risotto. But as delicious as it was, I had no appetite.

As Ryder walked around talking to people, I stayed seated at the table, moving my uneaten food around my plate. Tossing back a second glass of wine, I definitely appreciated the alcohol—particularly when Ryder's friend Benny made his way toward me.

With straggly hair and a long beard, his grungy style stood out from the pack. I hadn't met Benny at the wake the night before; he must have come and gone before I'd gotten there. While Ryder had pointed him out to me at the funeral, he hadn't had a chance to formally introduce us.

Benny reeked of marijuana as he approached the table. "Hi. I don't believe we've met."

"You're Benny," I said. "I've heard a lot about you."

I noticed him silently repeating my words before he asked, "What's your name?"

Surprised, I held out my hand. "Eden."

*Has Ryder never mentioned me?*

He took it. "And how do you know my boy Ryder? I've seen you with him all day."

Afraid of the answer, I asked, "Has he...not mentioned me?"

He squinted. "No. Can't say he has. I'm sorry."

A few seconds passed as I absorbed what that might mean.

"We're dating—have been for a few months."

Benny looked genuinely surprised. "No shit? Well, I'll have to grill him about that. I guess he's been holding out on me."

Feigning a smile, I said, "Yeah. Guess so."

"How did you guys meet?"

I gave the only answer that came to mind. "Online..."

"Really?" He stared over at Ryder and said, "Huh."

"What?"

"Oh, nothing. It's just that Ryder doesn't usually have to resort to that." He must have noticed the not-so-happy look on my face when he shook his head and added, "I didn't mean it that way. He just always has his pick of the litter wherever he goes."

That didn't make me feel much better. "Right."

"Sorry. I don't mean to be rude. I'm just surprised he did the online dating thing. You're obviously a catch. And I *obviously* don't know when to fucking stop talking. Jesus, I shouldn't have smoked just now." He wiped his forehead.

"It's okay." *I just know so much about you, and you know nothing about me, not even that I existed, that's all.*

He drank out of a random glass of water on the table. "You live around here?"

"No, I live in Utah."

"Utah?"

"Yes."

"Are you a Mormon?"

Inwardly rolling my eyes, I answered, "No, I'm not."

"Oh, okay. I know there are a lot of Mormons there."

"Right. So, of course I *must* be Mormon."

239

"Alright, I feel fucking dumb now. I've totally botched this convo. Sorry. I suck at life sometimes. I'm not good with social shit."

"It's okay. I'm not exactly good at it, either. Not to mention, I don't fit in here at all."

"What makes you say that?"

"Look at these people. I don't have money or influence. I'm just a girl from St. George."

"Well, I don't fit in, either, and I've been living here my entire life. So..."

That made me smile a little. "Ryder tells me you own a marijuana dispensary?"

"Yeah. I love what I do."

*I can smell that.* "I can tell."

"So, you flew in just for this?" he asked.

"Yes."

He looked over where Ryder was standing. "I'm really worried about him—how he's gonna handle everything that's gonna get thrown at him now."

"What do you think will happen at the company?"

He looked contemplative. "I don't know. My dad used to help run the studio. He always wanted me to get into it, but it was never my thing. Anyway, I know how much work goes into it just from watching him, and I don't think Ryder's going to be able to handle it all."

We sat in silence as our gazes fixed on Ryder for a while.

Then Benny turned to me and excused himself. "Well, I'm just about ready for another smoke. You seem really cool. It was nice meeting you."

"Nice meeting you, too."

As unintentionally insulting as Benny had been, he was much more laid back than anyone else here. He didn't quite fit, and that sort of made us kindred spirits.

After he left, though, the reality of our conversation hit me. Ryder had never mentioned me to him—one of his best friends. Was he ashamed of me? I'd never thought that before, but what other explanation could there be? I felt myself losing faith.

After Ryder wrapped up his conversation, he headed toward me.

He took a seat before grabbing my hand and kissing it. "Hey. Sorry for leaving you for so long."

"It's no problem."

I wanted so badly to ask him why he'd never mentioned me to Benny, but I refrained. This was not the time to push guilt on him or start a conversation about our relationship. He had just buried his dad, for Christ's sake. I'd have to hold my feelings in.

But quietly, the realization that he'd been keeping us on the down low put me in a different state of mind. I had to keep my guard up, not get my hopes up about anything. Ryder was surely going to need space over the next several weeks to deal with things at the studio. He was also going to be approached by Mallory, who planned to profess her undying love to him—a secret that was killing me, but was not mine to tell.

Later that afternoon, Ryder and I lay together in his living room. He had turned on the electric fireplace, and we were decompressing from the day's events. I was positioned be-

241

tween his legs with my back against his chest on the chaise lounge. I could feel the rise and fall of his breathing.

He'd been quiet for a while when he said, "The last time my father and I spoke, he told me he loved me and was proud of me. That wasn't something that happened very often."

Turning around to look at him, I said, "You almost wonder if his soul could sense something."

He tightened his grip around me. "Yeah. It's weird."

"And beautiful at the same time."

"The only reason I called him was because of my conversation with Ollie."

"That's right. I remember you saying that."

"So, I'm grateful to Ollie for putting that suggestion about movies in my head, because otherwise I wouldn't have spoken to Dad, would never have had that last moment with him."

"I'm so glad you did." After a moment, I said, "Ollie's been worried about you."

"Shit. Really?" He scooted up a bit. "Can I call him? Is it too late?"

"Not at all." I reached for my phone on the coffee table. "He doesn't go to bed for another hour."

I dialed my home number and put it on speakerphone.

Camille answered, "Hey! How's it going?"

"It was a long day. I have Ryder with me. You're on speakerphone—just letting you know."

"Thank you for the warning." She laughed. "I might have said something stupid." Her tone softened. "Very sorry for your loss, Ryder."

"Thank you, Camille. I appreciate that. And thank you for taking care of Ollie so I could have Eden here with me."

"My pleasure."

"Where's the big man now?" Ryder asked.

"He's in his room, but I'll hand him the phone. Hang on."

You could hear the muffled sounds of Camille talking to Ollie before my brother came on the line.

"Ryder?"

"Hey, buddy."

"Are you okay?" Ollie asked.

"Yes. That's why I'm calling. I wanted you to know you don't have to worry about me. I'm gonna be okay." Ryder glanced over at me and smiled before he said, "Thank you for letting me borrow your sister for a couple of days. Having her here has really helped."

"Eh, no problem. I haven't even missed her that much."

I chuckled. "Thanks a lot, Ollie."

"Okay, maybe I miss you a little."

"I know you miss me, silly. I'll be back tomorrow afternoon, okay? Be a good boy for Camille."

"Ryder?" Ollie said.

"Yeah?"

"Maybe your parents can meet my mom now."

Ryder smiled. "That would be really nice, wouldn't it?"

"You believe in Heaven, right?"

Ryder took a deep breath in, seeming to ponder Ollie's question. "I believe our loved ones are still with us after they pass. I don't know if there's another place that they all hang out together, or if they become a part of us in some other way, but I do believe there's more than this life, that they're still around. In fact, I've talked to my dad a lot in the past couple days."

"Has he talked back?"

Ryder closed his eyes and grinned. "No. But I feel like he can hear me."

"Cool. I'm gonna try talking to my mom."

"You should. I bet she'd like to hear from you."

"Thanks for the tip, Ryder."

"You're welcome, buddy. We'll talk soon, okay?"

"Okay."

After he hung up, Ryder lay back down and said, "It was nice to hear his voice."

"I know he's been dying to talk to you."

Ryder brought me in close to his body again. "What time is your flight tomorrow?"

"Noon."

"We'll have breakfast together before I take you to the airport."

"Okay. That'll be nice."

We lay in silence for a while longer before he said, "I saw you talking to Benny at the restaurant."

I licked my lips. "Yeah. I introduced myself. He didn't know who I was, didn't realize you were dating anyone." I couldn't help admitting that.

"I'm sorry I never had a chance to tell him about us."

"That's okay. I can understand why you might be a little ashamed of how we met."

"Whoa." Ryder turned me around to face him. "That's not it at all. I am *not* ashamed of you, Eden. Fuck. Don't *ever* think that." He tightened his grip on me. "Benny is very cynical and a smartass. I didn't feel like dealing with the tasteless jokes that would inevitably come if I told him the full story. And I didn't want to lie to him about how we met, either. So, I was figuring out how to handle it. He's an old friend, but he can be a bit of an idiot sometimes. I put off telling him only because I wanted to do it justice. Honestly, the main reason he doesn't know is that we haven't been speaking all that often the past few months. He's been off doing his own thing. I feel really shitty that you thought I was ashamed."

I felt ridiculous for having let it upset me. After all, he'd introduced me to Mallory as his girlfriend, and his housekeeper, Lorena, had known right away who I was. I guess I was just being sensitive.

"It's okay. I get it. I told him we met online."

"That must have confused him. He knows I've never done the online dating thing."

"Yeah, he was *totally* confused."

I looked over at the clock on my phone. It was getting late. My time here was almost over, and it made me panicky inside. Ryder could apparently see that in my face.

"What's wrong? Something else is bothering you. I know it."

"No," I lied.

"Eden..."

I couldn't let myself bring up Mallory. It was too much. So I did my best to relay my feelings without getting into a messy conversation about his ex.

"I know the next several months are going to be hard. I just want you to know I'll be here for you in whatever way you need me. I don't expect anything in return. You need time to figure out what direction your life is going, and that includes how I fit into it. That also means I need to proceed with caution, knowing that—"

"Are you trying to break up with me or something?" The look of concern on his face was growing by the second.

*Like I could ever willingly let you go.*

"No. I care about you so much...and that's why I want to give you time without pressure to figure out what you really want."

"I want *you*." He grabbed my hand and threaded his fingers through mine. "Where is this coming from?"

"My logical mind? I'm sorry. I told myself I wouldn't bring up our relationship while I was here. It's not appropriate, given what you're going through. I don't think we should be talking about this right now."

"Don't worry about that. I can handle it. And don't ever apologize for telling me what's on your mind. I'm just trying to figure out exactly what you're getting at." Ryder sat up, then lifted me to straddle him.

I looked deeply into his eyes and said, "After all of the time we've been seeing each other, we're no closer to knowing what's going to happen between us long-term. I'm really scared to lose you, but at the same time, I want to be realistic. We can't live with our heads in the sand. At some point, something's gotta give. Being out here has made me realize how much of your life I miss out on— pretty much all of it. It's just not possible to keep doing what we're doing forever."

His expression became less rigid as a realization seemed to come over him. "You're right. This isn't really fair, is it? I've never promised you anything...because a part of me is afraid I can't live up to what you need. And with my father passing, it's just made my future even more unclear. The only thing constant is how I feel about you. And I want that to be enough, more than anything."

If only that were enough.

"I have no doubt that you want to be with me," I clarified. "I guess what I'm trying to say is I know you need time to figure out your life. And I want to give that to you without you having to worry about losing me. I'll be here for you until you figure it out. I don't expect that to be tomorrow, or next month, even. But we *do* need to figure this out. We can't live in limbo forever."

*Plus, the longer I have you, the harder it's going to be to lose you.*

He placed his hand on my chin and caressed it with his thumb. "You're right. It's not fair. I promise to figure it out. I just wish I knew what that entails. Thank you for giving me time."

I opened my eyes at 5:30AM. Ryder had a tough time getting to sleep last night. He'd finally fallen asleep around three in the morning, and he was now completely out.

I couldn't get our conversation out of my head. He'd vowed to make a conscious effort to figure out where things stood between us. And I believed him. But that meant the clock was ticking. That terrified me, because I couldn't see any conclusion that wouldn't mean me getting hurt. It felt like the end of us was near.

Since I wasn't able to sleep, I slipped out of bed and headed downstairs. I hadn't spent any time outside on Ryder's property, and I thought it might be nice to watch the sunrise over the city in the distance. Because Ryder's house was up high, you could see the Los Angeles skyline.

After making some coffee, I took it outside and sat on a grassy hill out back. I closed my eyes and let the morning breeze blow into my face. It was so quiet and peaceful. Ryder had a gorgeous garden featuring rosebushes and exotic flowers, along with some sculptures. If I lived here, I would be outside every day, meditating and soaking in the beautifully landscaped scenery.

A rush of emotions hit me. More than anything, I wished I could stay here. It killed me that I couldn't continue to be here for Ryder when he needed me—especially this week when he'd be bombarded at work. I knew he was still so confused and stressed about what to do with the studio.

Unable to control it, I started to cry. Placing my head between my knees, I let myself unleash all of the feelings I'd kept inside these past couple of days.

A few moments later, a voice startled me. "Everything alright out here?"

I turned to find Ryder's housekeeper, Lorena, walking toward me. Dressed in an all-white uniform, she was petite with medium-length black hair, probably in her later fifties. I knew she was really important to him, so her presence made me a little nervous. It felt like the closest thing to meeting his mother.

"Did I scare you? I have a habit of doing that to house guests." She snickered.

"I heard about your cowbell," I said, managing a smile.

"Ah...he told you about that, eh?"

"Yes." I wiped my eyes and held out my hand as I stood up. "We didn't get a chance to talk at the funeral."

"I've known about you for a long time." She gestured to the grass. "Please, sit."

She took a seat next to me.

I turned to her. "He talks to you about me?"

"Yes, he does."

That made me feel even more foolish for getting upset about Benny.

"How much did he tell you?"

"I know you show your boobies and your cha-cha for a living."

"Okay." I laughed nervously. "So, everything then."

"Yeah. I used to tease him about it, until he came back from that first trip. Then I could see how serious he was about you. After he told me everything, I realized why you do what you do. So I stopped being a judgmental wiseass."

Her honesty was refreshing.

"I can understand why you were skeptical. Some days I can't even believe what I do for a living. But hopefully it won't be forever." I picked at some grass. "So, how could you tell he was serious about me?"

"Because Ryder came back from that trip a changed man. I can't even put my finger on it. I could see it in his face, I guess. It was like new life had been breathed into him. And that spoke volumes about you. Plus, he told me all about your sweet little brother. I'm sorry I ever judged you. You're supporting your family."

I really liked this woman. "Well, thank you for saying that."

We both looked off into the distance. "He mentioned you've been with him since childhood?" I asked.

"Yes. He's like a son to me. I care about him a lot. And I can tell you do, too."

"I guess it's obvious..."

"Your tears don't lie."

She could see right through me.

"I'm in love with him." Amazed at my own admission, I added, "That's the first time I've ever said it out loud."

"Does he know that?"

"I haven't said it in those words. I don't want to say them until I'm sure he feels the same. And this hasn't exactly been the opportune time to address it."

"Why don't you tell me what's really going on?"

"What do you mean?"

"The reason you were crying just now."

I looked down for a moment. "I'm afraid to lose him."

"Why?"

"Can I tell you something in confidence?"

"Depends on what it is, if it affects Ryder."

"It's about his ex...Mallory. I assume you know her?"

"Yes. She lived here for a couple of years."

*That's right.*

"So you knew her well, then?"

"Not as well as you would think. We were never close. She respected me, but I don't really think she *liked* me."

"What makes you say that?"

"I don't think she appreciated having me around. I think she found a housekeeper who shows up every day to be intrusive. She would look at me funny when I'd be folding Ryder's underwear, stuff like that. She didn't seem to understand that I'd changed his *diapers*, never mind folding his underwear. I never felt completely comfortable when she was living here. But after a while, I realized it wasn't necessary to feel comfortable, as long as Ryder was happy. He seemed to be, until they broke up. But I never felt she was right for him." She arched her brow. "Anyway, what about her?"

I needed to let it out. "Mallory cornered me at the wake—in the bathroom. She wanted to inquire about how serious Ryder and I were. She said she thought I should know she planned to tell him she was still in love with him. She wants to get him back and asked me not to say anything, given all the stress he's under. I agreed that it was best not to bring it up, but I've been dying inside, feeling like I'm about to lose him."

Lorena's eyes widened. "Shit. She had some nerve pulling you aside like that."

"Yeah. But I'm worried. I don't trust that he doesn't still have feelings for her."

She nodded. "Let me tell you something about Ryder. All that boy has ever wanted is to be loved. He loved Mallory, but she broke his heart. I'm not so sure he's going to be able to forget about that, no matter what she tells him. And don't be so quick to discount his feelings for you. You didn't exist in his life when all of that went down."

"Okay, but here's the thing—it would be so much easier for him to be with her. She doesn't have any baggage."

"The hell she doesn't. She left him and got engaged to someone else. That's emotional baggage."

"Okay. Yeah, that's true."

"I like you for him, Eden. You know why? Because I've never seen him happier. I've long given up the dream of Ryder marrying one of my nieces." She laughed. "So I'm rooting for you. And I'm gonna give you a little advice, too."

"Okay..."

"Don't be reactive to your fears. Don't distance your-self or change how you treat him because you're afraid of losing him. Don't let someone else invade what you two have. Be there for him, and always be that girl he fell for. If it's meant to be, it will. With his only family gone, more than anything right now, Ryder needs people around him whom he can trust. And believe me, there aren't many." She shrugged. "And hey, if he takes her back, he's not the one for you anyway."

Her words gave me a boost of confidence. "You're right, Lorena. You're very wise."

"Well, there's got to be some benefit to getting older, right?" She smiled. "You're a lot like me—a strong, inde-pendent woman who does what she needs to do to support her family. My ex-husband...took off on me and left me to raise my son alone. I was determined to find a job. I kept getting turned down, but I went after anything and everything I could find. Somehow, I ended up on Ryder's parents' doorstep. That changed my life. His mother hired me because she said her intuition told her to. I had no ex-perience and didn't deserve the job. But thirty years later, here I am. They have taken care of me very well. And I've tried to return the favor." Lorena sighed. "Anyway, I will always have respect for women who do whatever it takes to fend for themselves and their families. And that's you."

I wanted to hug her. "Thank you. I appreciate you say-ing that."

Suddenly, Ryder's deep morning voice came up from behind us. "The one morning I decide to sleep in a little, and the two women in my life are conspiring against me?"

"I was just telling Eden here she needs to treat you right, or she'll have to answer to me." Lorena winked at me.

"Pretty sure it's the other way around. You'll be the first to kick my ass if I ever fuck things up with her."

"You know me so well, *mijo*."

Lorena stood up and brushed off her white pants. "I'll go make you guys breakfast."

Ryder shook his head. "You don't have to do that. I got it, Lorena."

"Spend time with your lady. You only have a few hours before she has to leave. I've got it."

She was already halfway to the door when he hollered after her, "Thank you."

I watched as she disappeared inside. "She's so nice."

He narrowed his eyes. "Really?"

"Why do you sound surprised?"

Sitting down next to me, he said, "Lorena doesn't normally come across as *nice*. She's pretty tough on most people, but I think she really likes you. She respects you."

"She only respects me because of how you speak of me, because *you* respect me."

"I do." He grinned. "You know, I reached over for you in bed when I woke up and freaked out for a second that you weren't there."

That made my chest hurt, because I knew he still needed me so much, and I wouldn't be next to him when he woke up tomorrow.

"I've been out here watching the sunrise."

"I would've loved to do that with you. You should've gotten me up to join you."

"You needed your sleep."

"I would never choose sleep—or anything else—over watching a sunrise with you."

I took his hand. "I wish we had more time together. I hate feeling resentful of my life, but that's exactly what I am right now. I resent having to leave. I'm not ready."

"I'm sure as fuck not ready to let you go, either." He leaned in close. "I need to make love to you before you leave."

"We should go back to the bedroom after breakfast, then." I stared at my refection in his eyes. "I'm sorry if last night was a little tense. I didn't mean to put added pressure on you."

"You said what needed to be said. Don't be sorry about that." He moved behind me and brought me to his chest as he cradled me. "Let me hold you," he said before locking me in with both of his legs. "Do you have to work tonight?"

"Yeah."

"Can we talk at the normal time? At midnight?"

"Of course, if you're up for it."

"I'll be looking forward to that more than ever. I need it before having to face work tomorrow."

"You're not taking any time off before going back to the office?"

He sighed. "I can't. I need to start figuring things out. My father would've expected me to step into action, so that's what I need to be doing. So, back to business in the AM. Although, I did cancel the China trip."

I rubbed my hands over his arms wrapped around me. "I'm so proud of you. I've been meaning to tell you that."

He held me tighter. "I suddenly really want to skip breakfast. The only thing I want to eat right now is you."

Lorena stuck her head out the door and yelled, "Hope you're hungry!"

He flipped me around, then spoke over my lips. "I'm fucking starving."

Later that morning, Ryder insisted on paying for parking at LAX to accompany me inside. When he'd taken me as far as he was allowed to go, we stopped and stared at each other.

"You know what I wish?" he asked.

"What?"

"I wish we could fly to Catalina Island right now and run away from everything, have a quiet few days together. I want that more than anything."

"That sounds like a dream."

He had stars in his eyes. "Someday we'll go there. We'll figure out a way, even if I have to pay Camille a shit ton of money to watch Ollie." He grabbed my face and brought my lips to his. "Fuck. I don't want to let you go." He pulled me close and held me. We rocked back and forth for a while.

As hopeful as he was making things sound with fantasies of trips to Catalina, I was still terrified of the coming weeks.

*What if this is the last time he ever holds me like this?*

It was technically possible. I held him tighter, cherishing his smell and the warmth of his body.

"Goodbye, Ryder."

"Goodbye, baby. Be safe."

My heart dipped a little, wishing he'd said the three words I longed to hear. But he didn't.

As I tried to walk away, he kept holding my hand and wouldn't let it go. He suddenly pulled me back into him and planted the hardest kiss on my mouth. My bag dropped to the ground as I ran my fingers through his hair and accepted everything he gave me with every inch of my soul.

I had to pry myself from him, wiping tears from my eyes as I walked away, hoping I would get to experience that kind of kiss with him again.

## CHAPTER 25

*Ryder*

A week after my father's funeral, I was still no closer to determining the future of the company.

There were only two things keeping me going: nightly chats with Eden and daily emails from Ollie. I couldn't imagine how alone I'd feel without them in my life.

And I sort of did...a thing.

I knew Eden wasn't comfortable if she knew I was watching her during her show. So I created a fake profile so I could log in and "spend more time" with her without making her nervous. My new screen name was *AssLover433.*

Not only would I watch her while logged in under that name, but when I wanted to amuse myself, I'd interact with her and ask her really stupid questions. The best was when she'd complain to me during our midnight chat about how annoying AssLover was. In those moments it took everything in me not to bust out laughing. I would tell her eventually, and I was certain we'd have a good laugh about it. In the meantime, I was having too much fun.

As I sat in the middle of yet another board meeting—this time on a Saturday—to discuss the fate of the studio, I decided to check my email.

*A message from Ollie Shortsleeve using Voice-Text300:*

*Dear Ryder,*

*Can you call me? I need your help. It's important, but don't sound weird if Eden picks up. Please call soon.*

*Ollie*

That was odd. He never asked me to call him. My heart began to pound.

Excusing myself from the meeting, I walked down the hall and outside to the rear of the building. The sun was blazing as I dialed Eden's house number.

After a couple of rings, she picked up. "Ryder?"

"Hey," I said.

"What's up? I wasn't expecting you to call me."

"Well, technically, I'm not calling for you. Ollie asked me to call him."

"Really? Okay. He's just in his room. Hang on."

After a pause, I heard her say, "Ollie? Ryder's on the phone for you."

"Can you go back in the kitchen?" he asked her.

"Why? What don't you want me to hear?"

"Just...please?" he begged.

Eden sighed, and then I heard him come on the line.

He whispered, "Ryder?"

"Hey, buddy. Everything alright?"

"No."

"What's wrong?"

"Something is wrong with me."

"What do you mean?"

"Something...happened. And I don't know what it is. I want to know if *you* know what it is. And I can't tell Eden."

My pulse sped up, thinking maybe someone tried to touch him. "Okay. Talk to me."

"I'm kind of embarrassed to tell you."

Adrenaline ran through me. "Don't be. You can tell me anything."

"Promise me you won't tell Eden."

"Well, that depends on what it is."

"You *can't* tell Eden," he insisted.

"Okay. Okay. What's going on?"

"I think I'm bleeding."

"Bleeding? Well, then you need to tell your sister."

"I can't!"

"Why not?"

"I was...touching myself. My, um, penis. Because it felt good. I do that sometimes. And I think I went too far. I felt something come out of there. I think it's blood. There was a lot of it. It was sort of...hot."

*Oh shit.*

I had to sit down on a bench.

*Damn.*

*Isn't he a little young for that?*

*Nah. I was about twelve when it happened to me.*

*Ollie is eleven and a half.*

*Shit.*

*Alright.*

Just to confirm, I asked, "Did this stuff come out when you finished doing what you were doing?"

"Yes. Right at the end."

I took a deep breath and rubbed my eyes, silently laughing a little. "Ollie, listen, you're fine, okay? There is absolutely nothing wrong with you."

At that moment, one of the board members came through the revolving doors. He must have been looking for me.

"There you are. We're all waiting for you. I've got a tee time at four, so—"

"I need a minute," I barked. "I'll be in there soon."

He looked annoyed as he nodded and went back inside.

"Sorry about that. Okay, so as I was saying, what you did is completely okay. *Totally* normal."

"Why was I bleeding, then?"

"It wasn't blood. It's something else called semen."

"Demon?"

"*Semen.* It's something that comes out of your penis after you finish doing what you were doing."

"But it's *not* normal. It's never happened to me before. And I've been doing this for, like, six months."

"Once it happens the first time, it happens every time. It starts around puberty. So this was just your first time, or maybe the first time you noticed it or something. It means you're getting older."

"You bleed every time you do it?"

"Yes. Well, not exactly. Again, semen is not blood. It's different—it's sort of a whitish color. Blood is red. I know you don't know the difference, but they're different substances. And it doesn't mean anything is wrong with you. Just the opposite. It means your body is working the way it's supposed to."

"So what do I do?"

"You don't have to do anything. But when you know you're gonna...you know, *finish* next time, make sure you have a towel handy. And know that Eden's probably gonna figure it out if she does your laundry."

"I was really scared," he said. "I thought I was dying."

I chuckled. "No, buddy. You're good." Then it hit me. "Don't they have health class at your school? They should be teaching you this stuff."

"Next year."

"Okay. Well, if you have any questions, you can come to me."

"I Googled bloody penis and got scared."

"Oh, man. Yeah. Don't do that. I can imagine the stuff that came up."

"Anyway, thanks, Ryder."

"It's no problem at all. You got me out of a stressful work meeting. I needed to take a break from my problems anyway."

If the people upstairs in the meeting only knew what I was out here discussing.

I was just about to let him go when he asked, "Can I help you with your problem since you helped me with mine?"

That made me smile. "I wish."

"Does it have to do with your dad?"

I looked up at the sky. "Yeah, buddy, it does. When my dad died, he left me with the power to make some decisions about how his company should be run. And without him here, I'm not sure what to do, not sure what he would have wanted."

"Ask an adult for help."

"What?"

"That's what my teacher always says. When you're really stuck, ask an adult for help."

"You do realize I *am* an adult, right?"

"Yeah, but there's got to be someone who knows more than you, who can help *you*. Like, an even bigger adult."

A few seconds passed, and then something in my brain clicked. His words struck a chord.

*Of course.*

*Of course!*

Why hadn't I thought of this sooner? I couldn't do this alone. I never could. The answer on how to proceed wasn't going to come from me or any of those fools upstairs; they were only in it for themselves. There was only one person who could help me. And I was going to have to beg him.

*Ask an adult.*

"Ollie, you're brilliant, you know that?"

"Sometimes I am. But I thought I was bleeding demons out of my pee pee. So, not all of the time."

"Thank you for meeting me," I said.

Benny's father, Benjamin Eckelstein, Sr., led me out to his back patio where a pitcher of lemonade sat on the table. He wore a white tennis uniform. I'd called him right after hanging up with Ollie and asked if I could meet him at his house this afternoon.

"Of course, son. I've been expecting to hear from you."

That surprised me. "Really?"

He put his hand on my shoulder. "Yes, but I didn't want to be presumptuous in assuming you needed my help. If you didn't ask, I wasn't going to offer. I figured you were waiting for the dust to settle a little."

Benjamin had at one time been my father's right-hand man and business partner. He'd retired a few years ago at the age of sixty-six and was perhaps the only person who had the knowledge to advise me on next steps at Mc-Namara. I silently thanked Ollie again for bringing him to my mind.

Mr. Eckelstein poured the lemonade. I watched as a couple of fresh lemon slices fell into his glass along with the liquid.

"Tell me what's happening, son."

I rubbed my hands together to gear up for my proposition. "Well, obviously, you know Dad left me with enough voting rights to make the decision on how the company should proceed without him. As much as I would love to step in and take over where he left off, the reality is, I'm not qualified. We'd been working to get me there. But I'd say we were probably five years away from me being ready to take over."

He shook the ice around in his glass. "Well, it takes a strong person to admit that. I think many people in your position would just assume power and wing it. I respect you wanting to put the company first."

"My father would be freaking out right now. I know for a fact he didn't trust any other person to take over his spot. The only reason I've been tempted is so it doesn't go to someone else. The only person Dad would have trusted besides me...is you."

He nodded. "Okay, I'm listening."

"I need your expertise. I don't know if you'd be willing to come out of retirement for a little while to help me keep the company afloat, but I think that's what I need. I know that's a lot to ask and—"

"Absolutely, I would."

I blinked in surprise. "Really?"

"One-hundred percent. I thought you'd never ask. The truth is, retirement isn't all it's cracked up to be. I'd be lying if I said I didn't miss the business from time to time. I never thought I'd have a reason to return—or quite frankly, that anyone would want me back after being gone. I'm old, but I'm not *that* old. I'm still younger than the president of the United States. There's no reason I can't go back to work."

"So, you'd be willing to return for a while?"

"Yes, but I'd make myself co-chairman alongside you. I think it's important to continue what your father started, which is grooming you for the position. That was his dream. Unless that's not what *you* want."

It was always hard for me to admit I had doubts about that.

"Can I be brutally honest, Ben?"

"Sure, you can."

"I don't know what I want. There are some days I fantasize about selling my shares and doing something altogether different. But I've always wanted to make my father proud. That's the driving force behind everything I've ever done. Now that he's gone, I think I have some serious decisions to make. Life is short. And I need to be sure running the company is what I want for the long haul."

Benjamin finished off the last of his drink before setting the glass on the table. "As a father, let me give you my perspective." He poured lemonade into another glass and slid it in front of me. "We all want what's best for our kids. Ultimately, what's best is what makes them happy, despite our own personal dreams. Case in point, instead of making movies like I wanted him to, my son is a legal pot dealer, for Christ's sake. That doesn't make me love him any less. Maybe over the next year, one of our goals can be helping you figure out what you want—whether that's running the studio or something else. But in the meantime, let's not waste any time getting the place back up and running."

I could've kissed him. Maybe that sounded weird, but I was too happy to care. "You sure about this?"

"Your father was a good friend to me. This is the least I can do for him."

"Ben, you have no idea what peace this brings me. I don't even know how to thank you."

He stood up from his seat. "No time for thanks. Let's go to my office and get to work."

## CHAPTER 26

*Eden*

I'd just gotten Ollie to sleep when a call from Ryder lit up my phone.

I answered. "How did you know I was thinking of you?"

"Hey, beautiful," he said.

"This is earlier than you normally call me."

"I know. I just missed you. I couldn't wait until midnight." His voice was low and smooth—he sounded like sex.

Since leaving California, I'd cherished every conversation with Ryder more than the last. Tonight my heart was feeling particularly full, and I couldn't put my finger on why. It was so good to hear his voice.

"Where are you?" I asked.

"Home. Doing nothing. But earlier today I went for a jog through Runyon Canyon, and I kept thinking about how badly I wished you were with me."

"I wish I could have gone with you, too."

"Benjamin told me to take the afternoon off. We've been working overtime lately on the reorganization. He thought I needed a break. Can you believe that? That's one big difference between him and my father. Dad never took breaks. Benjamin encourages them."

"I bet your Dad is tickled you're working alongside his old friend. How is everything going with that?"

"He's been a godsend. Seriously. Benjamin is so smart. He's been gone from the industry for a few years, yet he jumped right back in the saddle. You'd never know he went away."

"I'm so glad he agreed to come back."

Things were silent for a bit before Ryder groaned. "I'm so horny. I'd give anything to fuck you right now."

"Don't say stuff like that to me. I can't handle it. I miss your body so much," I said.

"It's really tough being away from you. But I plan to come out there in a couple of weeks. So it won't be too much longer."

My body buzzed at the prospect of getting to see him soon. "I'll be counting the days, then."

"My hand is getting sick of me using him," he grumbled. "I've never masturbated so much in my life."

"Well, your hand should meet my hand. They can lament."

Ryder laughed before I heard the sound of a doorbell in the background.

"Shit," he said.

"What's up?"

"Someone's at the door. I don't feel like dealing with anyone tonight."

"Want me to let you go?" I asked.

"No. No. Hang on. Let me just see who it is."

A few seconds later, I could hear him talking to a woman.

Then Ryder said to her, "Excuse me a minute."

An uneasy feeling came over me. "Who is it?"

"It's, um, Mallory."

My heart thundered against my chest. "Mallory?"

He whispered, "Yeah. I'm not sure what she wants."

"Is this the first time she's come to see you?"

"Yes. I haven't seen her since the funeral."

*Shit.*

*Shit.*

*Shit.*

*This is it.*

"I see."

After I let out a long, panicked breath into the phone, he asked, "Are you okay?"

I was too worked up to bother pretending. "No, not really."

"Want me to tell her to leave?"

It felt like my throat was closing. "How are you gonna do that?"

"I can make up any excuse if her being here is upsetting you."

My breathing accelerated. "No. Talk to her. Get it over with."

"Get what over with?"

I didn't answer his question. "I'm late for my show anyway."

He let out a long breath into the phone. "Okay...same time tonight? Midnight?"

"Yeah. Same time," I breathed, pulling my hair as I paced.

I could hardly catch my breath as I hung up the phone.

The room felt like it was spinning. *This was it*. This was the moment I'd been fearing. Mallory was going to tell him she loved him. He'd be caught off guard and confused. Old feelings would come flooding back. I'd be able to hear it in his voice later, and so would begin the gradual demise of our relationship. That, of course, was my worst fear played out in two sentences.

*Please be honest with me, Ryder.*

Checking the time on my phone, I realized I really was late for work. I had no idea how I was going to put on a strong face tonight.

I needed to let it out, so I did something I almost never did. I looked up to the ceiling and channeled my mother.

Palm to palm, I held my hands together. "Hey, Mom. It's me, Eden. I know it's been a while since I've spoken to you. I just really need you right now. I wish you were here to give me advice. I know you'd tell me to put on my big-girl panties. You'd assure me I don't need a man to make me happy because you never did."

I started to change my clothes while continuing to speak to her.

"For the longest time, I assumed my life would always be lonely, especially after Ethan left. But meeting Ryder has made me realize why Ethan had to go—because my feelings for Ryder are stronger than I've ever felt in my life. I'll never regret what he and I have shared, even if it ends tomorrow."

I sat down at my vanity and began to brush my hair.

"I'm asking for your help. At this moment, I'm very afraid of losing him. Just send me strength. I know I'll be okay no matter what, because I've inherited your independent streak. But being okay with being alone doesn't mean I can't *want* what you never had—stability and true love from a man. I've spent the past four years taking care of Ollie and never once thought I needed anyone to take care of *me*. I don't financially. But emotionally? It feels damn good to be cared for. It's hard to lose that once you have it."

I looked up again.

"Anyway…I know Ollie's been talking your ear off lately, ever since Ryder gave him the idea. I hear him sometimes. He doesn't realize I listen. I hope you're as proud of our little guy as I am. I'm trying like hell, Mom. I hope I make you proud, too." Blowing a kiss, I said, "I love you."

My heart felt filled to the rim with love for Ryder that had nowhere to go. I hoped I didn't have to hold it inside forever. I so wanted to release it.

I reached into my jewelry box for one of my mother's old necklaces. The charm on it was a Celtic symbol signifying strength. Placing it around my neck, I locked the clasp and straightened the chain.

It was time to go to work.

## CHAPTER 27

*Ryder*

Mallory took a seat on my couch. She looked extremely nervous as she chugged down the last of her iced green tea until it was gone.

"What brings you by, Mallory?"

"Were you in the middle of an important call?"

"I was talking to Eden."

It looked like it pained her to ask, "How is she?"

She was gearing up for something.

"What's going on, Mal?"

"A lot." She patted the seat next to her. "Will you sit down next to me so we can talk?"

I took a seat on the couch, specifically keeping my distance.

She ran her hand along the microfiber of the sofa. "I've missed being in this house. This was my home for so long. And it still feels like home to me." She looked around as if she was reminiscing. At one point, she closed her eyes.

She moved closer, her leg almost brushing mine. My body went rigid. Her nearness was unsettling, and I couldn't figure out if it was because of an instinctual physical awareness or fear.

She blew out a shaky breath. "I have so much to say. I don't know where to begin."

"Just start anywhere, then."

Rubbing her palms along her knees, she nodded. "The night I ran into you at The Grove was really telling. There I was with the man I was supposed to marry, and the moment you said goodbye and walked away from me, I found myself aching for you. Seeing you after such a long time brought home the fact that I hadn't gotten over you, not even a little bit. I've come to realize that my jumping into another relationship was an attempt to forget all of the pain I caused. The truth is, I've never gotten over you at all."

My stomach felt uneasy. Now I knew exactly where this was going.

"That night, Aaron kept grilling me. He wanted to know why I was acting so strange, so preoccupied. I admitted that seeing you had affected me. Every day after that was worse than the next. I finally admitted I didn't love him the way I needed to." She stopped to look at me. "Aaron and I broke up because I'm still in love with you."

At one time I'd longed to hear those words. This was definitely bittersweet—but too late.

I couldn't help feeling a little defensive, too. "I'm sorry...I'm just really perplexed. Surely you can understand my confusion, given some of the things you said before you moved out."

"I know what I said—blaming you for things that were never your fault, for what happened with our son. It took a lot of therapy and balancing my out-of-whack hormones to see clearly again."

The fact that she'd been in therapy was news to me. She certainly hadn't gotten help when we were together, despite me urging her to.

"I'm glad to hear you finally went to see someone."

"My therapist made me realize my negative feelings were misdirected at you. I'm so sorry for blaming you. And I'm sorry for the words I used as weapons. I couldn't continue to live my life without you at least knowing how sorry I am."

"Is that why you came here? To apologize?"

Mallory got down on her knees in front of me—an awkward and desperate sight that broke my heart a little. Because as much as she had hurt me, I knew she was hurting, too. And I believed she was sincere. I believed she still loved me and regretted pushing me away.

"I came to ask you to give me a second chance...to give *us* a second chance before it's too late. I still love you so much. I can't imagine spending my life with anyone else."

This was incredibly surreal. I'd never imagined Mallory would come back, begging for another chance. And I certainly would have never imagined I would feel so... *numb* toward her. But what surprised me the most was the fact that all I could think about in this moment was Eden—how much I *loved* Eden and how hurt she would be if I were to leave her.

Hearing Mallory says these things forced me to face my true feelings. It could never work with Mallory or anyone else as long as I loved Eden.

*I love Eden.*

*Fuck.*

*I really love Eden.*

It was never clearer to me than in this moment. How ironic that it took Mallory coming back to make me realize exactly where my heart was. Maybe that's how it works sometimes. It was only when I was given what I'd *thought* I wanted for so long that I realized what I'd grown to *actually* want, so purely and organically over the past several months. My love for Eden had been simmering for a long time, but right now it felt like it was exploding out of me.

I thought long and hard before addressing Mallory. But there was nothing to do but be honest.

"I'm so sorry for what we lost, especially *your* loss as a mother. Of course, I know you weren't in your right mind right after the miscarriage. And there's no need to apologize for anything you said to me. I don't blame you for any of that." Nudging her up off the floor, I said, "Please, sit. I need you to hear this."

I waited for her to return to her seat on the couch before I said, "I waited for you to come back to me for a long time—two years. There were many nights I prayed to God that you would say the exact words that just came out of your mouth." Taking her hand in mine, I said, "I cried over losing you and mourned the loss of our baby and our relationship, asking why over and over and never getting an answer. Losing you was undoubtedly the biggest heartbreak of my life, and a part of me will always love you."

*Here comes the hard part.* "But the thing is...now I know why things had to end between us. We weren't meant to be together, Mal. People who are meant to be together don't break as easily as we broke. But more than that, I've found the person I'm meant to be with—and it isn't you. I'm sorry."

There was just no easy way to say it. And I felt a mix of emotions—sadness for Mallory and peace in knowing my heart now truly understood what it wanted.

A tear fell from her eye. "You really love this girl... Eden?" She wiped it away.

I didn't have to think about my answer. "Yes. Very much."

"She told me she cares about you, too. I just didn't think things were really that—"

"What?" *Mallory spoke to Eden?* "She told you? How?"

"I talked to her in the bathroom at your dad's wake. I told her I'd planned on getting you back and I still loved you. I asked her not to tell you about our conversation."

"She *knew* this was going to happen?"

"Yes."

Now it made sense, Eden's strange mood the last night she was in California.

And her comment on the phone tonight: *"Get it over with."*

*Fuck.*

She thought she was going to lose me to Mallory.

I had so much explaining to do, so much I needed to say to Eden. And it couldn't wait any longer.

"I'm really sorry, Mallory. Like I said, I can't tell you I don't love you anymore, because that wouldn't be true. A part of me will always love you and hold the time we had together close to my heart. But I know the right person is out there for you somewhere."

It took several minutes for Mallory to compose herself. She finally stood up and said, "This girl better treat you right. She has no idea how lucky she is. No idea."

After another moment, she moved from her spot.

"Take care of yourself," I told her.

I walked her to the door and watched as she got into her car and drove away.

By the time a couple of hours had passed, my heart was bursting with the need to talk to Eden, to tell her I loved her. It was long overdue.

Mallory had forced me to search inside myself. I'd been so consumed by the aftermath of my father's death that I hadn't been able to pay attention to what I was feeling.

Fuck, I *needed* to tell her. Now. But she was right in the middle of her show, so I *couldn't* talk to her.

The need to see her, though, was unbearable, especially when she might be thinking she was about to lose me. I needed to make sure she was okay. So I decided to turn on her show and watch for a while.

When I called up her page, Eden was sitting with her legs crossed, just talking and answering questions. She looked okay, not sad or anything, so that calmed me down a little. And my pulse definitely slowed any time I logged in and found her *not* naked. Thank God her clothes were on.

One of the questions someone typed in for her caught my attention.

**Luke893: Have you ever been in love, Montana? And how can you tell if you're really in love with someone?**

She was still in the middle of answering a different question, so I wasn't sure if she had seen that one. But I waited anxiously for her response.

After about a minute, she said, "Have I ever been in love, Luke wants to know."

My heart pounded as Eden inhaled and closed her eyes.

*Say yes.*

"I most definitely have been in love, Luke. All I can say is...you just know when you love someone. But the most telltale sign is if the thought of losing them scares you more than anything. You spend years just fine on your own and then—boom. Someone comes along, and you realize you can no longer breathe without them. It's...terrifying."

And if I'd had any doubt she was referring to me, she added, "Let's just say, your question is very timely tonight."

I couldn't let her go on another second thinking she was about to lose me. I needed her to know how much I loved her, how much she had me.

I typed frantically.

**I love you so much, Eden. I'm so sorry I haven't said those words before tonight, but I've felt it for a very long time. You're my person. And you're not going to lose me—not for any job,**

**not for any other woman, not for anything in this world. You are a gift from God who came into my life just when I needed you most. I want to spend the rest of my life showing you just how much I cherish you. Please forgive me for taking so long to realize that I cannot live without you.**

When she finally noticed the comment, the look on Eden's face wasn't what I'd been hoping for. It was an expression of shock...confusion...maybe disgust?

Then it hit me.

*Fuck.*

*Fuck!*

*Fuck!*

I'd just professed my love for her logged in as *AssLover433*! She had no way of knowing it was me—probably thought I was a whack-job stalker.

*Nice, Ryder.*

*Nice!*

I rubbed my hands over my face. *Okay, think.*

I typed.

**Eden, it's Ryder. Please don't hate me, but I created this account so I could watch you without you getting nervous about it. It's me— been me all along, fucking with you from this account. (Was gonna tell you about it eventually so we could have a laugh. Never got around to it. Whoops!) I got a little ahead of myself and forgot I wasn't logged in as ScreenGod just**

**now. I'm losing my mind because I needed to tell you how much I love you before you spent another second thinking we were in trouble. I know why you were worried. And you were wrong, Eden. It's not her. It's you. It's always been you. I love you. I meant every word I just said. I love you so much. So fucking much, baby. You have no idea.**

I immediately purchased a thousand coins and dumped them into the pot to request a private chat.

Eden's hands were shaking as she covered her mouth. Her voice trembled. "I'll be right back, everyone."

**CHAPTER 28**

## Eden

*What the what?*

I couldn't switch over to the private chat room fast enough. My entire body was trembling.

When Ryder's gorgeous face lit up my screen, the look in his eyes matched the beautiful sentiments he'd just typed.

I couldn't wait to say the words. "I love you, too. Oh my God, Ryder. I love you so much."

"I love you," he said again. "I love you. I love you. I love you. I'll never be able to say it enough."

"Say it again."

His eyes were glistening. "I love you, Eden Short-sleeve."

I wiped tears from my eyes. "You really shocked me tonight."

"Mallory told me what she said to you at the wake, and now I realize that's what's been bothering you. You've been holding your breath, waiting for the other shoe to drop. I also realize now that you had no reason to have confidence in me, because I never gave you a solid reason to believe in my feelings for you."

I had to know. "What happened with her tonight?"

"She came by and told me she wanted me back, that she loved me—everything you were expecting. I felt almost nothing while she was pouring her soul out to me. I was numb, and that's because every inch of my heart is filled with you. It's been slowly filling up from the moment I laid eyes on you."

I started to cry harder.

"Are you okay?"

I sniffled. "Yes. I'm just really happy."

"I know your mind is probably going a mile a minute, still wondering how we're gonna make this work. But we *will* make this work. When something is worth fighting for, you don't wait around to figure out logistics. You say yes, you accept the gift you've been given, and you figure out the rest later, because life is too damn short to be unhappy."

"What are you saying?"

"I'm saying, fuck the job, fuck everything else—I want to be with you. That's my priority. And I want to be a part of Ollie's life, too. Not just from a distance, but every day. And not just as a friend but as family. Because that's how I feel about you—both of you. You're my family, the only family I have."

I wiped my eyes again, overwhelmed with emotion. Then I started to laugh as the reality of what he was saying set in. "What? You're gonna move into my tiny house?"

"Yeah, maybe. Fuck it. That's for the three of us to figure out. It won't happen overnight. But in the meantime,

I'll come visit more often, and the goal will be deciding where we'll settle, whether that's L.A. or St. George. Maybe both. I know you don't want Ollie to leave his school. We'll figure it out, even if I have to commute every weekend for a while or indefinitely—that would be worth it. There is nothing that matters more to me than you, Eden. Nothing."

I felt like I could finally exhale. Looking up at the ceiling, I said a silent prayer to my mother, thanking her in case she had something to do with this.

*Thank you.*

"I can't believe you were AssLover all along. I can't even be mad at you for that."

"I had a lot of fun with it."

"Oh, I know. I was there!"

We'd decided we weren't going to say anything to Ollie about Ryder's upcoming visit. This one was going to be particularly epic because Ryder and I planned to tell Ollie about our commitment to each other.

Ollie and I were hanging around the house after dinner. I knew Ryder was set to arrive any minute, so I was feeling very antsy.

At one point, I noticed Ollie carrying a large pile of towels into the laundry room. Had he been hoarding towels? That was odd. He never took care of his own laundry. While perplexing, it made me happy to think he was taking some initiative around the house.

My heart jumped for joy when Ryder texted me that he was outside.

Ollie had returned to his room, so I quietly opened the front door and leapt into Ryder's arms.

His kiss felt warmer, more intense than ever, and I knew that was because for the first time I was tasting the man I knew truly belonged to me.

"How was your flight?" I whispered.

"Too long. I couldn't wait to get here." He looked beyond my shoulder. "Where's Ollie?"

"In his room."

When he arrived at Ollie's bedroom door, Ryder started to make his cricket sound.

Ollie jumped. "No way!"

"Hey, buddy." Ryder embraced him.

"You didn't tell me you were coming!"

"That was the whole point—to surprise you."

It warmed my heart to see the look on Ollie's face as they hugged. He was so at peace whenever Ryder was around.

"How long can you stay?"

"How long do you want me to stay?" Ryder asked.

"Is that a trick question?"

He laughed. "What if it wasn't?"

"What do you mean?"

"If it wasn't a trick question, how would you answer it? If you could choose, how long would I stay?"

Without hesitation, Ollie answered, "I would say forever."

"Well, I'm gonna stay longer than I normally do this time. And I'm gonna figure out a way to be with you guys more, and I don't have any plans to stop coming back. So that sounds kind of like forever to me."

"Are you serious?"

"Dead serious. I love your sister very much. And I love you, too. I want you to know that."

Ollie's eyes opened, something he only did when he was either stressed or really excited. It made me want to cry.

"You really mean that?" he asked.

Before Ryder, my brother had only known the men in his life to disappear. It meant so much to me that Ryder would be setting a different example.

Ryder placed his hand on Ollie's shoulder. "If there's one thing you know about me by now, I hope it's that I don't say things I don't mean."

Ollie nodded. "Yeah."

"You know, Ollie, people who can see are sometimes able to look into each other's eyes and tell when someone's being sincere. I know you can't do that, but I can show you something else." Ryder took Ollie's hand and placed it over his heart. "Feel that?"

"Your heart. It's beating really fast."

"It's beating like this because I've been wanting to say these things for a long time, but I was scared to. I was so nervous to admit that to you—not because I'm unsure, but because I was afraid you wouldn't believe me. I'm in this for the long haul, if you want me to be."

"Yeah, I do." Ollie reached for him. "I love you, too, Ryder. Like, more than anything—besides Eden."

They embraced, and Ryder shut his eyes tightly as if to soak in those words.

"You love me more than Gilbert Gottfried?"

Ollie pretended to have to think about it. "Yeah, I think so."

"I'll accept that one-percent doubt."

After they broke their hug, Ollie asked, "Does this mean you're moving here?"

"I can't move completely yet, because I still have a lot to figure out at work. But I'm gonna try to come every weekend, if that's cool with you."

"If we lived in California, you wouldn't have to do that."

"I know, but your school is here, and that's the most important thing."

Ollie shrugged. "Says who?"

"Your sister. And you feel that way, too, right?"

Surprised at Ollie's question, I addressed him, "You used to say you'd never want to move from St. George."

"That was before Ryder. I love my school, but if I had to choose between the two, I'd rather have Ryder around every day. It's not even a contest."

*Wow.* I guess I underestimated his feelings.

"There are a lot of considerations," I said. "You know this house inside out, and if we moved, you'd have to get used to an entirely new layout. We'd have to find a school that was a good fit for you. That takes time."

Ryder could see the look of concern on my face. I was sure he knew this talk of moving was starting to stress me out. It wasn't that I didn't want to move to California. I wanted that more than anything.

As if he could read my mind, Ryder came up behind me and rubbed my shoulders. "We've got all the time in the world. We can start by keeping an eye out for schools in California, though."

"Or keeping an *ear* out," Ollie corrected.

Ryder smacked his forehead. "You got me, kid. We'll keep our ears and noses out. If the right fit comes along, we'll make a decision together about moving. And even if we find a good school, you can change your mind. That's okay, too."

"It will be a team decision," I said.

Ryder glanced over at me. "Yeah, a family decision."

After Ollie went to sleep that night, Ryder seemed on edge as we retreated to my bedroom. We hadn't discussed whether or not I'd be working tonight, although my plan was to skip it.

"Are you okay?" I asked.

He seemed very tense. "There's actually something I want to talk to you about."

My heart sped up a bit. "Okay..."

"This is hard for me, because I normally consider myself a strong person, but when it comes to you, all bets are off. I'm jealous, out of control, a little crazy."

"What's going on?"

Ryder took me by the hand. "Come here. Let's sit." He sat on the bed with his back against the headboard and pulled me to straddle him. His face turned red as he let out a long breath. "I don't want to share you anymore, Eden."

It didn't take a rocket scientist to figure out what he was getting at. "You want me to stop camming..."

"Here's the thing. I don't want you to stop if it truly makes you happy. But if it doesn't make you happy? Then, yes. I want you to stop." He ran his hand along my body.

"Because this is mine, and I don't want anyone else to have it anymore—even virtually."

This clearly wasn't easy for him to bring up.

"You've been wanting to say this for a while, haven't you?"

"What right do I have to tell you what to do? None. All I can tell you is how I feel. I know that sounds hypocritical, because your job is how we met, but the more I grow to love you, the harder it is for me to accept sharing you."

I wanted to quit camming more than anything, but this wasn't just about no longer taking my clothes off. The camming was my livelihood, and giving it up meant becoming dependent on Ryder, something I'd vowed I'd never do.

"I really want to be able to say yes."

"What's your hesitation?"

"I don't want to have to rely on you. And without that money coming in, I will."

"What's wrong with leaning on someone else for a while—especially someone who has the means to support you? You've been independent for a long time. It's okay to let someone else help you, especially if they love you. This isn't charity, Eden. You finding a different career would benefit me just as much as you. In a way, it's me being selfish and using my money for my own benefit—for my own sanity. Look at it that way, if you want. Let me buy some sanity."

That did help me see the situation a bit differently. "Love is about sacrifice, isn't it? I guess I'm still getting used to not only that concept but the idea that someone would love me enough to want to take care of me."

"I wouldn't be supporting you forever, because I know you wouldn't let me do that, even though I might want to. So just let me get you on your feet, so you can do something you want to do, that makes you happy and doesn't make me want to kill half the male population of the world."

That made me laugh, but I knew he wasn't kidding. And I'd made up my mind; I wasn't going to continue doing something that made him miserable. It had been different before we were truly committed, but being in a relationship was about sacrifices. Ryder was already sacrificing a lot of time to be with me, and I needed to take this plunge, despite how scary it seemed.

There was only one thing left to say. "Okay."

Ryder seemed surprised at how easily I gave in. "Okay? Like, you're done? Just like that?"

"Yes. Cold turkey. I'll post a message on my page tomorrow and cancel my account."

He buried his face in my chest. "Thank you. Thank you. Thank you."

"You know, it was a big deal what you did earlier, using the word *family* around Ollie. I know you wouldn't do that unless you absolutely planned to stick around. That helped it sink in how serious you are about this. So, this is a two-way street. I wouldn't have the courage to leave camming if I wasn't certain you were here to stay."

"I am, baby. I love you so much."

I looked around at all of my props. "Whatever am I gonna do with all of this shit?"

He sighed. "Some of it I think we should burn. Other things, like the lube, we can put to good use."

With each second that passed, I became more relieved about leaving my job. "Oh my God, I never want to see another dildo for as long as I live."

"No more sacrificing bananas," he joked.

I cackled. "No more telling men how to dress themselves. No more talking like a baby to men wearing diapers."

His eyes widened. "Hold up. What?"

"Oh yeah. I didn't tell you that one?"

"No!" Ryder shook his head and laughed. "Also, no more dumb questions from AssLover."

"Aw, I loved AssLover. He was so…*special.*"

"Until he professed his love—that's when he crossed the line. You should've seen the look of horror on your face when you thought he was the one saying all those things."

"I can't even be mad about anything that went down that night. I was so relieved to find out I didn't have a delusional stalker, *and* that our feelings are mutual."

Ryder looked up into my eyes. "You know, I spent a long time feeling like I didn't belong in my own skin. I had the perfect job, the seemingly perfect life, yet I was never happy. Happiness cannot be found in *things.* I know that now. I never felt truly happy until I met you. And Ollie just adds a layer to that—one I didn't even know was possible. I've realized making him happy makes *me* happy. And it doesn't take much, because he appreciates the little things. I'm learning that the little things *are* the big things. He's taught me so much about what's really important. All I need is this little family we have. Thank you for letting me be part of it."

I couldn't kiss him hard enough as I planted my lips on his. "I don't know that it even felt like we were a complete family until you came into our lives, Ryder. It always felt like Ollie and me against the world. Now it's the three of us, and that feels complete."

His eyes searched mine. "I want you to feel safe with me. I know you're not used to trusting men. I wish there were a way for me to prove how serious I am about this. But only time will show my commitment. And I look forward to proving every day how much I love you. There's nothing I wouldn't do for you or that boy. I would move mountains for you."

When it came to Ryder's promises, I would soon discover moving mountains could be taken both figuratively and literally.

## CHAPTER 29

*Ryder*

I hoped she didn't think I was crazy. I'd been wrackling my brain for the past few months, trying to figure out how to move Eden and Ollie to Los Angeles without majorly disrupting Ollie's life.

I'd figured out the education component. There was a prestigious school for the blind, The Larchmont School, about twenty minutes south of where I lived. I'd spoken to the headmaster, told her a bit about Ollie, and she seemed to think the school would be a good fit. They'd offer comparable services to what he was used to in St. George, as well as other programs he might never have had access to in Utah. Of course, there was a waiting list to get in, but if ever there was a time to use the McNamara name, that was it. She seemed willing to bend the rules and allow him a spot if we wanted it.

However, there was still the issue of Ollie's day-to-day situation at home. It had taken his whole life to know his house well enough to be pretty independent. I didn't want him to have to start from scratch in my gigantic house.

There was only one solution that made any sense to me, and I decided to throw it out there during dinner one weekend in St. George. Ollie was in his room. I didn't want to bring it up in front of him and get his hopes up if Eden ended up dead set against it.

Pushing aside my plate, I cleared my throat. "So, I was thinking...what if we physically *move* this house to L.A.?"

Eden, who'd been drinking water, stopped mid-sip. "What? *Move* this house?"

"You heard me right."

Her eyes were practically bugging out of her head. "Can you do that?"

"Yes. People do it all of the time. It's small enough to actually move. I measured it out and made some calls. I already own an empty lot that would be perfect. I was originally thinking of putting it on my main property, but it's too hilly, and the movers wouldn't be able to get the house up there."

Eden's mouth hung open. "I don't know what to say. I wouldn't have thought this was even a possibility. That's got to cost a fortune."

"Don't worry about that. The peace of mind will be worth it. I can't put a price on getting to have you guys with me, not having to travel back and forth."

"This is seriously doable?"

"Yes. I've been talking to a lot of people this week about it. If you agree, I'm gonna have the moving company come out in a few days to take their own measurements and confirm before we mention it to Ollie. But I need your okay first. You'd have to really *want* to move. Talking about it is one thing, but doing it is another."

"You're sure Ollie would be guaranteed a spot at The Larchmont School?"

"Yes. The headmaster gave me her word on that. But you'll need to talk to her, too—make sure you approve of it before we confirm."

She took a moment to ponder, then smiled. "This sounds a little nuts, but I love the idea of moving the house. It's the last thing keeping us here."

My body filled with excitement at the prospect of having everything I needed and wanted in one place. "I was hoping you'd say that."

Eden beamed. "You did say you'd move mountains for me. I guess this proves it."

Six months later, our dream became a reality. We ended up waiting for the school year to finish in St. George before we bit the bullet and moved our house all the way to California.

It was quite a journey and took several days because the truck carrying the structure had to crawl on the highway.

We'd apparently been the talk of the neighborhood as spectators lined up to watch while the workers settled the structure onto its new foundation.

After that, it had taken some time before we could actually move in.

Now that we were inside, Ollie kept pointing out how sometimes he would forget we'd moved at all, because everything was the same, aside from his school.

Thankfully, he was loving his new teachers and slowly making friends. Eden and Ollie moving to L.A. was the best decision we could have made for ourselves—not only because Ollie was adapting well, but because Eden was finally moving on with her life, having just enrolled in the music program at Cal State. She'd decided what she wanted to do, which was to follow in her mother's footsteps and become a music teacher. And while I was helping her with the tuition, she insisted on contributing, taking a waitressing job at a high-end restaurant. She was proud that she'd gotten it on her own, without my connections.

I was still running the studio alongside Benjamin, and we'd made no plans to change that anytime soon. He'd given me a commitment of at least another year. I was still deciding whether I wanted to sell my shares or eventually run the company. I was so thankful Benjamin had given me the time to make that decision.

Perhaps the biggest difference since Eden's move was Lorena's changing role in my day-to-day life. We'd determined that there was no better person to help us with Ollie while we worked—or in Eden's case went to classes. Let's face it, there wasn't much housekeeping to do in our little place anyway, so Lorena became a trusted set of eyes we so desperately needed. She and Ollie got along well. He appreciated her humor, as I always had, and she was even teaching him Spanish.

Having Lorena's help also made it possible for Eden and me to have some semblance of a normal relationship—one that involved having sex in private and going out on actual dates. I still kept my bigger house, though the long-term plan was to sell it and build another house based on the layout Ollie was familiar with, except bigger. We would then take our time, allowing him to get used to it before we moved in.

Hanging on to the big house came in handy, though, because Eden and I would sneak over there at night while Lorena stayed with Ollie as he slept. We would frolic in the pool, have sex in the shower as loudly as we wanted, and do whatever we damn well pleased. Afterward, we'd head home to be there when Ollie woke up in the morning.

A little while after the move, one of our favorite ways to spend a sunny weekend became taking a ride out west to Malibu with a cooler full of food and drinks.

Eden and I were alone in our room, getting ready to spend the day at the beach with Ollie on one such afternoon when I brought up something that had been weighing on my mind.

"Have you given any more thought to what the doctor said?" I asked.

Eden put down the beach blanket she'd been folding and bit her bottom lip. "We can bring it up today, if you want. You know how I feel about this. I've always believed anything like that should be his choice with no pressure."

"You're right. There's no sense in even thinking about it further if we haven't talked it over with him."

She wrapped her arms around my neck. "I love you for wanting to look into it."

"I'd do anything for you and him. You know that. I don't want him to ever feel like I didn't do enough when I could've helped."

When we arrived in Malibu, it was shaping up to be the perfect beach day—not a cloud in the sky and just the right amount of current. The ocean had become Ollie's favorite place—the relaxing sounds of the waves, the feel of the water, and the texture of the sand. It was sensory overload. It was therefore an ironic place to broach the subject we were about to put forth.

Ollie and I had just come back to the shore to have lunch. As we sat down on the beach blanket, I looked over at Eden before I addressed him, "Can I talk to you about something?"

"You don't usually ask me permission."

"You're right. But this is important."

He shrugged. "Okay."

Eden moved in closer to sit next to him and placed her hand on his leg. I took in some of the salty air before I started talking.

"I feel guilty sometimes that you can't see the things we can, even though I know you don't feel like you're missing out because not seeing is all you know. I sometimes have to stop myself and understand that your experiences, while not the same as ours, are not necessarily *less*. They're just different. But because we care so much about you, I want to make sure I do everything in my power to help you live your best life. I feel like that's my responsibility, my calling."

Eden unwrapped a sandwich and handed it to him. He took a bite and ate quietly while I continued.

"So, I went to speak to a doctor, a world-renowned eye specialist, one my mother used to see, actually. Eden came with me, and we took all of your medical records. He let us know that there are some experimental surgeries available now that weren't around when you were younger. He said we might be able to look into some of those if you were ever interested. Nothing would be guaranteed, but if they could help you see, even a little..."

The breeze blew Ollie's longish hair around. He stopped chewing and opened his eyes. I suspected he was stressed.

"We don't have to talk about this if you don't want to, Ollie," I said.

"No, I'm listening," he answered.

"I never want you to misinterpret why I looked into this. There is absolutely nothing wrong with the way you are. I want to make that clear. I'm not looking to *fix* you in any way. I just want you to know there isn't anything I wouldn't do and no amount of money I wouldn't pay to try to help you see if you decided you wanted to take that chance."

After some silence, he asked, "What else did the doctor say?"

"He said he didn't think it would be possible for you to see fully, but that one of these experimental surgeries might allow you some limited vision—like seeing shadows and movements, things like that. He said we couldn't expect a miracle, and there was also a chance that even if you qualified for the surgeries and went through with one or more of them, they might not work at all. So there would be a lot to consider. You by no means have to make any kind of a decision right now. I'm just throwing it out there."

"Okay," he said.

"I'm not gonna say anything else, because this day is supposed to be about relaxing and enjoying the beach. I'll always be looking out for you in any way I can."

He nodded. "Because you're my brad."

*Brad?*

"Your what?"

"Like my brother and my dad. Brother-dad—brad."

My mouth curved into a smile. "I've never heard you say that before. Is that what you call me?"

"It is now...if you want."

I could feel my eyes starting to well up. "Of course, I want to be your brad. I love it. I think it's the perfect name."

He took another bite, then spoke with his mouth full. "Me, too."

## CHAPTER 30

**Eden**

Ryder seemed really anxious tonight, and I couldn't figure out why. I'd gotten a rare night off from waitressing, and he'd brought me to one of his favorite restaurants in downtown L.A., but he was really aggravated when the table he'd reserved wasn't ready when we arrived.

"What the fuck good is calling ahead if you have to wait?"

"It's okay, baby," I said, rubbing his back.

Nothing calmed him. "No, it's not."

We'd been particularly busy lately, and it had been a while since we'd gone out to eat alone. With my busy school schedule and work, most of our spare time was spent hanging out with Ollie.

As frustrated as he was, I couldn't help thinking how handsome he looked in his fitted navy sweater and dark jeans that hugged his ass. He smelled particularly delicious, and the truth of the matter was that I'd much rather have spent this time alone at the big house, screwing his brains out. But he was insistent that we go out tonight.

If I thought Ryder's mood couldn't get any worse, I was wrong.

A man and woman approached us.

"Hey, Ryder."

"Phil...good to see you."

They shook hands, and the guy's lady friend stood just behind him, smiling.

The man gestured to her. "This is my wife, Helena."

She nodded once and glanced over at me. "Nice to meet you."

Ryder pulled me close. "This is my girlfriend, Eden."

Phil squinted and tilted his head as he looked me over. "Are you an actress?"

"No, I'm not."

"Really? You look awfully familiar."

"Nope, never been an actress." My pulse started to race as I became a bit paranoid.

Phil was insistent. "Are you sure? I could swear I've seen you on camera."

Ryder's eyes darted toward him and lingered in a murderous stare.

*Shit.*

*No.*

*Could he recognize me?*

Anything was possible. I'd worked for two years as a cam girl through a popular site that got millions of hits. This guy having caught one of my shows was not out of the realm of possibility.

"Have a good night," Ryder suddenly said, ushering me away from them.

"What are you doing?" I asked as we headed out the door.

"We're getting the fuck out of here."

When the cool night air hit us, I turned to him. "Do you think he recognized me from the site?"

"I have no clue. But I didn't like the way he was looking at you."

Gripping his sweater, I brought him into me. "It's okay."

"No, it's not." He looked at me intensely. "None of this is okay. Waiting all night for a table, the way he was fucking you with his eyes—none of it."

*He's pissed.*

"None of those things matter to me," I soothed. "I'm just happy to be out with you, so happy to finally be in L.A. and for the life you've given me here. I'm so happy, Ryder, that none of these little aggravations matter. So please be happy with me tonight."

"I *am* happy. I'm so freaking happy I don't even know if I deserve it sometimes."

He dropped to one knee and looked up at me.

My heart pitter-pattered. "What are you doing?"

"I wanted tonight to be perfect. I really did. I had this elaborate plan, and it involved the perfect dinner and the perfect evening. The perfect timing. Everything was going to be perfect. But you know, nothing has ever worked out perfectly at first when it comes to us. But that doesn't matter, because damn it, we're *perfect together*. Things don't have to be perfect as long as I have you. You and Ollie are why I get up each morning. You've made me realize I could never be happy before because I was looking for happiness in all of the wrong places: my career, my social status. None of that shit matters. All that matters is having people in your world you love more than anything, who give you a reason to live. I want to spend the rest of my life with you, Eden. Will you marry me?"

I covered my mouth and jumped around in excitement. "Yes! Of course! Yes! Yes!"

The sounds of the city seemed to fade as Ryder stood and placed a gorgeous round diamond ring on my finger before lifting me into his arms.

He spoke into my ear. "I feel like I totally fucked up that proposal, but I don't even care because you said yes."

"It could have been so much worse."

"Oh yeah?"

"Yeah, you could have done it logged in as AssLover or something."

"That's true. Very true."

Ollie has always been afraid to fly. So when Ryder suggested we travel to New York City to get married, I was hesitant, knowing how much anxiety that would create for my brother.

But Ollie eventually agreed, because quite frankly, Ryder could convince him to do anything.

When it came time for our flight, I watched as Ryder held my brother's hand and gave him a play by play of what was happening. As the plane ascended, Ollie looked terrified, feeling the swift motion. But by the end of the flight, he had a huge smile on his face. I was proud of him for overcoming his fear.

Lorena had accompanied us to New York, and the four of us spent an action-packed several days touring the city and eating our way through the neighborhoods with the best food.

The week culminated in a private wedding ceremony at City Hall, followed by dinner at Tavern on the Green. It was exactly the type of affair we wanted—intimate, yet full of love and laughter from the people we held closest to our hearts.

Ryder had a special surprise up his sleeve for Ollie on the very last day of our trip. He'd rented a car and we'd just dropped Lorena off at the airport. She had to get back a day early for a baby shower.

We were driving down the expressway when Ollie asked, "Why are we leaving the city, and why won't you tell me where we're going?"

I turned around from the passenger seat. "It's a surprise."

"I don't like surprises."

"I think you'll like this one," I said.

Ryder looked over at me and smiled. Oddly, the entire timing of our wedding and New York trip had been planned around this one last thing.

We finally arrived in Long Island. Ryder pulled into the parking lot of the comedy club and shut off the car.

As we entered the building, Ryder spilled the beans at the ticket counter.

"Three tickets for Gilbert Gottfried, please."

Ollie jumped. "No way! What?"

The woman at the counter quickly put a damper on our excitement. "We can't let him in. This is an eighteen-and-over club."

Ryder took her aside. "Listen, my son is blind, and he loves listening to Gilbert more than anything. This was supposed to be a surprise for him. We know some of the stuff isn't appropriate for his age, but we teach him right from wrong, and listening to Gilbert just gives him so much joy. I—"

"I'm so sorry, sir. But I can't break that rule. I'll lose my job. And I like having a roof over my head."

Ryder nodded. I knew he was devastated for giving Ollie false hope.

Even though Ryder was silent, Ollie could sense he was upset.

"It's okay, Ryder. I know you meant well."

We were back in the middle of the parking lot, but Ryder refused to get in the car. My gut told me he had no intention of backing down.

"Stay here," he said.

I knew he didn't want to give up on this, but I had a feeling he was going to be sorely disappointed if he tried to go back in there and convince them again.

He was gone for several minutes before he came back and took Ollie by the hand. "Come on."

The look of excitement on Ollie's face was priceless. Ryder snuck us through a side door before handing a wad of cash to a mysterious man. We were somewhere behind the stage in a hallway.

The three of us sat down on the ground and huddled together as the show began. I was prepared to flee if necessary, but no one ever came around to kick us out.

The sound from where we sat was crystal clear, and Ryder and I watched Ollie's face as he laughed at all of the jokes. The trespassing was well worth it. We couldn't see Gilbert, but that was just fine. We experienced the show just as Ollie did.

As we headed back to the city that night, Ollie was on cloud nine. I let him sit in the front next to Ryder while I sat in the back.

"This was the best week of my life," he said.

I had no doubt he meant that. This was his first big trip away from home. Not only did he get to hear his idol perform live, but he got to be part of Ryder and me solidifying our union, which in turn made us officially a family.

Ryder turned to him. "I'm glad, buddy. Pretty sure this is the latest you've ever stayed up, too."

Ollie's next statement came seemingly out of nowhere.

"I don't want the surgery."

Ryder slowed the car and looked over at him. "What made you think of that right now?"

"I've been thinking about it a lot lately—not just right now. I figured I'd tell you."

Ryder looked back at me through the rearview mirror. "Okay..."

"I don't want you to think I'm ungrateful."

"Of course not, Ollie," I said.

"It's not that I don't want to *see* you guys. But the doctors don't even know if the surgery will work. I'm scared to make something worse when I'm happy the way I am."

After a few seconds of quiet, Ryder reached over and placed his hand on Ollie's leg. "That's all the explanation you'll ever need to give."

Back at the hotel, Ollie was asleep in the suite off of our room when Ryder joined me in bed.

"Today was pretty freaking amazing," he said.

"For so many reasons."

"Yeah. I'm really proud of Ollie for his honesty. I've learned so much about life from him—and from you."

Life was so strange. One little moment could change everything.

"Imagine if you hadn't clicked on my violin photo. I wonder how different our lives would be."

Ryder pulled me close. "I could never have imagined how much my life would change with one click of a button, that I could find this kind of love online."

"Blue skies." I grinned. "Like the song I was singing when you found me—it's been nothing except blue skies since that day. I think I'm finally living those lyrics."

He smiled wide. "That's right, baby. That makes two of us."

**EPILOGUE**

# Ryder

"She's so beautiful."

I never thought I'd look at a girl on a screen with such admiration again. But it had happened twice in one lifetime.

I mean after all, in a weird way, wasn't this how it had all started? Mesmerized, I watched as she moved around gracefully. Her big, beautiful eyes were clear as day, her lips like a perfect bow.

*Holy shit. Is this really happening?*

"Tell me what she looks like," Ollie said. He almost never asked that, never really cared to know such things. But apparently this was the exception.

"Well, I think she has your nose. Eden's nose, too."

His mouth curved into a satisfied grin. "Really?"

"Yeah." I smiled.

"What else?" he asked.

"It's hard to tell right now," Eden said, her giant belly slathered in goop. "But in two months, you'll get to hold her and trace that little nose with your fingers."

Suddenly, she started moving her arms and legs faster. It appeared my daughter was trying to dance. It was amazing what you could see in 4D.

"Looks like she's performing for an audience," the ultrasound tech said.

Eden looked over at me and squeezed my hand.

I winked. "She gets that from her mother."

# ACKNOWLEDGEMENTS

I always say that the acknowledgements are the hardest part of the book to write and that still stands! It's hard to put into words how thankful I am for every single reader who continues to support and promote my books. Your enthusiasm and hunger for my stories is what motivates me every day. And to all of the book bloggers who support me, I simply wouldn't be here without you.

To Vi – I say this every time, and I am saying it again because it holds even truer as time goes on. You're the best friend and partner in crime that I could ask for. I couldn't do any of this without you. Our co-written books are a gift, but the biggest blessing has always been our friendship, which came before the stories and will continue after them. Last year challenged us, but I'm proud to say we are still rearing to go onto the "next!"

To Julie – Thank you for your friendship and for always inspiring me with your amazing writing, attitude, and strength. This year is going to kick ass!

To Luna –Thank you for your love and support, day in and day out and for always being just a message away. Here's to many more Florida visits with sangria and tostones!

To Erika – It will always be an E thing. I am so thankful for your love and friendship and support and to our special hang time in July. Thank you for always brightening my days with your positive outlook.

To my Facebook fan group, Penelope's Peeps – I love you all. Your excitement motivates me every day. And to Queen Peep Amy – Thank you for starting the group way back when.

To Mia – Thank you, my friend, for always making me laugh. I know you're going to bring us some phenomenal words this year.

To my assistant Mindy Guerreiros – Thank you for being so awesome and handling so much of Vi's and my day-to day stuff. We appreciate you so much!

To my editor Jessica Royer Ocken – It was such a pleasure working with you for the first time on this book. I look forward to many more experiences to come.

To Elaine of Allusion Book Formatting and Publishing – Thank you for being the best proofreader, formatter, and friend a girl could ask for.

To Letitia of RBA Designs – The best cover designer ever! Thank you for always working with me until the cover is exactly how I want it.

To my agent extraordinaire, Kimberly Brower –Thank you for all of your hard work in getting my books into the international market and for believing in me long before you were my agent, back when you were a blogger and I was a first-time author.

To my husband – Thank you for always taking on so much more than you should have to so that I am able to write. I love you so much.

To the best parents in the world – I'm so lucky to have you! Thank you for everything you have ever done for me and for always being there.

To my besties: Allison, Angela, Tarah and Sonia – Thank you for putting up with that friend who suddenly became a nutty writer.

Last but not least, to my daughter and son – Mommy loves you. You are my motivation and inspiration!

# ABOUT THE AUTHOR

Penelope Ward is a *New York Times, USA Today* and *#1 Wall Street Journal* bestselling author.

She grew up in Boston with five older brothers and spent most of her twenties as a television news anchor. Penelope resides in Rhode Island with her husband, son and beautiful daughter with autism.

With over 1.5 million books sold, she is a twenty-time *New York Times* bestseller and the author of over twenty novels, including *RoomHate* which hit #2 on the *New York Times* bestseller list and #1 on the *Wall Street Journal* bestseller list. Other *New York Times* bestsellers include *Gentleman Nine, Drunk Dial, Stepbrother Dearest, Neighbor Dearest, Cocky Bastard, Stuck-Up Suit, Playboy Pilot, Mister Moneybags, Rebel Heir and Rebel Heart* (the latter six co-written with Vi Keeland).

Penelope's books have been translated into over a dozen languages and can be found in bookstores around the world.

Subscribe to Penelope's newsletter here:
http://bit.ly/1X725rj

# BOOKS BY PENELOPE WARD

Gentleman Nine

Drunk Dial

Mack Daddy

RoomHate

Stepbrother Dearest

Neighbor Dearest

Jaded and Tyed (A novelette)

Sins of Sevin

Jake Undone (Jake #1)

Jake Understood (Jake #2)

My Skylar

Gemini

# BOOKS BY PENELOPE WARD & VI KEELAND

Rebel Heart

Rebel Heir

Dear Bridget, I Want You

Mister Moneybags

Playboy Pilot

Stuck-Up Suit

Cocky Bastard

Made in the USA
Columbia, SC
21 July 2020